Sign up to my newsletter, and you will be notified when I release my next book!

ISBN-13: 9798371564832

D1521487

JACK BRYCE

To whomever invented thongs.

Chapter 1

James took a deep breath of clean forest air as he wiped the sweat from his brow.

It was time for a break.

He squinted up at the sun as he placed his axe against the sturdy trunk of a tree. With a satisfied sigh, he sat down — his back against the tree — and took a moment to appreciate the silent beauty of the forest.

He only recently moved into his cabin in Tour County, but he already felt more at home than he ever did in the city. This was the place for him; somewhere he could make his own place without the rat race of city life trying to pull him in.

But he had to work hard for it. Felling trees for lumber, making repairs on his property, and befriending the locals — although that was often more fun than work — were all high on his agenda.

But so far, it was all worth it.

He took a sip of water from the bottle he had brought, then unpacked the lunch Sara had prepared for him: sandwiches with sliced sausage, cheese, and tomato. The food was savory, the ingredients fresh, and James bit down with relish, washing it all away with fresh and clear water, which was a blessing on this warm, late summer day.

As he relaxed and ate, his eye fell on his axe, leaning against the tree trunk.

He had bought it at Lucy's general store a few days ago, but the edge was already getting blunt from the hard work.

No surprise there, James thought. *I've been taking down trees for two days nonstop.*

He needed lumber for his project; he wanted to expand the cabin.

At first, he had planned on only building a workshop. But his magical powers gave him the means to scale up his expansion. He was going to build an additional room on the north side of the cabin that could serve as a separate kitchen. Doing so would free up the current living room and kitchen combination, allowing a dedicated living room with more space to relax.

The new wall on the north side would double as the wall for his lean-to workshop.

On the west side, he would build an expansion that would double the sleeping room in size.

It was an ambitious plan, but his magic would ease the hardest part of the job — preparing logs and boards for the walls.

When James finished his sandwich, he picked up the axe and ran his thumb along the edge. When he felt how blunt it actually was, he shook his head.

One tree in particular had been rough on the tool. Sturdy and old, and with James's lumberjack skills still burgeoning, the blade got notched pretty bad...

This won't do...

But he hadn't brought anything to sharpen the tool

with.

As he considered the blunted edge, a strange but familiar sensation rose inside him. It was a powerful combination of arcane might and willpower — the foundation of his newly discovered magical abilities.

The sensation heralded the coming of an ancestral memory. Those memories allowed him to acquire new magical spells by tapping into the collective knowledge of his ancestors — the High Mages of the House of Harkness.

James pushed away all outside influences, focusing only on the edge of his axe, visualizing it as it should be — sharp, keen, honed to perfection.

And as he pictured this, he willed it with all his intent, bending his resolve to the desired result: a sharpened blade.

Magic burgeoned within him — mana blazing in his core — until the power almost overwhelmed him.

And then, just as Sara had taught him, he turned all that intent inward to seek the ancestral memory that would help him fulfill his task.

The light around James intensified, as if someone dialed up the sun, and mists seemed to billow up from the very earth to envelop him, to carry him away to some distant place where an ancestor of his Bloodline had applied the kind of magic he was now looking for.

It was a beautiful experience — something that made James at one with the many generations that went before him, carving their own paths in the world to achieve happiness.

He let those mists rise and envelop him, and they took him through the vast spaces of time — to learn and to improve.

When James opened his eyes, he found himself in the forest still.

But it was a different forest — all pine under a gray sky with a bleak and distant sun.

And all around him rang the laughter, chatter, and voices of men. The steady thrum of axes biting into wood underscored this cacophony, almost as if it were a rhythmic beat.

With a smile on his lips, James followed the sound through the massive boles of towering pine trees. The traces of men working lumber were everywhere — stumps, the branches of limbed trees, and the beds of needles on the forest ground.

With every step, the sounds grew louder, until James broke out of the tree line.

He came upon a clearing surrounded by a ring of massive pine trees. Some men were chopping and sawing at the trunks of the pines. Others held ropes tied to the branches and pulled at them, making sure that — once felled — the tree would fall in the direction of their choosing. And then there were men relaxing, taking their breaks as they sat on freshly cut logs, eating and drinking and laughing.

They could not see James, of course. In these visits to his ancestral memories, he was little more than a ghost. He could pass through solid objects and remained unseen and unheard. Here, James was a spectator; he could not influence the past.

He studied the men for a while, and soon enough learned that they spoke English in a similar fashion to how he himself spoke the language. In addition, their dress appeared simple but relatively modern. They wore winter outfits — thick coats, sturdy workman's pants and boots, and they shielded their hands and heads from the cold with gloves and hats.

These facts led him to believe that this ancestral memory did not go back for centuries. He had had those before, where men dressed in furs and leather spoke in a language he did not understand.

Finally, James's eye fell on a familiar face.

Throughout the ages, it seemed, the men and women of James's lineage — the House of Harkness — had always had similar features. James recognized those features from the mirror: keen eyes of an emerald hue and a mop of dark, thick hair with a will of its own.

One man with such features sat alone at the edge of the clearing, running his thumb along the blade of his axe almost exactly like James had done a few minutes ago.

Or rather, as James would do many years in the future...

The man looked hardy, weatherworn, as if he had a life full of hardships behind him.

"Oi, Beckett!" one man — the team leader — called out, and James's ancestor rose to attention.

Well, this can't be too long ago, James thought. *He has the same surname as me, after all.*

"Aye?" his ancestor called out.

"I need you and your axe up here," the team leader said. "We need a big flow of logs down Go Home River before the sun sets."

The team leader looked at a few of the other men still lounging. "Come on, guys," he exclaimed. "Damn break is over!"

The whole clearing came to life as burly men — lumberjacks, all — hopped to their feet, jostling and joking as they took up their peaveys, saws, and axes to resume the work.

But James's eyes remained fixed on his ancestor, who rose slowly, made sure no one was watching, and turned his back to the group of men picking up their work again.

When he was sure that he remained unseen, the man gripped his axe with one hand, the other hand hovering over it as he closed his eyes and focused his will on the blade.

Then, almost a whisper, the words nearly drowned by the din of the lumberjacks, James's ancestor spoke the magical words that James wanted to learn.

"*Vanbotta tod skerp.*

"*Bawerckinghe, maacken. Kraft.*

"*Vanbotta tod skerp.*"

The man opened his eyes, looked at the axe, and ran his forefinger over the blade — first along one side, then along the other.

His touch sharpened the axe as well as any tool, man, or machine could. All grime and dirt was gone. Even the notches in the blade from the intensive use had disappeared. It was as if the blade had only just been forged.

With a smile, James's ancestor turned around and rested the axe on his shoulder as he walked over to his fellows, exchanging a joke with a man in passing.

And as the men resumed their work, the memory already faded away, the mists of time rising to take James back to his own place in his own world — to his own time.

Chapter 2

James's eyes shot open.

He had returned to the same place, back in his own time. He knew from experience that only a few minutes had passed while he explored his ancestral memory.

And in those minutes, he had learned a new spell.

A smile formed on his lips as he rose to his feet and picked up his axe.

He would write down the magical words and the circumstances in which he learned them later in his Grimoire. He kept meticulous track of these things, because it was not the magic alone that interested him.

Learning magic was his primary goal, but James loved learning more about the history of his family. He had not been close to his father, and he knew little about his own ancestry — about the trials and tribulation of the House of Harkness.

But first, he wanted to test his new spell.

James copied the acts of his forefather, holding the axe in one hand and letting his other hand hover over it as he focused his willpower on sharpening it.

When the mana gathered in his veins, he spoke the words of power of the Sharpen spell he had just learned:

"*Vanbotta tod skerp.*

"*Bawerckinghe, maacken. Kraft.*

"*Vanbotta tod skerp.*"

The magic blossomed in his veins, and when he ran his finger along the edge of the blade of his axe, his potent magic restored the tool to great sharpness, as his ancestor's magic had done in the vision.

James also noticed this spell was not as intensive to use as some of the others he had learned.

Although it was difficult to quantify mana, it was clear to James that it was an expendable resource that renewed with rest and good food. So far, he hadn't run into his own limits when casting spells, but that didn't mean he had none.

Like any new skill acquired and practiced, it would take time for him to find the boundaries...

And then, of course, try to move them.

With his axe sharp and a smile on his face, James turned back to the job at hand — felling trees for the planned expansion of his cabin.

He stopped short.

A fleeting shape in the forest.

Something darted and weaved through the trunks, then disappeared.

"What the..." James muttered.

He narrowed his eyes and found comfort in the firm grip of his axe. He thought he recognized some part of the shape. Did he see legs and a tail?

Either way, someone was watching him.

James intended to find out whom.

He shouldered his backpack, took his axe in hand, and strode forward, He crouched low as he followed in the direction the skittish shape had taken.

James kept his bearing as he ventured deeper into the forest. He had not gotten another glimpse of the limber shape, but he believed he was going in the right direction.

His pace slowed as he entered a wilder area where the trees competed for sunlight, leaving the scraps for the bushy and thorny undergrowth. There was no sound but the creaking of branches and the rustling of leaves in the wind.

In a place like this, James could have been the only human being on earth.

He stopped to listen for sounds — anything that might indicate where the other was hiding. But he heard nothing.

He started walking again, and the underbrush grew thicker and taller with every step. He was now deep in the dense wood, and he found no trace of the shape that he'd been pursuing.

Looks like I lost the trail, he thought.

Still, he wouldn't give up just like that.

He continued walking, and after a few minutes, he

was certain that the other eluded him.

Who was it? he wondered.

He remained fairly certain that the shape had been watching him — or rather, following him — but he saw no face or defining features besides legs and a fluffy tail.

Just as he turned around to get back to work, there came a rustling from the undergrowth, and a branch snapped.

"Oops," someone muttered — a female voice.

James whirled around. His sharp gaze found a pretty little face hidden away in the shrubs.

She peeked at him with large eyes — one blue, the other green — from under an unruly mop of ginger hair.

Two cute fox ears crowned that pretty head, now folded back as the fox girl regarded him.

Kesha.

"Hey there," James said, raising his hands to calm her.

At that, she bolted off.

She was quick, but James saw her now. He called out again, then gave chase to her as she careened through the forest.

He wanted to speak to her, wanted to ask her why she was following him around. To him, the fox girl posed yet another mystery of the woods of Tour County, and James loved a good mystery…

She was fast, though.

James had to put in everything he had to keep up with her. And carrying a backpack as he ran didn't make it any easier.

She darted through the undergrowth and between the tree trunks with the grace and speed of…

Well, of a *fox*.

Soon enough, the distance between them increased, and James feared he would lose her again.

"Please stop!" He called out after her. "I am not going to hurt you!"

But she ignored him and kept running, her three fox tails — ginger with white tips — billowing behind her as she cleared bushes and ditches with impressive leaps. Her long, coppery hair flew behind her as she ran, and the bouncing of her firm butt in her tight shorts added to the allure of the fox girl.

Kesha disappeared behind the next row of trees, and James took off after her, hoping that he wouldn't lose track. But she was faster than him — at least in the forest — and he was by no means slow.

As he rounded a turn, James caught sight of Kesha's slender back as she leaped over a ditch. As she landed on the other side, he saw her lean over to look behind her, to check if she had already lost him.

And in that moment, she tripped on a root and fell.

She went down with a fox-like yip, a blur of shapely and fair-skinned limbs.

This was James's chance.

He dashed forward, cleared the ditch with a powerful jump, and landed right beside her as she rolled onto her back.

She looked up at him with big eyes, and an expression of pain contorted her beautiful face as she reached down to grab her knee. It was scuffed, bleeding.

"Let me help with that," James said as he kneeled down beside her.

She recoiled, crawling back on her elbows with fear in her heterochromatic eyes.

"It's okay," James said, raising both hands, palms outward in a calming gesture. "I promise I'm not going to hurt you."

She blinked once, watching him with apprehension as he studied her wound.

It was nothing big; she had only grazed her knee on the hard soil. But it would need cleaning and something to cover it.

His eyes met hers again as she lay on her back, propped up on her elbows. She was beautiful — even though she was wild. Her body was fit, her long legs toned, and the crop top she wore revealed a flat stomach with slight muscle definition.

And how could she not be fit? Kesha lived alone in the woods.

She was Lucy's daughter, but judging by what Lucy had told him, the two of them had grown apart, and Kesha had taken to living in the wild by herself.

Apparently, that had had some impact on her social skills and trust of strangers...

"I need to clean this wound," James said. "And I'll need to put a Band-Aid on it as well. You're lucky that I don't go out into the forest without first aid supplies."

She pressed her lips into a thin line, not speaking, but she didn't stop him or try to run away again.

"Come on," James said, nodding in the direction of a moss-covered log nearby. "You can sit down over there while I patch you up."

He stood, holding his hand out toward her, and she slowly allowed him to pull her to her feet. Once she was standing, he held his hand out for her again so that she could steady herself against him as they walked together through the thick underbrush.

Her arm was warm against his, and she shuddered when they first touched. Still, she clung to him for stability.

Together, they walked over to the moss-covered log nearby.

Kesha sat down, gently guided by James, and a little moan of pain escaped her.

"Easy now," James said. "Just relax." He kneeled down in front of her.

Still wary, she leaned back, hands splayed on the surface of the log, as he gently lifted her shapely leg to inspect the scrape.

He gave a nod. As he had expected, it was not serious. It only needed cleaning and a little care, and it would heal on its own.

He pulled a small bottle out of his bag, uncapped it, and used a cotton swab to apply disinfectant.

As he dabbed it on the wound, Kesha gave a snarl and tried to pull her leg back.

"Easy, easy," James said. "I'm cleaning the wound to make sure he doesn't get infected, okay?"

She followed his every movement with a wary gaze, but let him continue.

As James cleaned her wound, he wondered how wild the fox girl had become in nature. After all, if she was Lucy's daughter, she would have been born and raised in civilization — probably in the house above the general store where Lucy lived now. All Lucy had told him was that she had left some time ago to be closer to the wild.

Apparently, she had taken the wilderness to heart.

When James finished cleaning the wound, he applied a Band-Aid and offered her one of the spare water bottles from his pack.

"Here," he said, handing the bottle to her. "Have something to drink."

She shook her head, still watching him as if he might strike out at her at any moment.

James sighed. "Look," he said. "I'm not going to harm you. I'm actually helping you. What more proof of my good will do you need?"

She bit her lip, doubt flaring in her pretty, multicolored eyes as she looked him over.

He offered the bottle again. "Here," he said.

She took it, screwed off the cap, and drank.

"So, you're Kesha, right?" James asked.

She flinched at the sound of her own name and stopped drinking. Some of the skittishness returned to her posture, but James wasn't going to let up.

"I'm a friend of Lucy's," he said. "She told me you lived out here."

A muscle in her cheek pulled as she studied him.

"Look," James said. "I'm just trying to be friendly. If you ever need any help out here, you can come to me, all right? I live in the cabin, a little farther down that way." He gestured toward the southeast, in the rough direction of the cabin. "Even if it's only food or drink you need, okay?"

She remained expressionless.

"Just don't let me find you in Corinne's chicken coop again, okay?"

At that, she finally let go, losing her attitude for a moment as she gave an amused snort.

He grinned, straightening himself as he popped his neck muscles. "Oh, you think that's funny?"

Her expression softened, and she gave him a smile. "Maybe a little," she replied.

The first word she had spoken to him... She had a light voice, sprightly, as if the rustling of the undergrowth and the gentle breeze of summer itself lived within her.

She looked down at her knee — at the Band-Aid. "Thank you," she muttered.

"Don't mention it," he said, glad that she was finally speaking. "So, what were you doing out here, anyway? Why were you watching me?"

She frowned. "I wasn't watching you," she said.

"Okay," he said. "Then what were you doing?"

She bit her lip, eyes darting left, then right. "I, uh... I was... Well, maybe I *was* watching you." She wrung her hands together in her lap. "I... I didn't know if you were a threat. I saw you before... At Corinne's. And you had a gun."

He nodded. "Yeah, Corinne thought there was a fox paying nightly visits to her chicken coop, and she asked me to chase it away. Turns out she was half right about that."

Kesha chuckled. "Yeah... Half right is true, I guess."

"Listen," James said. "I'm all for living in the wild and getting in touch with nature. But you shouldn't get your daily dose of poultry from Corinne's chicken coop, okay? The poor girl's working her ass off to make sure that she doesn't lose the farm. It's a hard time for her. I'd rather you come to me when you're hungry and can't find anything in the wild, all right?"

She nodded slowly, keeping her enchanting eyes on

him. "It's just that... Well, chicken is *so* good."

He laughed and shook his head, placing his hands on his sides. "I can get you chicken from the general store if you like it so much," he said. "In fact, it'll likely be the same chicken as the ones you can get from Corinne's coop. Only this time, she will actually make some money on it."

Kesha chuckled and cocked her head to study him. "Are you Corinne's lover?"

He grinned and gave a light shrug.

There was no point lying to anyone about what he thought of Corinne, and he had resolved to be honest in this new life he had begun out in the woods of Tour County.

"I would say that we're dating. If it's up to me, we will be lovers, yeah." He studied the fox girl to gauge her reaction, but she only gave a slight twitch of her long, furry ears as she considered his words.

"You are very honest," she said, keeping her eyes on him, some kind of new interest flaring up in them.

"Yeah," he said. "I've had heard a fair share of lies in my life. I've no interest in more."

They remained like that for a moment — Kesha sitting on the log and James standing in front of her, hands on his sides. At length, she stirred and spoke again.

"The cabin used to be empty," she said, cocking one ear as she studied him. "Why are you living there now?"

"I inherited it from my father," James said. "I came down to Tour County to inspect it, and I fell in love at once. So I decided to stay and live there. It needs some work — especially to make it a little more comfortable. But I have the time and the will; I will turn it into a nice home."

"Home," she muttered, almost as if the word were something alien to her and she was trying it out for size.

He chuckled. "Try it sometime," he said. "A home is a nice thing to have."

She smiled up at him, a big and sincere smile that warmed him. Then she gestured at the surrounding forest. "I have a home," she said. "You see it all around you."

She didn't sound particularly convinced of that herself.

"You sleep out here?" James asked. "In the wild?"

She wagged her head. "Well, I make a kind of shelter for myself. I don't like to get wet when it rains, and the woods are cold at night — even in summer."

He considered those words for a moment, trying to

picture the pretty fox girl out in the wild at night, sleeping under a shelter of branches and leaves.

There was something romantic about it, but he also expected she was lonely.

"How long have you been out here?" he asked.

"A few years," she said. She then considered his question a little deeper. "I count two winters."

"Must've been rough," he said, folding his arms over each other.

"At times," she said with a light shrug. "But I prefer it that way. Life in town was... not for me."

He decided not to press on that. He hoped to get to know Kesha better in the future, and there would be plenty of time for the fox girl to explain why she liked living out in the woods.

"Well," he said. "If you ever tire of it or would simply like to spend the night by a warm fire, you'd be welcome at my cabin."

She laughed and cocked her head slightly. "But we don't know each other?" she said. "Do you always invite strangers over to your house?"

He shrugged. "You're Lucy's daughter," he said. "Lucy is a dear friend of mine. Anything I can do to help her and her family would be my pleasure."

She narrowed her eyes. "A dear friend, hmm?" she

purred.

A smile touched his lips, but he decided not to elaborate on that. If she wanted to know more about him or his relationship with Lucy, he would be happy to tell her... in due time.

She folded one leg over the other, and the movement distracted James. She was pretty, limber and fast, and when his eyes shot up again to meet hers, he was fairly sure that she had noticed him watching her.

But she just smiled at him, and she didn't seem to mind.

James cleared his throat and scanned the area. A couple of squirrels scurried up a tree trunk nearby, their bushy tails bobbing up and down. Birds flew overhead, squawking loudly at one another.

"So," he said. "If you've been out here for that long, why did you start going after Corinne's chickens only recently?" He turned his gaze back to her, keeping her pinned with it. "I mean, it would stand to reason that you would've gone after them a long time ago, right?"

That question seemed to unsettle her a little. She shifted her weight on the log, but she said nothing.

"Any reason?" he pressed on. "Maybe your other food sources ran out?"

She shook her head, apprehension in her posture

again. "I don't like to talk about it," she said.

"I can't help you if you don't," he said.

She shot him a look, and her skittishness returned in force. Her toned body was coiled up, ready to bolt again.

"It's... It's not because of you," she said. "But..."

Loud chatter came from behind, interrupting the fox girl, and James whirled on his feet.

It was just one of the squirrels, chasing the other up a tree in some kind of forest critter game.

James chortled before turning back to Kesha.

But the log she had sat on was empty now. The only trace of her passage deeper into the forest was the slight trembling of a branch she had touched while running off.

She's a skittish one, James thought as he peered through the branches and the foliage.

For a moment, he considered giving chase again, but he did not want to scare her off. After all, the first contact had been made now, and she probably wouldn't recoil as she had before when they ran into each other again.

It would probably take some time to build up a relationship with her, but he was certain that running after her would now be detrimental to that desire.

With a shrug, he let her go for now, picking up his axe and backpack before getting back to work.

Chapter 3

After a long day of satisfying work, James returned to his cabin.

He had managed to cut several trees, building up on his stockpile of lumber for his project. In addition, he had dragged every one of those logs to the cabin.

He still needed to finish clearing and leveling ground for the actual construction, but it was good to have stockpiled some of the resources he would need.

After arranging everything and covering the logs with a piece of tarp — it was unlikely to rain, but he wasn't going to take any chances — he headed over to the nearby creek, shrugged off his clothes, and washed himself.

He was feeling quite good about the day's work, and he enjoyed the fresh, cool water on his skin. As he scrubbed himself clean of sweat and grime, he reflected on Kesha.

He was glad that they had gotten along despite their rough start; it would be nice to speak with her more often. As a denizen of the forest, he expected she had knowledge about the magical nature of Tour and the surrounding woods.

And maybe in time, they could become friends — even more, preferably.

When James finished his bath, he toweled himself off and returned to the cabin. The griminess that resulted from a hard day's work had now gone and made place for that satisfied sensation of slight fatigue after a pleasant bath at the end of the day.

He felt even better when he found Sara on the porch in front of the cabin.

The cat girl was on hands and knees and had not seen

him coming. She was busy — focused on the wooden floor of the porch.

She wore a tight skirt that would've been short even standing up, but now that she was on all fours, it had hitched up to reveal a cute pair of striped panties. The fluffy tail going back and forth — almost hovering over her — completed the picture.

Smile on his lips, James walked over to her to see what she was doing.

She was so engrossed in her activity that the normally very perceptive cat girl still didn't see him coming. That gave them a chance to peek over her shoulder.

A terrified squirrel was looking up at her from between the floorboards.

A soft meow came from Sara's mouth as she cocked her head, left ear twitching, and tried to wriggle a few fingers in between the floorboards.

"That poor thing," James said.

Sara almost jumped a foot in the air, then looked over her shoulder, still on all fours, and smiled. "James!" she said. "I was just, uh..."

"Getting dinner?" he suggested.

She laughed. "No, silly," she said. "Of course not! I wouldn't eat a squirrel... It's more for playing, I suppose?"

"I don't think the scroll enjoys the game," James said.

A wicked grin surfaced on her lips. "Well, then it should have stayed away from our cabin, shouldn't it?"

James laughed. "You are ruthless," he said, leaning forward to give her a pat on her shapely butt. "Ruthless and delicious. I've been looking forward to seeing you all day."

She gave a naughty smile before she rose to her feet, further ignoring the squirrel — to the little rodent's great relief.

"I've missed you too," she said. "Are you still planning to head out to the city tomorrow?"

That made James's expression drop a little. A nice day in the forest had made him forget all about the meeting with his father's attorney and his brother about winding up his father's inheritance.

The prospect of leaving Tour wasn't a very nice one; he enjoyed himself here, and a return to the city — however short — was as if he were interrupting the pleasant enchantment he had submerged himself in.

But there was other stuff he had to take care of as well. Things he had to make sure that were in order before he could take up permanent residence at the cabin.

Sara cocked her head slightly as she studied him, her

left ear giving a single twitch. "You're not looking forward to it, are you?" she asked.

"Not really," James said. "But what needs to be done needs to be done."

She smiled and stepped forward, placing a slender hand on his shoulder. "Why don't you try to think of it this way?" she said. "You came to Tour — to me — to escape that life in the city that you no longer wanted, right?"

He nodded. "Yeah," he said. "That's right."

"Well then," she continued. "Let this little trip to the city be a reminder of the reasons you left. Wouldn't that be a good idea? You go down there once again to see and to confirm that you made the right choice by coming here?"

He smiled, stepping forward to take her up in his arms. The moment he enclosed her in his embrace, a low purr rose from the base of her throat.

"I'm already one hundred percent sure I made the right choice by coming here," he said. "I don't need to be reminded of my past life to enjoy the present one."

He dipped his hand to her round bottom and gave it a squeeze, winning a little yelp from her.

"Besides," he added, his voice turning a little husky. "I'd much rather spend my time here with you."

She pushed herself up against him and gave a little wiggle of her delicious body as she fixed him with her gaze, a naughty light burning in her yellow eyes.

"You can do both," she crooned, her slender fingers raking through his hair. "We have the entire night to ourselves…"

He smiled and leaned in for a kiss, and the full and wet lips of the perfect cat girl met his, surrendering to the kind of passionate kiss that only lovers could share.

Chapter 4

James could hardly keep his hands off Sara as she cooked them dinner.

She purred her pleasure at his attention, playfully swatting away his hands when he distracted her from her work.

But as he stood behind her, his body pressed against hers, her tail curled around his leg, she slowly began to cave. She pushed out her bum, grinding it on his growing erection.

She giggled as his hand slipped under her skirt to give that bouncy rump a squeeze.

"James!" she protested playfully. "I'm trying to make us dinner!"

"I know what I want to have for dinner, baby," he whispered in her ear as he gave her a playful push with his pelvis, pinning her against the kitchen counter.

She bit her lip. "James," she purred. "You're so bad!"

Maybe that was so, but he could hardly help himself.

One of his hands roamed over her rump, still wrapped in the tight fabric of her skirt, while the other cupped one of her big breasts, his fingers exploring her stiff nipples poking against the fabric.

"Hmm," she hummed. "If you're not going to stop soon, this is going to get out of hand, baby."

"I want it to get out of hand," he said, rolling her nipple between his thumb and index finger.

She bit her lip. "Oh, that's good. That's... Ah, that's *so* good."

He kissed the gentle slope of her neck, tasting the slightly wild flavor of his cat girl familiar as she let her head hang, surrendering herself to him.

He curled his fingers under the hem of her skirt

before pulling the garment up. She gave a satisfied moan as she reached around and placed her soft hand on his crotch, caressing his erection through the fabric of his pants.

"Hmm, baby," she murmured. "I can't cook with this distracting me."

He chuckled. "Then we should probably take care of it, hmm?"

With that, James unzipped his jeans and slid them and his underwear down with one swift motion. His cock sprang forth, thick and hard, a bead of precum forming on the tip.

Sara looked at it over her shoulder, her yellow eyes wide.

"By the Elements," she breathed. "You'd think it's been neglected for years…"

He grinned as she playfully swayed left and right, making his cock slide over the soft fabric of her striped panties.

She wasn't wrong; they'd been having sex multiple times per day, but both of them were constantly lusting for more, unable to keep their hands off each other.

"Hmm, baby," Sara purred as she reached around again to grip his firm shaft, letting it slip between her butt cheeks, the tip pointing up. She gave him a naughty look over her shoulder. "I like the way it rubs up against my butt."

"It's even better when you're not wearing panties," he muttered, captivated by the sight of his firm cock in her dainty hand, pressed up against her striped panties.

As he spoke, he pulled down the collar of her shirt, making her ample breasts spilled out. He kneaded the warm flesh, and Sara moaned with delight at his slightly rough touch, once again pushing her butt out.

"Take them off, baby," she hummed. "Take them off for me, please."

His hungry hand slipped under the waistband of the cute panties and pulled them down, revealing Sara's round ass.

She pushed it up and out for him, standing on her tippy toes and giving him an eyeful of her pink, glistening pussy as well.

"You're beautiful," he muttered as he took in the delicious sight.

"Baby," she purred. "What about... What about the cooking?"

"Fuck the cooking," he grunted as he wiped the kitchen counter clean.

Pots, plates, and utensils clattered into the sink, and Sara laughed as he picked her up, flipped her around, and parked her pretty ass on the kitchen counter. Then he stepped forward, grabbed his firm shaft, and pressed it against her hot womanhood.

"Oh, James!" she purred, pushing her hips out. "Oh, by the Elements! I like it when you do that... Hm... Don't stop."

With a grunt of satisfaction, he complied, taking his cock in his hand and rubbing the swollen tip over her plump pussy lips, spreading the little bead of precum all over her tight pink pussy.

She mewled her pleasure as she reached down with one hand to part her lips and reveal her swollen nub.

James bit his lip hard as he let the tip of his cock slip up her tight pussy until it touched her clit.

Sara moaned with delight at the touch, throwing her head back, and he began rubbing little circles around her clit with the tip of his cock, his own arousal rising at the sight of his woman in heat.

His balls tightened up as he rubbed her sensitive nub, pressing his cock against her tight pussy. Sara pushed out her rump to meet him, giving him a view of her pretty butt as she arched her back to give him clear access to her glistening pussy.

"James!" she whimpered as he began rubbing faster. "Please, baby! Make me come!"

He gritted his teeth as he increased his pace, rubbing the tip of his cock harder against her little nub, feeling the heat and wetness emanate from her ready pussy.

Sara's body tensed, and in the moment that presaged her orgasm, her yellow eyes found James.

She bit her lip, then gave the cutest meow as her eyes rolled back and her tongue escaped her parted lips. A rush of heat flushed through her body as she came.

Seeing her like this gave James a sweet and silky sensation that made his entire being tingle, his knees almost buckling under his need to plow into her and make her his once more.

But he held himself in check, his breathing coming in short, quick bursts as he waited for her pleasure to subside, kissing her full breasts and licking the fresh sweat from her soft neck.

"Oh, baby," she moaned. "Put it in me, please! I want your love inside me. I want it to fill me up."

He did not need to hear that twice.

With a grunt of desire, he pushed up against her, ready to claim his cat girl once more...

James's hand slipped under Sara's skirt and hitched it all the way up to her waist.

She purred her delight, her nails raking his back. With a hiss of pleasure, he lined up his rock-hard cock with her dripping pussy.

He pushed hard, parting her walls — still tight from her orgasm — to invade her delicious womanhood. She purred and gasped and mewled as he sunk in one inch at a time.

Her legs curled around him, clamped him down, and her nails drew furrows down his back.

But that slight sensation of pain only heightened his pleasure. And as he sank in balls deep, Sara let out a growl, hugged him closer, and her cute canines nipped at his neck.

"Fuck me," she gasped in between nibbling at him. "By the Elements, fuck me good, James!"

She purred her delight as he pounded her hard, his hands cupping her full breasts. A soft cry escaped her, her fuzzy ears folding back as he squeezed those big tits while pushing against her cervix.

Her pussy clamped on his cock, her nails clawing at his back as his balls tightened. A grunt of pleasure came from his throat every time he slammed into her, their sweaty skin slapping together as he took her on the kitchen counter.

And as he rammed harder and deeper, she arched her back, pushing her delicious body against him, making him feel her soft breasts against his chest.

"Cum in me, James," she whispered. "I want to have your seed inside me."

He groaned at the thought of filling her tight pussy with his hot cum. And as he fucked her with all his might, his balls drew up, preparing for his climax.

"Fuck, baby…" he muttered. "I'm gonna cum."

"Yes," she hissed, surrendering to her delight, eyes squeezed shut. "I want you to fill me up and breed me. I'm yours, baby! Give it all to me!"

James bit his lip as pleasure gathered. He pushed as deep inside her as she could handle, winning a deep moan of delight from the delicious cat girl.

On the next thrust, James gasped for air as a warm rope of seed spurted from his throbbing cock, filling the cat girl's delicious, wet pussy — just like she wanted him to.

"Fuck," James groaned. "I'm cumming."

"Yes," she moaned. "Cum for me, baby."

He pulled her close, their lips meeting as they kissed passionately. Their tongues met, swirling around as he slammed into her again, filling her up with his seed.

He gave her a final thrust, and the intensity of his last wave rocked his world as more cum pulsed from his cock and flooded Sara's pussy, making her arch her back with another loud moan of pure joy as she clamped her legs around him.

His breath came hard as he gave a final sigh of delight.

"That was amazing," he managed to utter in between pants of pleasure.

Sara licked her lips and leaned back on the counter with a contented smile. "Exactly what I needed," she said, her voice husky.

He chuckled and placed a warm kiss on her neck.

"I could do this all day," he murmured as he reached up to wipe the sweat from his brow.

She giggled, squeezing her thighs while he was still inside her, winning another grunt of pleasure from him.

"So could I," she said, her voice teasing.

Then her gaze shot to the mess on the kitchen counter. "We'd probably starve if we did, though," she added.

James laughed. "A good way to go, if you ask me."

She laughed along with him as she relaxed the grip of her shapely legs and leaned back against the wall.

"Hm-hm," she agreed, then gave him a playful poke

with her finger. "Now get out of the kitchen," she said. "Let me finish the meal!"

He laughed, gave her another kiss on her soft cheek and pulled out, some of his seed already running down her thick thighs. He rolled his shoulders as he walked back to the couch in the living room and slumped in it.

Sara gave him a naughty look before she continued cooking.

To his great pleasure, she finished the job naked.

He knew that a delicious meal lay ahead, followed by some quality time cuddling on the couch together. After that, they would probably find themselves tempted to have another roll in the hay.

He sat back and relaxed, watching his love cook them a meal, all thoughts of going to the city tomorrow forgotten for now.

Chapter 5

The sun was setting over Lake Erie when James pulled his busted-up sedan into a parking lot on the north side of Cleveland.

He wrinkled his nose at the air — it was far from as crisp as in Tour — before he walked across a small bridge to an open grassy park with a large fountain in the center and rows of tall trees lining the perimeter.

A group of young kids played basketball at one end while several people sat on benches chatting and reading. A couple of dogs chased each other around the periphery of the park. The smell of food wafted from a nearby restaurant, where he could see families enjoying their meals.

The sensations were a little overwhelming after his time in the country, and it was strange to come back here.

He had been in Tour for only a week, but his life had completely changed.

For the better.

Smile on his lips, James made his way to the lawyer's office. As expected, a secretary told him the lawyer was running late for their meeting. She parked him in the waiting room while she went off to fetch a drink for him.

As he waited, an unreal sensation crept up on him.

All these people, he thought. *They have no idea about magic and dragons. Most don't believe in it, and those who do are most likely considered more than a little weird...*

He looked down at his fingertips.

But there is *magic in these,* he thought.

He could cast spells just by focusing his intent and speaking the words of power gleaned from... well, from ancestral memories. It wasn't like having a wand or staff. It was within him.

In his Bloodline.

Sara had been the one to teach him how to use magic. How to summon and control his power. Thinking of his cat girl beauty made him want to go back to the cabin as soon as possible.

But first I have to sort out this inheritance, he thought.

"Mr. Beckett?" the secretary said, interrupting his train of thought. "Mr. Craney will see you in a minute. Please follow me."

With a smile, James followed the woman through the glass doors.

The meeting room was small and sparsely but tastefully furnished. There was a table with six chairs, all wooden. The walls were bare except for some framed diplomas. The place brought a smile to his lips. Just a few days ago, he'd been here with the attorney, his brother, and his sister-in-law.

At the beginning of what would be a grand adventure...

At the indication of the secretary, James sat down at the table. She poured him a glass of water, and he politely declined her offer of coffee.

He took a sip of water and leaned forward, placing

both elbows on the polished wood surface.

When Mr. Craney entered, James rose from his seat. His smile faltered when he saw his two cousins and brother enter as the attorney held open the door.

James and his brother weren't exactly friends, but his cousins... His cousins hated James. And the feeling had grown mutual over the years.

And judging by their shit-eating grins, this wasn't looking good for James.

Craney gestured at the empty chairs, and everyone sat down. His cousins gave James smug nods as a greeting. James's brother just looked bored.

After they all settled in, the attorney cleared his throat. "Good day, everyone," he began. "First, let me welcome you all to my office. I apologize for the delay."

He paused for a moment to gather his thoughts. "Let's begin."

He nodded at the cousins. "My name is Charles Craney. I was your uncle's attorney, and today we are going to discuss the final aspects of the estate of Thomas Beckett."

At this point, my eyebrows were up.

"Discuss?" I asked. "As far as I know, I just need to sign for the cabin, right?"

The attorney cleared his throat. He adjusted his

glasses and continued. "Yes. But there are certain matters that need to be discussed as well."

He glanced at the four men in turn.

James frowned. Something was wrong. This wasn't right.

The attorney reached into a folder and withdrew a leather bound file. With a flourish, he placed it on the table. Then he flipped to the front page and removed a stack of papers from inside.

James picked them up. They were all legal documents.

"I am sorry, but I don't understand," James said. "What is the purpose of this meeting?"

His oldest cousin, Brad, spoke up. "Well, James, it seems our dear old Uncle Tom left us quite a mess."

"Things looked well enough to me," James said. "I mean, everything was in good shape when we discussed things a few days ago. Why would they be a mess now?"

Brad just smiled.

He was the biggest of James's cousins. And the meanest. A sparse mop of hair topped his head, while a pair of greedy eyes peered out from under bushy eyebrows. He was always trying to get something for nothing.

"It seems your father had some financial issues," the attorney explained.

James frowned. For all his faults, James's father had worked hard every day of his life. Money problems seemed unlikely.

Then again, money problems are also easy to come by...

"It appears your father lost money on poor investments," Craney continues. "There is also pending litigation against one of the companies he controlled. The other shareholders advise to settle. I would recommend the estate join in on the settlement. It doesn't look good."

"I'm sorry?" James said. "How much debt?"

The attorney cleared his throat. "Counting the settlement?"

James nodded.

"Uhm, I'm listing a four-hundred-and-forty-thousand-dollar debt," the attorney said. "About half of which is the settlement amount."

"That's a lot of money..." James muttered.

And it was... But by no means did it exceed the money his father had left behind, most of which had gone to James's brother and his cousins.

James's gaze swiveled over to his cousins. "Well," he said. "There should be enough to pay for all that, right?"

The attorney cleared his throat. "There is, but it would need to be settled with the remainder of the money to be distributed," he said. "You, uh, wouldn't stand to receive anything beside the cabin. You..."

"That's fine," James said.

All jaws at the table dropped at the same time.

"You... you are all right with that?" Mr. Craney stuttered.

"Yeah," James said.

The confusion at the table endured. His brother, normally so icy, showed a confounded expression that made him look almost like a cartoon character.

His cousins seemed wary, exchanging worried glances.

James laughed. He couldn't help it — couldn't keep it in. He saw what this was about now. They all expected he would get angry, money-hungry. They'd expected James would turn greedy and try to claim more for himself and try to get the others to carry the debt.

Like they would do if the tables were turned.

And then they would team up on him as they used to do when he was a boy. They would try to bully him or — if he persisted — make it as hard for him as possible to get more money out of this whole mess.

But James understood now that he differed from them.

He always had... But his time in Tour had brought out the differences even more.

He looked at each of them in turn.

"I don't care about money," he finally said. "I never did... But do you know what I *would* have liked?"

The others looked at him, still unable to speak.

A big drop of sweat formed on Craney's shining forehead.

"I would have liked it if you all cared a little bit more about dad and not just kissed his ass for money. I would have liked it if we had been an actual family."

Brad swallowed, his gaze darting left and right. James's other cousin and brother looked down at the table, unable to meet James's eyes.

"But that ship has sailed, hasn't it?" James asked, not expecting an answer.

And he didn't get any; the silence endured.

That was fine. James couldn't spare the time for their nonsense anyway. He had other stuff to take care of before he could leave the city again.

"So," James finally said, his voice growing louder as he turned to Craney. "Let's sign those papers and get this over with. I'm pretty eager to return home — to the people who actually *are* my family..."

James's old landlord gave him an easy time as James handed back the lease of his old apartment. The apartment had a few more scuffs and scrapes, but the old man had always been friendly to James. He was just a guy trying to make it in the city.

After James returned the keys, they exchanged farewells and shook hands.

"It was a pleasure, Mr. Beckett."

"Same here, Mr. Parnell."

With a nod, James walked away from the building, headed toward the parking lot where he had parked his old sedan. There was one more stop before he would return to Tour.

James got in, and the engine turned over on the second try. He drove southeasterly until he came to the sorting facility where he'd spent most of his days since dropping out of college.

He walked up to the building, pushed the door open, and headed on inside.

As usual, Derek was riding the guys. James watched

from the doorway as the overbearing man prowled around. He gave James's hard-working, soon-to-be-former colleagues a hard time whenever he caught them listening to music or their favorite audiobooks to make the work more bearable.

A workplace tyrant... There were probably thousands like him all across America.

Derek stopped when he saw James standing in the doorway. The man's face took on a mean aspect.

"Well, well, Mr. Beckett!" he exclaimed, making everyone look up to the exchange. "How good of you to finally join us!"

"Hello, Derek," James said.

Derek's expression turned to a scowl. "Don't you 'hello, Derek' me, you damn deadbeat. You were supposed to come in yesterday."

James took a few steps forward, and something in the way he moved must've ticked Derek off, because the man inched back.

Their colleagues all looked up.

James shook his head. "I called in my absence with HR," he said.

"Yeah? Well, they didn't tell me."

"Not my problem," James said, taking a few more steps forward. "And don't call me a deadbeat, Derek.

All you do around here is strut around like a peacock, trying to keep anyone from actually enjoying their job."

A few chuckles broke out around the sorting room. Derek's face turned red.

James noticed several of his co-workers had pulled their out their earbuds to observe the exchange.

"What the hell did you just say to me?" Derek demanded.

"I said you're a lazy prick, Derek. A petty excuse of a man."

Laughter. Someone in the back actually whooped. Derek whipped around, glaring, but he couldn't see the culprit. He turned back to James, a nasty grin on his face.

"For that, Beckett, I'm firing your ass. You're out, asshole."

Derek crossed his arms, satisfied, not knowing that this was the result James had hoped for.

"Good," James said, fishing his access card out of his back pocket. "Saves me the effort of handing in my notice and looking at your ugly face for thirty more days."

And with that, James flipped him off.

Unrestrained cheers broke out throughout the room.

"Woo-hoo, James!" someone shouted.

"Yeah, James!"

"You tell him, brother!"

With a big grin, James waved to his coworkers, hoping the exchange would give them the courage to stand up to workplace bullies like Derek, too.

Then he strode over to his desk and grabbed his stuff before heading for the exit.

The last thing he saw as he passed was Derek turning on his heel and stalking over to the group of workers. But the expressions that met Derek's fury were a little more defiant this time, as if everyone had realized that Derek couldn't fire them all at once.

James left the old sorting center with the biggest smile.

He had been looking forward to this moment. Ever since he decided he would stay at the cabin, he'd fantasized about it. He hoped the guys would find inspiration in his defiance and put Derek in his place. Surely, the job wouldn't be too bad for them if the manager wasn't such as ass.

But James was off to greener pastures.

He stepped outside into the bright sunshine and took a deep breath. The longing for his cabin, his companions, and the forest simmered deep within. He couldn't wait to be back. There wasn't much left for him to do here, so he ambled over to his car with his chin up.

Life was good.

James got in, started the engine, and backed out of the lot, headed back home, a smile on his face.

Chapter 6

For the third time in his life, James crossed the boundary into Tour County.

The first time had been with his father on their hunting trip — one of the few times the two of them had bonded. The second time had been a few days ago, when he was on his way to the cabin after becoming its owner.

On both occasions, crossing into Tour had been an exhilarating experience.

He rolled down the window to experience the freshness of the air, which was like a cleansing, as if it washed away the clinging odors from his body and mind. He took in the colors — brighter, more vibrant — and reveled at the transition.

And now that his magical talent had been awakened, James could sense it even better: Tour was different from any other town. As if it had a spirit of its own.

And then there were its inhabitants. No men lived in the village, only women, and the forest offered a home to sprightly and magical creatures, the cat girl Sara not the least among them.

Then there was Astra the Dragonkin, standoffish and fierce, but she was also curious about James. After all, he turned out to be the first High Mage in these parts in many decades.

And finally Kesha, the shy and wild fox girl whom he was just getting to know better...

Despite having just seen her, James wanted to meet her and speak to her again. He liked her — a lot. The wild aspect made her more charming, and as a Fae, she might teach him some useful things relating to magic.

A smile formed on James's lips as Tour dawned

ahead among the trees. He drove past Rovary's Lot and into the quiet town. Only a few people were out and about on Main Street. They were people James hadn't met yet.

Something I should remedy, James thought.

The general store was still open, even though it was getting pretty late. James had promised Sara he'd be home tonight, but he wanted to see Lucy as well, so he decided to stop by and see how she was doing.

He pulled into the lot next to the general store and killed the engine. He already saw movement behind the windows — probably Lucy cleaning up.

James stepped out of the car and into the balmy air of early evening, fresh and alive with the pines and the last hints of summer. He took a deep breath, letting his lungs fill with the wholesome air of the forest.

He glanced up at a deepening sky. The sun would set in about an hour or two. After that, nature would serve up a perfect night sky full of stars.

He headed over to the store. The bell chimed as he pushed the door open.

When Lucy looked up at him, he could see the lines of weariness. Still, a broad smile appeared.

"James!" she exclaimed. "This is a nice surprise!"

"Yeah," James said, pulling the door shut behind

him. "I just came back from the city, and I felt like seeing you."

"Hmm," she hummed. "Good! You were on my mind all day. Do you mind turning the sign on the door around? I'm closing up. Especially now that you're here."

He nodded and flipped the sign around so that the word 'closed' faced outward. "Kinda late, huh?"

She wiped her hands on a cloth and sighed. "It is."

He walked over to her, and she leaned forward on the counter giving him a peek down her bright red tank top with the words 'Lucy's Deals' written on it in fading print.

James gave her a kiss on her soft cheek, relishing in the sweet scent of her. There was a slight hint of her lavender perfume.

"So," he said. "What's bothering you?"

She gave a tired smile. "That obvious, huh?"

He laughed. "Hm... you look like you need an evening by the warm fire. What do you say I help you clean up here and you drive up to the cabin with me? Sara and I will cook you up something nice. We'll open a bottle of wine, and we'll relax. You can tell me all about your day."

"Oooh," she sighed, a measure of relaxation finally

seeping into her big blue eyes. "That sounds like heaven."

He gave her another peck on the cheek and nodded at the broom in the corner. "Hand that one to me, then. We'll hop to it; it'll only take a second if we do it together."

Doing the work together was fun. Lucy cranked up the music as James swept and mopped the floor. She sang well, her rich voice obviously practiced.

And when she swept past him, holding a crate filled with dry wares, he gave her shapely rump a pinch.

"No fair," she laughed. "I have my hands full!"

"In that case..." James said, lifting her skirt to take a peek at her lace panties.

"James!" she exclaimed, laughing, and she leaned into his hand so that he cupped a full cheek in his palm. "We'll never get the work done like this!"

He smiled and released his grip from her butt to finish the rest of the work. "I can't help it," he said. "You're a walking distraction."

"Should I go into another room?" she teased.

He poked her rump with the broomstick. "And let me do all the work?"

She yelped and laughed, skipping along to get back to her work.

After half an hour, the shop was spotless, and Lucy put away everything neatly before locking up for the night. When she was finished, she took a deep breath. Her shoulders relaxed, and she stretched.

She already looked a lot better and more relaxed than she had when he came in.

"Ready to head out?" James asked. "If we're quick, we might catch the sunset over the forest at the cabin after dinner."

She smiled and attached herself to his arm. "That sounds perfect!"

He grinned and kissed her as he pulled her along. "All right, let's head out!"

Chapter 7

James and Lucy drove up to the cabin together, passing by Corinne's barn on the way. There was no light burning this time, so James drove on. He would link up with the redhead later.

Lucy sat beside him as he drove, the window on her side cracked open to let in the balmy evening breeze.

The trees stood dark against the deepening sky, and

in an hour or so, the world would turn to rosy pink as the sun would set over the canopy.

They could both feel the magic radiating from Tour — the forest seemed more alive. Lucy's hand lay soft on James's thigh as they enjoyed the drive together.

James drove slowly through the forest, his heart beating faster as the cabin drew closer. The trees grew thick as he turned onto the trail that led to his cabin, their branches interlocking overhead, like nature's own network — everything connected and alive.

The car shook and jostled on the rutted trail, and James supposed he'd need to get a vehicle with some off-road capability in time, once he got the money for it.

He would do that even if his High Magic would let him *fly*; he loved driving. It was something he wouldn't give up.

As they neared the cabin, the trees thinned and gave way to a clearing. James parked in front of the cabin. A cozy firelight peeked out from between the boards of the shutters.

No place like home, James thought.

The door creaked when he pushed it open, and the rich fragrance of the forest hit him. He walked over to the passenger side and opened the door for Lucy.

"Welcome to the palace," he joked. "Shall we,

madam?"

She hopped out with a chuckle and hooked her arm through his.

Together, they walked up to the front door.

The cabin was simple: a single story wooden structure with a small porch. It stood slightly elevated, and the cellar beneath it was large and with stone walls.

It was almost as if it had been built on ancient stone foundations...

That was a mystery James hadn't discussed with Sara yet, and one he was eager to explore soon. He hadn't even seen the total expanse of the cellar.

Lucy's radiant smile blasted the thoughts from his mind. He gestured for her to enter as he pulled open the door. As they went inside, the delicious aroma of freshly cut herbs and vegetables tempted James's senses, causing his stomach to rumble loudly.

It was dinnertime.

Sara wore an apron that was a size too small. It hugged her tight body, and her little dress underneath was short, almost revealing the undercurves of her perfect ass. She'd cut a hole in it for her tail.

When James and Lucy entered, the cat girl pivoted with a broad grin that flashed her cute canines, but James's eyes were drawn to Sara's apron.

It read: 'eat the cook.'

James broke out laughing, and Lucy followed the moment she saw it, too.

"What!?" Sara said, big grin still on her plump lips.

It took a few moments before James recovered and could answer. "Where did you even get that?" he exclaimed, suppressing another bout of laughter as he wiped tears from his eyes.

The way she stood there, a big spoon in one hand, her plump body wrapped in that crazy apron, big yellow eyes fixed on him, was just too cute.

"I made it myself!" she said.

"You made it!?" James said. "That's amazing!"

"It's a spell," Sara said. "A simple one."

Lucy covered her mouth with her hands. "You know a spell to make *clothes*? God, I wish I could cast spells like that! Imagine how much easier life would be."

Sara chuckled as she smiled. "You have us," she said. "We can cast them for you."

Lucy smiled, then walked over to Sara to greet her with a hug. "That's so sweet of you," she said.

"Hm," James agreed, following Lucy. "I'd have to learn the spell first, though."

After James gave Sara a kiss on her soft cheek, he looked around. The cabin was nice and cozy, lit by a fire that crackled and popped in the hearth. A pot of pumpkin soup bubbled happily on the stovetop, filling the air with its savory scent.

"That smells delicious," James said, moving in to pat the cat girl on her round butt as he lifted a bottle of red from the countertop.

Sara giggled, her left ear giving its signature twitch as her tail found and brushed his leg.

"Thank you," she purred. "It's simple but filling. I baked fresh rolls earlier today to go with it!"

James kissed the tips of his fingers. "Perfect," he said, then took three glasses from the small cabinet above the stove.

"Go sit," Sara said, shooing them both away from the stovetop. "I'll serve you your soup when it's ready."

James took Lucy by her soft hand and led her to the couch and the armchair at the low table near the fireplace. She sat down on the couch and watched him with her big blue eyes as he poured three glasses of wine.

With a sigh, the blonde MILF leaned against the

backrest. "You were right, James," she purred. "This is just what I need."

He smiled, shooting her a glance from across the table. "And it's Saturday tomorrow," he said. "How about you spend the night here and open up a little later?"

She laughed. "Well, Mrs. Truncey is always there at eight," she said. "I don't want her to shuffle all the way to the store for nothing."

James nodded. "Fair enough. Tell you what: I'll get up with you early tomorrow morning and drive you down to the store, okay?"

She touched his arm and smiled. "That's sweet of you! Deal!"

He flopped down on the couch next to her and placed his hand on her thigh as he studied Sara's shapely backside while the cat girl stirred the soup with gusto. "Well, I might have an ulterior motive," James said.

Lucy laughed, folding one leg over another as she took a sip from her wine.

Sara began ladling the soup into bowls. A moment later she served up the delicacy with freshly baked rolls. The armchair was free, but Sara preferred to sit on the rug.

They dug in, each of them hungry after a hard day's

work. The soup was rich in taste, nice and chunky, and the fresh rolls were enriched with herbs — no doubt from Corinne's farm — which made them delicious even without the full butter Sara served with them.

They ate in silence for a while until James's mind went back to the cabin's seemingly ancient stone foundation. He turned his eyes to Sara. "Sara," he said. "I have a question."

She looked up at him from her spot on the rug, yellow eyes wide as she chewed on a piece of bread. "Sure!" she said around a mouthful.

"Was there a building in this place before the cabin?"

She blinked. "Why?"

Lucy leaned in as well.

"Well," James said. "These foundations look really old."

Sara nodded. "They are!"

James grinned. "I was wondering if they might not be older than the cabin itself?"

She nodded vigorously. "They are," she said. "I've... Well, it's something we'll need to talk about. But yes, they're definitely older than the cabin. As you know, there is magic in Tour. I don't understand much of it... but your predecessor did."

James perked an eyebrow. "Predecessor?"

She nodded. "Hm-hm," she said. "Another High Mage used to live here. But... well..." She shook her head. "We should talk about it some other time. Soon, I promise."

It was plain to see she struggled to recall it, perhaps because the memories were hazy, but James understood they may be painful as well. He was curious — very much so, in fact — but he knew Sara well enough to understand that she'd come around to telling him on her own terms when she was ready.

He took another sip of his wine, then gave her a kiss on her head and leaned back against the couch, scratching Sara behind her ear as he did so. A low purr came from the cat girl.

"So," he said. "What do you girls say to this: we take dessert, something to drink, and a few blankets with us, and we head out into the woods to watch the sunset?"

"That's a great idea!" Lucy chimed in.

Sara nodded as well. "That sounds lovely," she said. "But we should bring a flashlight, too, for the way back."

James gave her a wink. "Great!" he said. "Come on. An evening stroll will do us good."

Chapter 8

It took only a few minutes to get the things together and put on a pair of sturdy boots. The girls weren't really dressed for a long walk, but James knew a glade nearby — at the brook he got his water from.

With a beautiful woman on each arm, James strolled out of the cabin and into the darkening sky. The rosy glow was setting in, and they'd have to hurry if they wanted to catch it all.

A deep breath of forest air revived him, and part of him so thoroughly enjoyed the simple things here: just being able to walk out into nature, no one jostling him or bothering as he went his hurried way down busy streets, and being able to leave his door unlocked, knowing that his belongings — admittedly meager — were safe.

The girls giggled as he pulled them along under the rosy glow. They had to jump to cross the brook. James took the leap first, catching the women as they hopped from one side to the other, holding them a little longer than necessary after he caught them.

And they did not mind.

As they strolled among the trees of ages, James sensed more and more like a being of the forest, a spirit full of life and laughter, far removed from the humdrum of his past.

The glade opened up before them. Lush and green, it was almost as if nature had engineered it just for their enjoyment.

Sara stepped forward first, and James studied her hourglass figure with profound joy.

She stepped lightly, almost on her tippy toes, and something in her posture betrayed that she was of the wild — that she belonged here.

Lucy was less graceful and nimble, but James found joy in how she clung to him for guidance, her full figure pressed against his. He led her into the glade as Sara straightened herself at the center of the clearing, her cat ears straight and up.

"It's a lively night," Sara purred. "Many creatures are out."

Lucy looked around as if monsters might come jumping out at any moment. "Dangerous creatures?" she ventured.

"No," Sara whispered. "Curious creatures."

Lucy gave a relieved sigh, and James patted her on her butt before he unfolded the blankets they'd brought.

"This is such a perfect place," Lucy said. "I've lived here most of my life and there is still so much I've never seen before."

Sara looked over her shoulder, and the way the darkening world lit up her yellow eyes was nothing short of breathtaking.

"The woods around Tour are magical," she said. "They change, too... From time to time."

"Change?" James asked, eyebrow perked as he straightened out the blanket for them to sit on. "How do you mean?"

"Well," Sara said, then brought her finger to her lips to consider her words. "There are things out here that are not of this world, because this place is connected... to other places. And sometimes, those things shimmer through. It is as if they cast shadows in our world."

"That sounds kinda scary," Lucy said, once again checking the surrounding trees.

"It's okay," Sara said, and her smile was infectious. "You don't have to be afraid of the shadows. Most things out here are good. And if they are not..." She gave an almost predatory grin. "Well, we'll be able to handle them."

James laughed at that. He had little doubt Sara could handle herself if anything came up. "Well, let's just enjoy the sunset as it is. I'm sure we'll be fine."

Still, he remembered the stones that had appeared at Rovary's Lot on the first day he got to work chopping wood for Lucy. They hadn't been there before — at least, Lucy had never seen them, even though it was her lot. And she hadn't seen them again after.

He remembered, too, the vision he'd had there — running through the forest, being hunted, while a woman called out to him. It seemed to him now that it had been an ancestral memory, just like the ones that triggered his knowledge of magic.

But the woman's voice in that vision had been so similar to Sara's.

As he sat down on the blanket, his eyes roamed over Sara once more. There was still much mystery about her — still many questions left unanswered.

They sat down at the heart of the clearing, and Lucy reached for his hand as she graciously folded her legs under her.

"I want to thank you," she said, looking up at him. "Ever since I met you, I've been feeling a lot better about everything. Your optimism..." She smiled. "Well, it's infectious. I find myself waking up brighter and happier since we met."

Her lips trembled as she spoke, and James couldn't help but be touched by her words. He smiled at her in return, grateful for this moment.

"I'm happy to hear that, Lucy," he said. "It's the same with me. Life has gotten so much more meaning since I came to Tour and met you." He winked at Sara. "And Sara, of course. And Corinne."

Sara joined in with a gentle touch on Lucy's thigh as she leaned against James. The cat girl's soft fur tail stroked his lower back.

"I'm happy with both of you, too," she purred. "You're bringing life and excitement to this place. I haven't felt so rooted in this world for a long time."

The three of them were silent for a while, taking in the forest's beauty around them.

Overhead, a deep red rose from the west, as if the sky were on fire, and James was the first to lie back on the blanket, fold his hands behind his head, and simply let himself be ensorcelled by sunset — the most wondrous of daily occurrences.

The girls lay beside him, one clinging to each of his arms. Their hair spread out like a golden or charcoal-black carpet under their heads. The contrast between Lucy's blonde locks and Sara's dark hair almost rivaled the colors of the sunset.

He heard Lucy sigh, finally relaxing after a long day. A low purr rumbled in Sara's throat.

James closed his eyes and listened to their breathing. He was thankful for them, for his new life here.

At the same time, he was almost flush with excitement. There was so much to learn, so much to do. He couldn't imagine ever getting bored or fed up with it all.

And as he lay there, basking in his own happiness, reveling in the soft bodies pushed against him, his mind drifted to his plans for the cabin.

First, he wanted to complete the expansion on the

north side — a new kitchen and a lean-to workshop. He had plenty of lumber, and he had a Board Crafting spell to make the seasoned boards he needed for a the workshop. Still, a good deal of physical labor remained involved. The hardest part was building the log walls for the actual cabin — he wanted the actual expansion to match the rest of the cabin.

As he lay there, thinking about the task at hand and enjoying the sunset, resolve suddenly suffused him, and his mind began grinding like crazy, seeking a way to do the work ahead of him.

And with that rising intent, a mist of ages rose up from the depths of his mind. He recognized that unique sensation by now, and he surrendered to it.

He let the ancestral memory in.

Chapter 9

The sun was setting in James's ancestral memory as well.

Perhaps that made the connection of this memory to James's world and life easier. A similar time, yet in another age.

Seagulls screeched overhead as James blinked to adapt to the new vista. Behind him, waves hit the shore with the rhythm of time immemorial, and the salty aroma of the sea struck his nostrils with unrivaled intensity.

He looked down at himself, noted the transparency he usually experienced during such visions. He had found before — during a vision that brought him to a ship on a stormy sea — that no harm could befall him.

He looked around, for a moment enchanted by how the sea was colored pink by the setting sun. It was cold here; he knew it more than he felt it, and the beach was rocky and barren. A ship lay on it — a longship with a single mast, a dragon's head carved in its prow, the oars stowed away, and the ship itself shored up with rocks. The keel was still dripping.

A group of men and women stood around it.

Without knowing, James sensed they were adventurers. They set out from their distant home to tame a new land, to carve out a place of their own on this island. In the centuries to come, from their seed would rise a nation.

But now, they needed to survive.

The men unloaded supplies from the ship, and none spared his hands — even the children bore their burden. Clothes, tools, furs, hides, food, drink; they had brought much, knowing that it would take time before the land would yield its first crop.

As James walked over to them — unseen, because he was a specter in these visions — the group set out in a single file. They were a family; they helped each other. When one faltered, the others helped lighten their load, and although they knew hardship lay ahead, their eyes shone bright with optimism, full of the fire of explorers and adventurers, full of the brazen courage of those who go their own way.

It was similar to what James felt when he thought of his own cabin, his own place in the woods, and he supposed that optimism and adventurous spirit had linked this vision to him.

Excited, he followed the group.

Behind the beach lay a green valley, awakening from a long winter. Given a few weeks, the soil would be fertile here. The people had chosen well.

And they were not the first to have come. A large stack of lumber lay ready, and several hide tents sprawled around them. Furs and hides hung from tanning racks, and several figures had gathered at the center of this encampment — bearded men. Rough and strong, with axes hanging from their belts that were tools as much as they were weapons.

The reunion was full of life and laughter. Fathers held

their sons once again, and wives embraced long-lost husbands. They feasted, celebrated their arrival.

But one figure caught James's eye.

An elder woman, almost too old to have made the journey, shuffling in the back of the group. One man stepped forward and extended his hand to her. He was dark of hair with piercing green eyes — perhaps how James's father would have looked were he inclined to grow a beard and work out a lot.

"*Kohmt dan in meine armen, moehke!*" he rumbled, laughing in his beard. "*Wuthin's Aug kieckt dan eindlyck oppa ons wedermooting.*"

She hugged him, a mother's tears in her verdant eyes, and many of those assembled gave good cheer at the reunion.

But the man turned serious after the hug.

"*Enen storm kohmt, moehke,*" he said, then gestured to the north. "*Kon the ons helpen?*"

Storm clouds gathered in the north, lightning crackled with the menace of nature's fury.

The woman gave a single nod. She turned to the pile of lumber gathered at the heart of the encampment — raw, unworked logs. There lay many of them, limbed and ready for use, but they would be difficult to move. She raised her hands up to the sky.

Whether it was from potent High Magic or only a mere coincidence, the icy winds of this place picked up, hard-cutting and salt with the sea as the woman's matted gray hair danced around her weatherworn face like silver fire.

"Vanhoudt tod kervthoudt.

"Bawerckinghe, maacken. Kraft.

"Vanhoudt tod kervthoudt.

"Danoock, vanealders tod meinenwil.

"Brengang, furanderinghe. Kraft.

"Vanealders tod meinenwil."

James could sense the power rage within, and the winds swept up and raked her frail body as her bony fingers curled. Those gathered behind her — kinsfolk and friends — watched in awe as the old woman bent reality to her powerful will.

The lumber moved.

One log at a time, they rose from the pile. Wedges were cut into the corners, bark was stripped away, and a natural varnishing solution was applied. It was the same as with James's Board Crafting spell, but this one allowed the old woman greater control, because with simple motions of her hands, she placed those stripped and carved logs into a pile.

No, not a pile.

A wall...

James stood as awed as the others as the old crone built four walls from willpower and timber alone. The wall was tall and straight and massive. The logs would still need to be lashed together with ropes, but the wedges interlocked perfectly, making the whole thing stable and strong.

And all that in minutes.

Sweat beaded on the old woman's forehead as she continued her work, while her kinsfolk and friends shared their excitement. James wanted to see more — desperately.

How would she make the roof? The floors? What about shutters for the rough windows?

But reality already tugged at him, calling him back to his own time. He sensed his weight trickle away as if he dissolved into thin air.

As the image of these people — his ancestors — faded away, darkness overtook him, taking him away from this beach in a faraway land, a faraway time, and back to his own world...

Chapter 10

"James, are you okay?"

James opened his eyes to look into the concerned blue eyes of Lucy as the blonde MILF hovered over him.

Sara was beside her, their heads almost touching, but the cat girl had a smile on her plump lips.

"See?" she purred in her slightly exotic accent. "I told you he's fine."

Lucy shot him a crooked smile. "Yeah... but... Well, I never saw anything like that before."

James chuckled, then sat up and rubbed his eyes. The sky was still red — little more than a few minutes had passed. He smiled, and Lucy leaned forward to kiss him.

"I'm glad you're okay," she said. "It looked... strange."

"Was it a memory?" Sara asked, excitement ablaze in her yellow eyes.

James nodded.

Sara's lips parted with surprise, and her eyes widened. "Really? Did you learn anything?"

"Yeah," he said. "It was... a double spell. A woman made a wall from timber, carving and stripping logs and placing them with her High Magic."

Sara covered her mouth. "Compound magic!" she exclaimed. She hopped up on her knees, and her tail almost lashed James in the face as her left ear gave its twitch. "That's great!"

"Compound magic?" he prompted, pulling Lucy a little closer as the blonde still eyed him with some concern.

Sara nodded vigorously. "Yes, when High Mages combine two or more spells into one. It's an art that not many High Mages know, and even fewer master."

James quirked an eyebrow. "Is compound magic more powerful?"

She smiled. "Yes! It's quicker and less draining to combine magic and, therefore, more powerful. It gets more complicated, though, so that's why only some High Mages can do it. But you are talented! You should try it; I have faith that you can master it."

James nodded, his eagerness to try out this new technique rising.

Sara could see, because she laughed and placed a gently hand on his chest. "Not now!" she purred. "Try it tomorrow when you're well-rested and have daylight."

James smiled. "Okay, fair point. I'll practice tomorrow."

"But don't forget to record the spell," Sara said, arching a black eyebrow.

James nodded. He wrote down every spell and the circumstances in which he learned it in his Grimoire. He hadn't brought it with him, of course; he hadn't expected an ancestral memory out here tonight. They rarely came unless he tried to tap into one. But luckily, James had a way of getting his Grimoire.

He focused on the Grimoire in his mind, seeing the

leather-bound tome before him, covered in the emblems of the Eleven Elements of Magic: Time, Space, Fire, Lightning, Force, Water, Air, Life, Death, Blood, and Earth.

When James had the image firm in his mind, he focused his intent on it until a sharp pang at the back of his mind told him his will was focused.

Then he spoke the words of magic.

"Vanealders tod heer.

"Brengang, bestansvlack. Rhuimte.

"Vanealders tod heer."

He raised his palms, and the Grimoire appeared in them out of nothing. The weight pressed his hands down, and he couldn't suppress a grin at casting a magical spell successfully, even if it was a simple one.

Lucy giggled. "That never stops amazing me," she said, pushing herself a little closer against James.

Sara purred in agreement.

Both women looked on as James jotted down the words of his new Woodcraft spell in his Grimoire. As always, he added a brief description of the memory that gave him the spell. This was for his own interest; the little tidbits of knowledge of the trials and tribulations of his ancestors fascinated him.

When he was done, they enjoyed what remained of

the sunset. When darkness fell, James popped the bottle and poured the girls a drink.

They sat on the blanket, close to each other, watching him as he gathered firewood. Sara's eyes were big and full of admiration for him. Lucy just watched, bemused by his every movement. Now and again, the lusty blonde wetted her plump lips with a quick-darting tongue. The sight of his two beauties like that awakened more than a little lust in James.

When he'd gathered enough firewood, he made a neat little stack at the center of the clearing, using some inner bark for kindling. Then, he focused on a small twig in his hand, envisioned it burning, and spoke his words of power.

"Vanluket tod flamma.

"Furanderinghe, verneetigung. Vurra.

"Vanluket tod flamma."

Lucy's eyes widened as a bright and sprightly little flame sprang to life at the end of the twig. Sara purred her approval.

James crouched beside the fire and lit it with the twig, taking the time to make sure all the tinder caught. The thick aroma of smoke filled the air as the women watched him work, sipping their wine.

When the fire settled into a merry crackling, James

stepped back and gave a contented nod.

"James..." Sara purred

He looked over her shoulder to see the cat girl on her knees, leaning forward, arms pressing her ample breasts together as the deep cut of her cleavage allowed him a view of those big breasts he so loved. His blood began pumping a little faster.

Lucy sat next to her, biting her lower lip. She was leaning back on her hands, her legs spread slightly. And since she wore a skirt tonight, her position gave James a good look at those cute lace panties.

He cleared his throat. "Yeah?" he said, eyeing the women in turn.

Sara patted the blanket. "Come sit with us," she crooned. "We have a nice warm fire, and now it's *your* turn to relax."

"Hm-hm," Lucy agreed, giving him a bold-eyed look.

How could he resist that?

With a smile, he walked over to his women...

Chapter 11

Lucy scooted over, and James sat down between the two women. It was almost as if his magic turned them on more, because Sara practically threw her leg across his lap and straddled him, while Lucy pushed herself up and nestled against his side.

He wrapped his arms around Sara's waist and kissed her cheek.

Sara smiled and leaned in to kiss him on the lips.

Her scent, musky, sweet, and wild, filled his nostrils as her tongue darted into his mouth, and they shared a long, passionate, and loving kiss. Her tail wrapped around his leg and stroked it, and his hand climbed up to scratch her behind her ear, making the cat girl lean even more into their kiss.

As they parted, Sara licked her lips and smiled wickedly. She looked at Lucy and grinned, nodding for her to come closer.

The blonde bit her lip, her cheeks flushing. Being a supernatural creature with wholly different mores, Sara had no qualms about sharing her love with another woman — or women, even.

For Lucy, it still took some getting used to.

Still, the MILF leaned in, slightly hesitant, but every ounce of that hesitation vanished when — under Sara's approving purr — she kissed James deeply.

With a groan, James moved one hand from Sara's firm waist to Lucy's plump ass. He squeezed that delicious rump as Lucy's scent — with a slight hint of lavender — made him heady with desire.

Sara hummed. "Now," she said to James, "you can take off that shirt."

James smiled, his cock swelling in anticipation. He

grabbed his shirt by its hem and pulled it over his head. He tossed it aside, the motion making his muscles ripple.

The girls ogled his muscular chest and shoulders, exchanged a naughty look, and giggled. He sensed the heat of their gazes on him as he stared back at them.

Sara leaned into him again, kissing him with her tongue as she ground her full weight in his lap.

James moaned into her mouth, and his hand moved down. One was now on Lucy's round ass; the other on Sara's, and it was heavenly. He squeezed those delicious rumps — roughly — winning a squeal from both girls.

Lucy pressed herself against him, rising to her knees. "I want some, too," she cooed in his ear as he kissed Sara.

Sara broke the kiss, panting and grinning at Lucy. "You want some? Come on, then."

Lucy bit her lower lip, then moved in to join James and Sara's kiss.

Fuck, James thought. *This is too hot.*

Their lips met. Tongues swirled, exploring James's mouth, while hot lips kissed his neck and cheeks. His cock strained against the front of his jeans. God, he needed to get those off soon!

Lucy kissed James hard, her hands groping his body and exploring his biceps. Her nipples strained against the fabric of her shirt, and she pushed those big tits against James, mewling and panting with heat.

He slipped his hands underneath her shirt, squeezing those firm globes, kneading the soft flesh, pulling at the nipples until Lucy went completely mad with lust.

She gave a low moan as she pulled her hands back from James and freed her delicious MILF body from the constraints of that shirt, her big breasts bouncing free.

Sara, meanwhile, shimmied down from his lap to work on his belt buckle and his pants. As Lucy rose to her knees to let James suck on her swollen nipple, squealing with delight as he licked, sucked, and nibbled, the cat girl focused on freeing James's cock from its confines.

Sara tugged his jeans and boxers down his legs until his cock popped out, already hard. Her eyes widened, and she licked her lips as she took in the sight.

"Such a pretty cock," she purred as she closed a dainty hand around the base of his shaft and slowly pumped it. She shot a crooked glance at Lucy. "You're going to want a taste of this."

"Yess," Lucy moaned. She was watching Sara intently; it was obvious how much she wanted to play with it, to taste it. But for now, Sara got to enjoy it.

Lucy lowered herself, her breast popping out of James's mouth, and they kissed once again. James could feel the blonde MILF's need in the fire of that kiss; she was hungry for his cock. She was eager for it.

And damn, did he like that.

"I want to feel your cum on my skin again, baby," Lucy purred in between two kisses. "I want to taste it and be covered in it."

Fuck!

James's eyes drifted to Sara. The cat girl cradled James's balls with one hand, while the other pumped his shaft. She was going slowly, her touch featherlight, but the mischievous blaze in her yellow eyes told James she had dirty plans.

She grinned, then let go of his cock to pull off her tiny black dress, freeing her big, pale breasts. She wore a lacy black thong and stockings underneath, and the sight of her luscious body like that made his cock buck.

"Hmm, baby," Lucy purred, pressing her hot body against his.

Her hands slipped down her own delicious body to wriggle out of her tight skirt, finally revealing those cute lacy striped panties. There was a little bow on the front, and the way the tight garment hugged her pussy lips into a pretty camel toe made her look like a present indeed.

"Hm," James groaned. "I'm going to plow that pretty little pussy."

She pressed her lips into a thin line and arched her back so that her big tits pressed against him, giving him another chance to suck on her nipples.

"Baby..." she purred. "I need you inside me. I've missed it so much!"

That made James only hornier. With a growl of desire, he sucked on her tits, nibbled on her, and reveled in the sound of her panting in her unbridled lust.

At the same time, Sara cooed and purred from below, just before closing her plump lips around his shaft.

God, that feeling of entering his cat girl's hot mouth! There was nothing like it.

He pushed his pelvis forward, trying to sink even deeper inside her mouth. He felt the suction of her plump lips, her throat working in concert with her hand to make him crazy with pleasure.

Sara moaned around his dick, and she tickled his cum-laden balls. Then she began sucking harder and faster, which sent a jolt of pleasure straight up his spine.

His cock throbbed and twitched, and he couldn't help

but thrust his hips into Sara's mouth, fucking the cat girl's face as she sucked on his cock.

"Oh, yeah," Lucy muttered, almost breathless. "Look at her go!"

Sara's head bobbed up and down on James's cock, her tongue swirling and licking the underside. He knew this wasn't going to take long; the cat girl was giving him an amazing blowjob, and his pleasure already rose.

But then Sara stopped.

"F-fuck," James groaned.

He looked down to see Sara grinning at Lucy, a strand of saliva and precum connecting his cockhead to her plump lips. "You want his cum on you?" she crooned at the blonde. "Come down here."

Lucy bit her lip, shot him a naughty glance, then lowered herself.

Oh damn, James thought. *This is gonna be good...*

The two girls exchanged a look as they sat on their knees on either side of him, both undressed down to their panties.

Sara was the first to act. She grabbed James's throbbing cock with one hand. The other snaked to the back of Lucy and pulled the sultry blonde down. An excited sigh escaped the MILF before she submitted, letting Sara guide James's firm weapon between her parted lips.

And Sara wasn't gentle.

A dirty grin appeared on her full lips, her left ear giving a single twitch as she pushed Lucy all the way down. The blonde gagged on James's cock once, then settled into it with vigor.

James had to fight off his orgasm as Lucy's curvy body jiggled with every gag on his cock — those large breasts, round butt cheeks, and trembling thighs were enough to make any man shoot his load, but he had had some practice since he first came to Tour.

And so, he groaned his pleasure, relishing in the feel of Lucy's wet tongue sliding along his sensitive member. He held his load in and enjoyed the view.

Lucy's lips were wrapped around his shaft, her tongue teasing at the head, while her big tits bounced with each deep stroke into her throat.

"Yess," Sara purred. "Look at her go."

She gripped Lucy's hair in one hand, using the other to hold on to James's cock. She slid her fingers through the blonde hair, tugging it gently, then used her grip to pull Lucy off him, his cock leaving her warm mouth with a slurp.

Lucy yelped with need, her eyes still closed from her surrender to that dirty blowjob.

"Use your tits," Sara commanded her.

Lucy obeyed at once, shimmying back and leaning forward, her cheeks crimson framed by golden locks, and she bent over. James's cock — glib with spit and precum — slid between those big and firm tits, and it was like coming home to a bed of velvet.

"Fuuuck," James groaned.

Lucy bit her lip and began pumping. She worked her big tits up and down his cock, smacking them together to drive him wild. Her hands squeezed her breasts together, making James groan in delight.

"That's it," Sara purred, slipping a hand down the front of her thong. "The pretty little blonde wants your cum, James. You should give it to her."

"Hmm," Lucy moaned, still pumping his cock. "I want it, baby. Make me into your little cumslut."

Sara giggled and reached over to give Lucy's round ass a slap. "Cum all over her tits, James," she hissed.

There was no resisting this — not that James wanted to.

With a grunt that seemed to come all the way from his toes, his body tensed and his balls tightened. When the tip of his cock popped up from between Lucy's firm tits, a thick rope of cum shot out, caking Lucy's pretty face.

The blonde gave a yelp but, to her credit, didn't relent. She kept pumping those delicious tits around James's cock, sending him straight into heaven. And with every pump, a thick load of seed shot out from between her ample tits, splattering over her big breasts.

With a last squeeze from Lucy, James released a last gob of cum onto Lucy's chest before he was done.

"Damn," he groaned, popping his neck muscles as he looked at his handiwork; Lucy's firm breasts were glazed, dripping with a big load, and the blonde looked down at it with blazing cheeks and big eyes.

Sara purred with pleasure, reaching over to flick up some with her finger before having a taste. She then swiveled her yellow eyes to James and grinned.

"Wasn't that nice?" she crooned.

James chuckled. "You bet."

The cat girl then rose to her feet and shimmied out of her tight thong, showing him that pretty pussy with its cute triangle of black pubic hair. He couldn't get enough of that sight. And having her in stockings made the blood pump again.

Sara saw his cock twitch and grinned. "Good," she hummed. "Because I do not think we are done yet..."

Sara swung one leg over James, straddling him.

"Remember what my apron said?" she purred.

He grinned, eyeing her delicious body up and down. "Eat the cook?"

She bit her lip and nodded, a slight blush coloring her cheeks.

"Oh..." Lucy purred from below. "You're... you're getting hard again."

Sara shot Lucy a glance over her shoulder, threw James a naughty look, then turned around so that she sat reverse cowgirl style.

James licked his lips at the sight of her perfect, plump ass with the swaying tail above it, then placed both hands on Sara's waist to pull her onto his face. He was eager to do what the apron had said: he wanted to taste that silky soft pussy again.

She groaned when he pulled her onto his face, letting his lips graze her slick and hot pussy lips.

"Yesss, James," she moaned as her tail wrapped around one of his arms. "Oh, by the Elements!"

"Hmm," Lucy purred. "Is he good?"

"So good," Sara moaned. "Hmm... Come here. You... ahhh... You should rub your pussy on his cock... hmmm... that'd be so hot to watch while he... ahh... while he eats me out."

"O-okay," Lucy hummed, her voice heavy with lust.

James buried his face between Sara's thighs, winning another delighted moan from the cat girl. With his mouth pressed against her sweet and smooth pussy, he sucked on her labia, flicking his tongue over her clit before taking it into his mouth to tease and lick.

As he ate her out, Sara's hips moved to meet his tongue, and she squirmed in pleasure. He felt another weight settle on top of him.

Lucy.

"Take those off," Sara purred. "He should feel your pretty pussy against his skin."

James's heart banged against his chest as Lucy rose and wriggled out of her cute little panties. Lucy's slick heat pushed up against his cock — rock hard again — as the pretty blonde MILF sat down on him.

With a groan of delight, feeling the weight of two such pretty women on him, he devoted himself to Sara's tight little snatch.

The cat girl yelped and moaned as he teased her clit, squirming on his face, eager for more.

"James," she purred. "Oh... you're going to make me come."

He grunted as her firm ass squirmed on him. Lucy took his cock in her hand, moaned her delight as she pushed his firm rod between her plump and wet pussy lips without taking him inside.

She rubbed her pussy on him, slowly grinding up along his cock, and Sara let out an excited moan at the sight, her body shuddering with pleasure, her firm ass bouncing as she twerked a little on James's face.

"Rub... ahh... Rub your little clit, Lucy," she crooned. "I want to see you come, too."

"Hnn, fuck," Lucy squealed as she complied, rubbing circles on her swollen clit.

"Oh, yes, yes, yes," Sara whimpered, her hips moving faster now, her wet pussy rubbing on James's tongue like silk.

His own pleasure rose again, his balls tightening to spurt another load as Lucy rubbed his cock on her plump pussy lips. But he wanted nothing more than to penetrate her — for her to take that cock into her tight little snatch and let him creampie her as she came trembling.

And apparently, Sara had the same idea.

"Ohh, Lucy," she purred. "I want to see him fuck

you."

"Ahnn," Lucy moaned, gyrating and grinding on James. With the next circle, his swollen, sticky tip already poked in a little. "Fuck... Yes..."

"Sooo hot," Sara moaned, her body tensing as James licked at that dripping pussy, lapping up her nectar. Her orgasm was coming. "Uhnn... Begin with the tip."

"Oh... only the tip?" Lucy moaned, lining his cock up with her dripping snatch. Her eyes were begging for more, but she listened to Sara.

God, that feeling.

It was only the tip, but her pussy was so warm and welcoming, so tight as it milked him. Lucy was practically begging for a creampie, and James had to focus completely on eating Sara out to stop himself from cumming.

"It feels so gooood," Lucy moaned, taking another half inch.

James's head became clouded. He lapped at Sara's pussy, focusing on her clit, and her thighs clamped on him even as Lucy slipped his cock in a little deeper.

"Ahn..." Sara moaned. "That looks... oh... I'm coming. I'm coming, James! Don't stop! Fuck her! Cum in her! Put it in... Ah! Put it in, Lucy!"

With a mewl of delight, Lucy obeyed, unable to resist

her own desires any longer. She let James's cock slam all the way into her, ramming her cervix, and she began riding him with reckless abandon like an amazon, eager for that creampie. Her ass bounced and slapped on his cock with every move she made, her pussy clenching tightly on James in time with her movements.

His cock throbbed with pleasure and he could no longer hold back, not with that hot MILF riding him. He came with a roar, spurting deep inside Lucy and making her wail in ecstasy as her own handiwork on her swollen clit made her release.

"Yes," she moaned. "Cum in me!"

Sara mewled with delight as her orgasm crashed over her in waves. She came hard, her body quaking and shaking from the force of her pleasure. And the fact that James was cumming inside Lucy only made it better for her.

"Hnn," she purred. "Fill her up! Fill... ahh! Give her what she wants."

"Hmm," he groaned, face still buried between Sara's thighs as he spurted another jet of cum into Lucy's warm and welcoming pussy.

She slammed down on him again, milking his seed as eagerly as he shot it into her. At the same time, Sara practically collapsed onto him, a low purr rising from her throat.

"Ahh," James huffed as the quavering and shaking of their orgasms died down, "That was too good."

"Hmm," Sara hummed. "There's no such thing as 'too good'!"

"Delicious," a freshly creampied Lucy crooned as she rolled off James's dick and onto the blanket. "That was so hot."

James chuckled and gave her a wet slap on her round ass, enjoying the sight of his cum still dripping from her freshly pounded pussy. He then gave Sara a playful push, and the cat girl meowed as she slid off him, slipping to his other side.

Now, he had a girl on either side of him.

"We should do something with Corinne again soon," Lucy muttered as she nestled against James, a dirty promise hidden in her words.

"Or *to* Corinne," Sara crooned.

James laughed, then winked at Lucy. "Totally," he agreed as he reached for the bottle of red, eager for a drink.

"I like her," Sara hummed. "She seems a little shy, though."

"Well," Lucy said. "It takes some getting used to... *all this*."

James chuckled. "Yeah, I agree. I'll pay her a visit. She's game, but she needs to ease into it." He took a swig, then settled back on the blanket as the women snuggled up against him.

With sunset behind them, the stars came out over the clearing. Out here, you could see every one of them, and it was arresting in its beauty.

Some of the hot day's balmy warmth still lingered, and they'd have a few minutes to enjoy like this before it would get too cold and they'd need to get dressed.

Best enjoy it while we can, James thought.

Then, his gaze lowered — down from the stars to the tree line.

He had seen something move.

And now that his eyes fixed on the tree trunks and the bustling undergrowth, a grin appeared on his lips.

He hadn't imagined it; he saw something.

Or rather, *someone…*

And he was pretty damn sure there were blazing eyes watching them from the undergrowth.

One blue. One green.

And fuzzy fox tails, cute and perky fox ears, and a wild mop of ginger hair. A moment later, the bushes shook, and the figure took off.

Kesha.

She had been watching them.

He chuckled to himself, then pulled his two women a little closer.

Looks like I might want to have another chat with the fox girl, he thought.

James, Lucy, and Sara relaxed under the darkening sky for a while, basking in each other's warmth. They were all tired after the busy day and the physical activities. They needed rest to be ready for tomorrow.

The day would bring some exciting things for James. He would finish up clearing the land for his construction project.

And if he had some time left, he would begin felling the logs that he needed to raise the walls. He was thankful for his new spell, which would help him and make the actual construction of the wall significantly easier.

As he lay there thinking, the warmth of the day seeped away into the earth and the nightly cold settled in. When Lucy shivered beside him, the movement roused from his considerations. He patted her on her side.

"I think it's time we head back," he said. "We don't want to get too cold."

Lucy nodded. "You're right."

He helped Lucy to her feet first, and she leaned into him as she stood, wrapping her arms around his waist as she pressed her cheek against his chest.

"This was nice," she whispered. "I wish we could stay longer."

He smiled. "I know. There will be many more times like this; don't worry."

"I hope so," she replied, leaning her head on his shoulder as he helped Sara up.

Sara smiled as James pulled her to her feet. Once up, she kissed James deeply as she wrapped her arms around his neck. He kissed her back, his hands running over her warm body as they held each other tight.

"It was nice," Sara agreed, looking him deep in his eyes.

They got dressed in the dim glow of the fire James had built, shadows dancing on their bodies. Once they were done, they walked down toward the trail that led to the cabin.

James was thankful they had brought a flashlight, because the darkness in the woods was sudden and very deep. Lucy and Sara hung from his arms as he navigated the trail until they made out the cabin among the trees in the distance.

"When we're back," he said. "I'll make a fire so we can get nice and toasty."

Sara grinned and said, "Sounds good to me."

With that, they reached the cabin and stepped inside, closing the door behind them. The girls settled on the couch as James got to work on the fire.

They spent a few more hours talking and relaxing together until the fatigue of a long day finally caught up with each of them. James extinguished the fire before they retired for the night, but left the windows open to let the fresh scent of the pine forest in the cabin.

But once he lay in his bed with those two beautiful women — one on either side of him — it was difficult to actually sleep. By the gentle stirring of the women beside him, he could tell that they struggled with the same thing.

Once again surrendering to his need and theirs, James turned onto his side, smiled, and took Lucy in his arms while Sara gave an approving purr and let her warm hands roam over his body.

The night was not over yet.

Chapter 12

James was up early; he didn't need to set an alarm clock these days.

Beside him, Lucy and Sara were still sleeping, their delicious bodies outlined by the soft sheets under which they slept.

James didn't make a sound as he rose quietly from their bed and went about getting breakfast ready.

It wasn't much, just bread, cheese, sausage, coffee, and tea. But that would be a good foundation for a day full of hard work, both for him and his companions.

He would still have to solve the issue of refrigeration in the cabin. There was no electricity, so he would either have to get the cabin on the grid or come up with some kind of solution.

After all, what is life without bacon?

As he prepared breakfast, he heard the women stir in the bedroom. They giggled softly as they spoke with one another, and the sound brought a broad smile to James's lips.

At times like this, he still struggled to comprehend that this was his life now — that he owned his own little place out in the woods and had such lovely companions to share his happiness with.

He wondered if this was perhaps what his father wanted for him when he had made up his last will and decided to let the cabin in Tour County pass to James.

Perhaps this was even the life he had wanted for himself?

James had not seen his father as happy and relaxed as he had been during the one time they traveled to Tour County together on a hunting trip so many years ago.

It was almost as if they had escaped the dreariness of

city life together and escaped to some kind of magical place where everything was as it should have been — where father and son could bond without the constant strain of expectations for the future.

Whatever the case, James had decided to live this life to the fullest, to enjoy every moment of his newfound freedom and happiness, and to never take any of it for granted.

The smile was still on his lips when he finished preparing breakfast. He did his best to arrange the food on the small table in the cabin, but he had to clear out the wineglasses and the empty bottle from last night first.

Once he finished up, he had a table filled with the leftover fresh rolls that Sara had made, several cheeses of varying age and intensity. He also served sausage and a bowl with fresh vegetables — cucumber and tomatoes. He finished the breakfast table up with a pot of tea and coffee.

The only things missing were eggs, bacon, and orange juice, but he would get those once he got his refrigeration set up.

"My, my," Lucy purred as she came out of the bedroom. "This all looks delicious."

She stretched and smiled at him. She looked cute in

one of his old dress shirts she had pillaged from his wardrobe.

Sara was not far behind her, dressed in a t-shirt and a pair of panties. She licked her lips, and her tail gave an excited swish at the sight of the sausage. She was a meat-eater first and foremost.

In fact, James had been surprised that she had prepared a vegetable soup for them yesterday.

They sat down at the table together, and James poured the girls coffee or tea as they mulled over the selection he had prepared for them.

Predictably, Sara chose the sausage, combining it with a few slices of bread. Lucy made herself a roll with cucumber and tomatoes, then made one with cucumber, sausage, cheese, and tomatoes for James as he sat down between them on the couch.

"Hmm," Lucy hummed as she took a bite. "These are great rolls, Sara."

"They are," James agreed. "Who would have thought that a cat girl would be such an excellent baker?"

Sara's left ear twitched as she regarded James, and she chuckled. "Why not?"

James exchanged a look with Lucy, and they both laughed.

"I guess she's right," Lucy said. "Why not?"

James grinned and shook his head. "I guess I'm still struggling with cat stereotypes. I mean, I did catch you hunting mice in the cellar once, didn't I?"

Sara chuckled. "So?" she said, giving him a bold glance. "Are hunting mice and baking bread mutually exclusive?"

James laughed and threw up his hands. "All right," he said. "I give up. You're right. It's perfectly possible for someone who hunts small rodents for fun to still be an excellent baker."

Sara grinned and flashed her canines and him. "I will guarantee you this thing, James Beckett," she said. "You will see much stranger things than me in the days to come…"

James smiled at those cryptic words.

The truth was that he was looking forward to it — the idea of exploring the magical world of High Magic excited him more than anything else.

"Let's eat," Lucy said. "Before you guys get caught up in another discussion about magic…"

Sara and James laughed, then dug in.

While Sara, Lucy, and James enjoyed breakfast together, James filled them in on his plans for the day: clearing out more of the trees around their cabin so that he could start work on his planned expansion.

If he had any time to spare, he'd cut down a few more large trees, too.

The work was going to be hard, but James was looking forward to it.

"Well," Lucy said. "I have a full day at the store ahead of me. Corinne is due to come in with some pickled wares and dried herbs later today. And I have to think about the inventory for the upcoming fall."

James nodded. "That sounds like a full day." He shifted his gaze to Sara. "What about you?" he asked.

She gave a mischievous grin. "I don't have a job, James," she said. "You know that." She stretched lazily and curled up against him on the couch.

"Cats sleep," she purred.

He laughed. "I don't believe that at all," he said. "I'm sure you get up to a lot of mischief while the rest of us do our daily chores and our work."

She waggled her eyebrows as she ran a long finger with a sharp nail along the inside of his thigh. "Maybe," she said, letting the word trail off.

"But you and I should talk later today," James said.

He had not forgotten about the many questions he still had for the cat girl, and he intended to speak to her sooner or later.

She gave him a curious look, her left ear twitching. "Talk?" she asked. "About what?"

"The cabin," James said. "And a bit about magic as well."

Lucy giggled, her eyes shining with amusement as she watched the exchange between James and Sara. "Sounds like an exclusive topic," she said. "Maybe I should give you two an evening together?"

James grinned and leaned over to place a kiss on her soft cheek. "Maybe just one," he said. "But I would like to see you again real soon."

"Hmm, likewise," she purred before looking at Sara. "And you, too."

Sara winked at her before settling back against James's side, giving a soft purr as he scratched her behind her ear.

"But let's get you to the store first," James said to Lucy. "We don't want Mrs. Truncey to find a closed door, now do we?"

Lucy chuckled and gave James a peck on the cheek before she hopped to her feet.

"You're right," she said. "Let's go!"

Chapter 13

James dropped Lucy off at the general store before driving back to the cabin.

It was still early — before eight in the morning — and he enjoyed driving down Main Street with his window rolled down, letting the early warmth of the day roll in.

In a few weeks, the temperature would start dropping as Tour County neared the end of summer.

While James loved summer, he was looking forward to a winter at the cabin as well, provided he could get everything in order before the actual frost set in. After all, cold weather would make it difficult for him to spend a lot of time working outside.

He drove north until he came to Forrester Trail. As always, he kept an eye open for Corinne at the barn. This time, the doors were open, and a light shone inside.

Good, James thought. *I've been meaning to speak to her.*

He hadn't seen much of Corinne since the night he, Lucy, and Sara shared with her at the cabin. He knew she was busy; the farm wasn't doing too well. Still, he would like to see more of her.

He pulled up next to the gate in the fence that enclosed the redhead's property and parked his car.

As he got out and opened the gate, James saw Corinne heading outside and closing the barn doors behind her. She glanced over and smiled when she saw him and waved him over.

"Well, howdy there, cowboy," she said as she waited for him, one hand on her supple waist, the other hanging by her side.

The redhead wore loose-fitting coveralls with a tight white tank top underneath. Large work boots finished the image of the hard-working country girl, but she wore her beautiful ginger locks in two pigtails — a sight to make James's heart pound a little faster.

"Howdy yourself," he said. "I was hoping to catch you here."

Corinne laughed. "Well, ya did," she said with a wink. "And any day I get caught by the handsome James Beckett himself is a very fine day, indeed. How are you today?"

He laughed. "You're in a good mood, aren't you?" he said.

Her smile grew wider. "It is a lovely day," she said. "Not a cloud in the sky. And when I went out this morning to check on the chicken coop, I found that my feathered friends had suffered no casualties during the night."

She clicked her tongue and winked at him. "All thanks to you."

"Hmm," James hummed. "The fox girl left you alone, huh?"

She looked him up and down for a moment before her green eyes settled on his again.

"Looks like it," she said. "But to tell you the truth, I had to think about her a few times since I learned she was Lucy's daughter. I mean, the poor thing is out there, in the wild, with nothing to her name. Don't ya think we should help her?"

That was kind of her. Corinne could've harbored a grudge over the chickens. But instead, her heart went out to Kesha, and she wanted to help.

That kindness made her even more beautiful to James.

James smiled and nodded as he walked closer to her.

"I'm not sure if she wants to be helped," he said. "But if she does, then yeah... we should."

Corinne watched him approach with a smile on her plump lips.

"Maybe I should leave her a note, huh? Something like 'stay the hell away from my chickens and head on over to James Beckett's cabin if you're hungry.' Ya think that would work?" There was a teasing light in her eyes as she watched him come closer still.

James's heart made a little jump as the distance between them closed — ten feet, nine feet, five feet...

"Maybe it would," he said. "But I don't have any chickens."

One corner of her mouth curled up in a smile, then she pouted her lips a little, probably subconsciously.

"Plenty of *chicks*, though," she quipped.

Three feet.

"If that's so, then there's one more chick I'd like to add to my coop," James said, keeping his eyes on hers.

She laughed, shaking her head.

"You're a bad one, cowboy," she said, giving him a warm look.

She didn't move when he stood in front of her. James wrapped his arms around her slim waist, and she sighed as he pulled her in closer — complete surrender.

Their lips met on their own, without even a shred of conscious effort, and Corinne's delicious aroma swirled around him. Her scent was that of nature — a woman who was always outside and not afraid to break a sweat.

He surrendered to her delights, and his entire world consisted of her soft body pressed against his — still slightly shy and trembling a little — as they shared a passionate kiss.

"Hmm," she sighed when she drew back. "That was nice…"

James hummed agreement and brushed his thumb along her lower lip before fixing his eyes on hers. "I actually wanted to check up on you, Corinne," he said. "I hope the night before with Lucy and Sara didn't scare you off…"

She shook her head, still in his embrace. "No," she

breathed. "I can't wait to do it again."

James smiled and squeezed her tight. "Well," he said. "I'm happy to report that the others are eager to see you again."

She laughed, her eyes widening a little. "Really?" she said. "You really think so?"

"Oh yes," James assured her. "They were both talking about you last night and this morning, saying they can't wait to see you again."

Her grin broadened, making her freckles dance across her cute face. "That's so nice to hear," she said. "I'll admit I was afraid things would get a little awkward, y'know?"

James shook his head, keeping his hands on the small of her back.

"Lucy and Sara are not jealous," he said. "At least not of each other, and they won't be jealous of you, either. They get along great, so I'm sure you won't run into any problems with them. But I don't want to rush you into anything, Corinne," he added. "You take all the time you need. I only wanted to make sure you were okay."

"Hmm," she hummed, giving his butt a squeeze. "More than okay."

He laughed. "All right, consider me reassured."

He let his gaze shift to the farmhouse in the distance. It looked in need of repair, and the trees that flanked the driveway leading up to the front door told the tale of how long it must've stood there.

He looked back at her. "You need any help around the farm?" he asked, pulling back from the embrace a little.

"Well," she said. "I got harvest coming up soon." She shrugged. "If it gets too busy for me to manage, you could give me a hand. I'd be very grateful."

"Sure thing," James agreed. "I'd love to help."

She hesitated for a moment, keeping her gaze pinned on him.

"I can tell something else is on your mind," James said.

She laughed. "That obvious, huh? I must be like an open book! Well, to tell ya the truth..." She hesitated again.

James reached down to her plump butt and gave it a squeeze, winning a squeal from the redhead.

"Out with it!" he exclaimed.

She laughed and nodded. "All right, all right," she said. "The thing is... while I really like being with you and Lucy and Sara, it kinda of feels like things are going a little fast, ya know?"

She raised a hand to take some of the edge off. "Not that I want to slow down with you… But I want to… uh, I'd like to spend some time alone with just you, if you catch my drift."

That made a lot of sense. For most women James had known throughout his life, sharing their man would not be something they would easily consider — even if they got along well enough with the women they were sharing with.

Truth be told, he was looking forward to having his nights alone with his girls as well. Admittedly, time spent together was fun — a lot of fun — but being alone with someone usually offered a chance for more quality time and deep discussion.

"Of course," he said. "I understand completely. I was actually thinking that you and I should go on a date — just the two of us."

Corinne grinned widely and threw herself at him again, almost making him stagger back under the weight of her enthusiasm. "Yes! Please!"

He laughed. "Sounds like we have a deal," he said. "What do you say to a little swim at the lake?"

"Perfect!" she exclaimed. "Tell ya what: you come pick me up with your car, and I'll bring something to eat and drink for when we're done swimming. Will have ourselves a little picnic by the lake side."

"Sounds like a dream," he said, still holding her in his arms. "And it'll be just you and me. I got some work to do today, but how about tomorrow?"

She nodded vigorously. "I'd love that!"

He smiled and leaned in to give her a soft kiss on her lips. He had meant for it to just be a peck, but she pulled him in, pressing him close against her lithe body, and kissed him deeply.

Her sweet taste enveloped him as their tongues struggled for dominance, and he could feel his manhood rise to full attention, his mind swirling with images of how Corinne had looked naked, pleasuring herself as she watched him play with Lucy and Sara.

She pulled back, her eyes wide and hazy. "All right," she said softly, pushing her hips into him, so that her toned thighs rubbed against his cock through the fabric of his jeans.

"Gettin' a little excited there, cowboy?" She threw him a wicked grin.

He drew a deep breath. "Well," he said. "You got yourself to thank for that, cowgirl." He finished by loosening their embrace and giving her a rough slap on the butt.

"Ow!" she yelped, laughing.

"I'll see you tomorrow, then," James said. "Pick you up at eleven?"

She grinned, made her thumb and index finger into a gun, and mimicked shooting at him. "Ya got it, gringo," she said.

Laughing, James turned around and headed back to his car.

Chapter 14

James drove back to the cabin, eager to get started with the day's work.

Before he hopped to it, he enjoyed a quick cup of coffee in the cabin. Sara was nowhere to be found, but he expected she either roamed in the cellar or dwelled in the forest, likely in cat form.

Reinvigorated by the coffee, James headed outside,

took a deep breath of fresh air, and set to the task before him.

His first order of business was to finish up clearing out an area of land to the north and to the west of his cabin. He needed about five hundred square feet for his kitchen and workshop and two hundred square feet for the bedroom expansion. He had already cleared the trees, leaving a massive pile of firewood that would get him through the first cold weeks, but he still needed to chop those up when he would get some time.

After the trees, the next step was moving the larger rocks. This was another easy but intensive job. The trick was mainly to lift and move the rocks in a way that didn't cause unnecessary strain.

As someone who had done some physical labor before, James knew that proper lifting technique made all the difference in still having something of a back left once you hit fifty.

He tried to tap into his ancestral memories to see if he could unearth a spell for this job, but he came back blank.

I guess magic can't solve everything, he thought.

He'd need a plan, then.

Since he didn't have any heavy machinery, he had to rely on his wits and his strength. The smaller rocks he moved by simply lifting them — always from the knees — and piling them up near the tree line.

For the heavier rocks, he came up with a system that involved prying the rock loose, then wedging a plank under it — crafted with his magic from the lumber he had stockpiled.

Once the plank was in place, he would place an old tire beside it, then lift the boulder into the tire, using the board as a lever. Once the boulder sat snug in the tire, it was just a matter of tying a rope around it and dragging it out of the way.

It was a simple system, but it worked like a charm.

After a few hours of hard work, he had cleared enough land for his construction project.

Up next were the stumps. This was hard work, and James was thankful that only a few of them went truly deep. Either way, it cost James the better part of the morning.

Once he cleared out the stumps, he afforded himself some time for a break. His muscles ached and throbbed, and he felt exhausted, so he headed on into the cabin to grab some lunch.

He smiled when he found Sara had made him a few scrumptious sandwiches from the leftovers of breakfast. He made himself a fresh pot of coffee and took his food outside with him, and sat on the bottom step of the stairs leading to his porch, basking in the sunlight.

His stomach growled with healthy appetite, and he was quick to eat up and wash it all down with some piping hot coffee and a glass of water.

Smiling to himself, he sat back and allowed himself a few more minutes of relaxation.

This is the life, James thought.

Soon enough, he felt eager to get back to it. With renewed energy, he dedicated himself to his job.

Up next were the final two steps. Removing all the shrubs and bushes and leveling the land. If he worked hard enough, he could do it all before he lost the daylight.

With determination, he set to it.

First, he removed all the plant growth, which proved to be easier than digging up stumps. Most didn't have roots that went very deep. Oftentimes, he pulled the shrubs and weeds out using his heavy-duty gloves. There were a few that required the use of the shovel, but otherwise, he progressed swiftly.

Within two hours, he surveyed a clear swath of land of about five hundred square feet to the north of his cabin and another two hundred square feet to the west, adjacent to the bedroom. This was big enough for his planned expansion, with a little room to spare for stocking any excess lumber or other materials. The land was still rough, looking like an army had just marched over it.

All that remained was to level it.

James stood back from his work, stretching his aching muscles. It had been an intense afternoon so far. He was sweaty, tired, and thirsty, but he couldn't help feeling satisfied at how much he had accomplished.

He found satisfaction in doing the labor manually. The work brought him close to it all, to his cabin, to his creation.

He had a swift bite, made sure he drank plenty of water, and continued.

Leveling the ground wasn't as easy as clearing out the weeds and grasses. This was because James needed to make sure that he evened the surface properly, especially given that his expansions would be attached to the cabin. The cabin had a foundation of stone, and James wanted the bedroom, kitchen, and workshop to be level with that.

He did his work meticulously, first digging the soil with a shovel and breaking the big lumps until the entire plot was turned over. Next, he used a hoe to compact the ground, moving soil to sunken areas or holes where he dug up stumps and shrubs to level them. At this point, he also added bags full of a mixture of soil and sand that would serve as a top layer of soil.

Once this was done, James took a common garden rake and raked up the soil, breaking up whatever clumps remained with the teeth of his rake or — if they were a little more stubborn — the back.

The sun dipped toward the west when James stepped back from his cleared and leveled the plot.

He rubbed the sweat from his forehead with the back of his hand and leaned on his rake as he surveyed the fruit of his handiwork.

I'd be damned if that's not level, James thought.

He had a perfect plot, the top layer lighter than the rest of the soil around his cabin due to the leveling solution he had used. He took another drink of water and checked his phone: almost 6 pm.

That was a full day's work, and the last thing to do was to cover his plot with a tarp. After all, he would go out with Corinne tomorrow, which meant that he wouldn't be able to spend any time on his construction project. He didn't want to risk weeds or other plans retaking his little plot — and things grew fast in the summer.

James used stakes and some boulders he had cleared

earlier to keep the tarp in place. It wasn't rock-solid, but it would do for a day, as he was sure he would pick up work the day after his date with Corinne.

With the satisfied nod, he took a last look at the result of his hard work, then turned toward the cabin. He headed inside to grab a towel. He would go to the creek to wash up, change into something dry, and prepare himself for a nice, quiet evening.

He hoped Sara would be around after that, so they could have their talk.

Whistling and with a towel flung over his shoulder, James headed to the creek near his cabin. He was excited about his date with Corinne tomorrow; in fact, he couldn't wait!

As soon as he reached the stream, he stripped off his clothes and stepped in, enjoying the refreshing coldness of the water. The babbling creek wasn't deep at all, reaching no higher than his waist. But that was deep enough for him to fully submerge himself and wash his hair and make sure he was thoroughly clean.

In time, he would look into getting something like a

shower for the cabin. He enjoyed bathing out here in the forest. There was something primeval about it, like he was taking care of his body in the same way his ancestors once had. But come winter, it might be a little too cold.

Once he'd washed himself, he swished his arms through the water a few times and emerged, letting the water drip from him before wrapping the towel around his body.

With the sun on its way down, he relaxed for a moment, sitting on a large boulder that the little creek babbled close to. All around him was the lush green of summer, and the fresh scent of pine trees filled his nostrils as the gentle watersong of the creek calmed his mind.

It was beautiful out here, so peaceful and quiet, yet vibrant with life in its purest form. As he sat there, James doubted he would ever want to leave.

And the good part was that he didn't have to.

He had no obligations other than those to himself and his loved ones. Sitting here in the westering sunlight, James was profoundly happy that he hadn't fought his brother and his cousins over his father's inheritance. They probably thought he was crazy, but he just laughed at it all.

Not crazy, he thought. *Just free…*

He enjoyed his moment of quiet in the waning warmth of the day for a few minutes before he toweled himself down and got to work, washing his clothes in the creek.

Now, most things about his new life were perfect, but this was a job that he didn't really enjoy. Even if you did it in the most beautiful place in the world with the most beautiful women by your side, doing laundry would still suck balls.

Maybe High Magic can help me here? James thought.

That wasn't a bad idea. He blinked and took a step back, still naked except for the towel wrapped around his waist. He had arranged his clothes on the boulder that he had sat on just a minute ago, ready to wash them one by one.

But what if…

He grinned to himself, then focused on the pile of laundry. With High Magic, intent was key. To trigger the ancestral memories from which he could glean the secrets of magic, he had to focus his intent. When his magical energy — mana, Sara had called it — would backlash into pain, he needed to turn it inward and search his ancestral memories. He needed to find those who had gone before him and achieved the same effect.

James focused on the pile of clothes. He tried to visualize them clean and dry, ready to be worn again, smelling fresh like spring flowers or a field of grass under a carpet of morning dew.

The fire of magic began to burn at his core.

The power waxed and rose, but James didn't channel it into a magical formula — after all, he didn't know the one he needed yet. So instead, the mana just pulsed through his channels without purpose until it transitioned into a light aching. And as that fire raged within, growing in strength by the second, James turned his power inward, calling upon the might of his Bloodline — the House of Harkness.

He knew his ancestors, even though he did not know their faces. They remained there at the back of his mind, trailing back into the shadows of time, reaching into years uncounted.

And as he consulted their featureless faces, known and unknown at the same time, he visualized cleaning and cleanliness, rituals as old as time, and tried to couple them with locations.

He thought of huts, of hovels, of castles, of ships, then of the babbling brooks and creeks that he himself washed his clothes in.

And from ages past, a vision rushed on.

Space and time became nothing, and James once again climbed the branches of his ancestral tree to learn of the past so that it might serve him in the present.

Chapter 15

Blood leeched into the cold, uncaring soil.

This was the first thing that James saw as he manifested in his vision.

Several men sat by a stream. They were pale, with bags under their eyes that stood wide in fear. Their dress was that of a time long past — waistcoats and three-cornered hats. But they were dirty, bloodied, stained as if from battle. One man lay against a tree, motionless and white as death, bleeding.

There was also one man in a red coat, on his knees, his hands behind his head, as he regarded what James assumed to be his captors with fear in his eyes. One of the other soldiers seemed to be in the middle of interrogating him.

James's first instinct was to step forward and intervene, but he realized right away that no one saw him. He wasn't really there — he was a spectator.

"Let me do away with this traitor!" the interrogating soldier snapped at the man in the red coat as he drew a knife from his belt. "Your King won't save you now!"

"Peace, Leighton," one of the other soldiers said. He was a grim man with long black hair tied back into a ponytail. Green eyes blazed with the fire of the forest from under dark, bushy eyebrows.

The man reminded James of the image he saw in the mirror every day.

His ancestor.

"We should bring him back to Ward at the siege camp," James's ancestor continued. "Let the boys over there sort him out. Not our jobs."

The interrogating soldier still had fury on his face. The knuckles on the fist that gripped the knife were white. He flashed a furious glare at the man sprawled against the tree.

"And what of Smith?" he demanded. "What shall we tell his wife? His children?"

"We shall tell him he fell defending their freedom," James's ancestor snapped. "Now think with your head, man." he turned to address the rest of the group. "The British are just over the hill. They are waiting. What does that tell us?"

One of the soldiers cleared his throat. "They want to use the cover of night to move the supplies?"

James's ancestor nodded. "Dead right," he said. "That gives us time... Time to get back to the camp. Ward needs to know. These supplies must never make it to Boston. Every shipment of munitions that makes it to the city prolongs the siege, prolongs the war, and will be the death of more good men like Smith."

The other soldiers nodded in agreement. Even the belligerent one that insisted on killing the prisoner now clenched his lips together and gave a grim, determined nod.

"They stand between us, though," one soldier commented, his accent Irish. "If we go 'round the lobsterbacks, we shall come late, aye?"

"Right you are, Neil," James's ancestor said. "We

can't go around them."

"So what are you suggesting, cap'n?"

James's ancestor rose to his feet. "Undress the redcoat," he said. "He and I shall swap clothes. For a single night, I shall be a turncoat, in all but heart. That will give me a chance to sneak past the British formations and make it to Ward's line."

The other soldiers exchanged glances. It was clear to James that they considered this a risky venture indeed. But the pieces of the puzzle fell in place for James now.

This was the Revolutionary War.

The man in the red coat was just that — a redcoat. And if he remembered his history lessons well enough, this might be the siege of Boston, at the beginning of the war that stood at the cradle of one of the world's greatest nations.

It was a little overwhelming — so different from the more anonymous visions he had had of the distant past.

Much closer.

And apparently, the House of Harkness had endured even in those days.

James's ancestor stood by as the other soldiers stripped the redcoat of his clothing, leaving him only in his longjohns.

"It's a more than a wee bit dirty," the Irish soldier,

Neil, said. "You might draw unwanted attention, cap'n."

James's ancestor gave a nod. "I'll take this to the creek and clean it, make sure it's nice and up to their standards."

"Then you'll be drenched," Neil mumbled, shaking his head. "Not sure about this plan o' yours, cap'n. The lobsterbacks will notice something off about you."

"I have a solution," James's ancestor said. "An old family recipe to clean and dry. Just give me a few minutes, eh?"

The other soldiers watched with doubt on their faces as James's ancestor disappeared among the trees in the direction of the babbling brook. Heart pounding in his chest, James followed.

At length, the man found the gentle lapping waters. He stood there for a moment, looking around, making sure that no one was watching him.

Unaware that he had a spectator from the future.

Then, when he had ascertained that he was alone, the man placed the redcoat uniform on a large boulder that hugged the course of the brook. He gave one last look around to reaffirm he had no onlookers, then raised his hands over the bundle of clothing.

He shut his eyes, and James could sense the swelling

of magic in his ancestor's chest. He was growing more sensitive to magic, detecting with more ease as his own practice grew stronger.

With the voice of a commander, James's ancestor spoke the words of power:

"Vansmetta tod reinigt.

"Furanderinghe, herstellinghe. Wasser.

"Vansmetta tod reinigt.

"Danoock, vannatta tod droock.

"Furanderinghe, herstellinghe. Vurra.

"Vannatta tod droock."

And as the man spoke the first segment of the magical formula, the uniform grew wet, drawing water through arcane means from the gently babbling brook behind it. But the effect was more than just drenching the uniform. The water went deep, deeper than it should have been able to without soap or a cleansing solution.

The blood and the dirt just washed out, dripping down the sides of the boulder before it seeped into the thirsty earth.

Then, James's ancestor reached the second part of his magical formula — another compound spell of High Magic — and in an instant, the clothing turned dry. There remained not a wrinkle or a trace of the garments having been wet. It was spotless now. In fact, the clothes seemed almost so spotless that James wondered if the British wouldn't notice that more than they would notice a dirty uniform.

But apparently, his ancestor was satisfied.

He flashed another look around him, and even as he did so, James felt himself turn lighter. Already, the vision was fading — now that it had taught him what he needed to know.

As the man disappeared among the trees, the stolen uniform under his arm, James gave him the last look as he faded back through time and space.

In his heart, he wished his ancestor Godspeed, even though that would not change the course of affairs.

After all, history was already written.

Chapter 16

With a gasp, James returned to his own place and time.

He blinked once, taking in his surroundings. Very little — if any — time had passed.

Still, the vision had left him a little disoriented and a lot excited. The feeling of having seen things from a perspective that he himself never experienced made him feel as if he were a child again — discovering new worlds and people in the pages of his books.

It was amazing. From warriors to homesteaders, his ancestral line contained everything, and he was almost as excited about learning of his ancestors as he was about mastering High Magic.

He shook off the disorientation, then summoned his Grimoire with the simple spell he now knew by heart.

The book appeared in his hands, and he sat down, taking a few minutes to write down not only the formula of this new spell to clean and dry but also the circumstances under which he had learned it.

When James was done, he dismissed the Grimoire and finally focused on the pile of clothes.

He visualized them clean and crisp, free of wrinkles as if they were new, and the magic blossomed in his chest. He raised his hands, like his ancestor had done, even though he wasn't sure that was necessary, and spoke the words:

"Vansmetta tod reinigt.

"Furanderinghe, herstellinghe. Wasser.

"Vansmetta tod reinigt.

"Danoock, vannatta tod droock.

"Furanderinghe, herstellinghe. Vurra.

"Vannatta tod droock."

The mana blazed in his core, and the water of the

brook suffused the garment, cleaning it more deeply than any laundry machine or cleaning solution could. And when James moved to the next part of his formula, the clothes turned dry and neat, as if they just been ironed by someone with lifelong experience in making sure that garments looked absolutely immaculate.

This is amazing, James thought.

He chuckled to himself as he let go of the arcane energy and stepped forward to gather his clothes.

Then a sound behind him made him freeze.

He turned around, body ready to spring, and met the wide hazel eyes of a wild creature of the forest.

What the hell...

"O-oh," the creature stammered as she took a step back.

And she was definitely a she...

In a split second, James's eyes roved over a body that was only half human at most.

The top half was decidedly human female, except for the pair of floppy ears and, above them, the pair of antlers that poked out of an unruly mop of chestnut brown hair. She wore a flimsy top and a matching loincloth that had been made of leaves and some kind of plant fiber.

Even though the garments did not appear very durable, James's had to appreciate that great craftsmanship must have gone into making it — it was intricate and it fit her slim body well.

But from the waist down, this woman was furry. Soft, chestnut brown fur with white spots covered her shapely but powerful legs, and she had hooves instead of feet. As she half turned away, ready to bolt should James prove a threat, he discerned just the cutest little white tail poking over the edge of her loincloth.

If anything, she resembled a doe, a female deer.

"It's okay," James said, making a calming gesture at the sprightly creature. "You just startled me, is all. I mean no harm."

Her tail twitched slightly, and there was something jittery about her movements as she regarded him with the biggest hazel eyes he had ever seen in his entire life. He was still naked, but she didn't seem to mind at all.

And she wasn't running yet, but she wasn't talking to him either.

Skittish, James thought.

He held up his hands as he spoke. "I'm James Beckett," he said. "I live in the cabin over there."

He jerked his thumb in the cabin's direction, and she crouched low at his sudden movement, almost bolting off between the tree trunks.

"Relax, relax," he added.

She sniffed, cocking her head a little.

"What's your name?" James asked as he studied her petite figure. Like he would expect from a doe girl, she was lean and built for speed. Her breasts were nice, firm handfuls, and her waist and shoulders were narrow.

Her hips and thighs, though…

Hot damn.

"Hind," she said. Her voice sounded small; her words quick. "I am called Hind." She was curious, but ready to jump at a moment's notice.

"Hind," James repeated, sampling the name. "That's a beautiful name. You live around here?"

She took a step back, still skittish. "Maybe?" she muttered.

That made James chuckle. Any creature too honest to lie about even such a simple question had to have a sweet heart. But his laughter put her on edge again, and she took a careful step back.

He didn't want to see her leave, but he had to admire the way her hooved feet found a perfect balance on the uneven flooring.

I bet she's quick, James thought.

"I was just bathing in the creek here," James said, continuing the conversation to prevent her from hopping off.

"Are you the one who has been building?" she asked.

He blinked. "Yeah," he said. "Yeah, I'm building over at my cabin. I'm expanding the bedroom and kitchen and building a workshop."

"It's very noisy," she said, cocking her head as she studied him. "What's a workshop?"

He laughed. "A place to make more noise."

At that, a slight smile graced her plump lips. "Do you like to make noise?" she asked.

There was some kind of maddeningly sexy innocence about her line of questioning, about the way she stood there with her head to the side, about the little twitch of her tail and her ears as she studied him.

Something wild and pure that called out to the most base needs of James's soul.

He cleared his throat, trying to get the dirty thoughts to leave his mind.

"It's not really about the noise," he said. "I plan to make a nice home for me and my... Well, I guess my family. If it bothers you, you're welcome to drop by and we can discuss it. I want to be neighborly."

"Neighborly," she repeated, as if the word was the strangest thing she ever heard, her hazel eyes drifting over his naked form without shame.

Wow, this is a real wild one, James thought.

"Very well," she said, still studying him with her big hazel eyes. "I will come by when it bothers me. And what about my friends, the squirrels?"

"Uh, what about them?"

She took half a step closer, still slightly crouching, as if ready to spring. "Can they come by when it bothers them? Will you be neighborly to them?"

"Uh, sure," James said. "I don't speak 'squirrel,' though... or whatever it is that they speak."

Now it was her turn to chuckle. She covered her mouth and narrowed her eyes at him as if he were a child trying to fool her.

"Squirrels don't speak," she said.

He returned her smile and stood a little straighter. "Well," he said. "Then I guess *you* will have to come speak to me on their behalf whenever they are bothered by my noise, won't you?"

She considered that for a moment and nodded once. Then she shook herself and looked down at him.

"Thank you," she said.

"For what?"

"For inviting us to visit your house so that we can all be neighborly," she said, and James still remained unsure if she actually understood what the word 'neighborly' meant.

Still, he smiled and nodded. "You're welcome anytime."

Her eyes were still narrowed, and she gave him another look.

"How did you clean those things?" she said, pointing a long, slender finger at the pile of clothes on the boulder. "Were you speaking magic to them?"

"Speaking magic?" He echoed. "Yeah, I guess so."

"You're a Mage?" she asked, cocking her head to the other side as she took another half step closer.

Her proximity distracted him. She didn't seem to notice that the flimsy clothes she wore revealed a lot, but left him wanting to see much, much more.

His eyes dipped down to those delicious thighs and — although he never would have thought it before all this — the fur on her legs was pretty hot in its own unique way.

"Yeah," he said. "I'm… I'm a High Mage. A fledgling one, I suppose. I'm just starting out."

"Interesting," she said, studying him with renewed

curiosity.

He opened his mouth, not sure what he was going to ask, when a branch snapped behind her. In less time than it would take James to blink, she drew herself up, threw him a last glance, and bounded off into the forest without another word.

And for a moment, as he stood there in befuddled silence, he thought he saw a pair of red eyes study him from the undergrowth.

And then they were gone.

Strange...

He cleared his throat, gathered his clothes, and headed back to the cabin.

Chapter 17

The deer girl, Hind, was still on James's mind as he made his way back to the cabin.

The woods around Tour were full of fascinating creatures, although some of them were skittish or shy — like Kesha the fox girl or Hind.

James took their wariness as a sign that they were kind but careful. And he was certainly interested in getting to know them better. He expected that he would. After all, she seemed very interested in his ability to use High Magic.

As James approached the cabin, the sky above the canopy darkened. To his delight, a warm light shone out from the windows of the cabin, telling him that Sara was home.

Good, James thought.

He wanted to have a talk with her by the fire tonight and learn a little more about the world he was fast becoming part of.

He opened the door to the cabin and stepped inside. The delicious aroma of the fire met him, and he took a deep breath, reveling in the homeliness of it all.

"I'm home, baby," he called out.

"I'll be out in a second!" Sara's reply came from the bedroom.

With a smile on his lips, James sauntered over to the couch and sat down, giving his weary muscles some time to recover. It had been a long day working outside to level the ground for his construction project, and he felt that satisfying strain on his muscles as he stretched and yawned.

A few moments later, Sara appeared in the doorway, wearing a short pink dress. She was smiling at him, her bright yellow eyes shining like a pair of polished gemstones.

"How was your day, baby?" she asked.

He beckoned for her to come over. "It was good," he said. "I got a lot of work done, but I'm hungry as hell."

She came over to him with feline grace, and he drank in the sight of her beautiful and curvy body and the way every step made her ample breasts bounce a little.

With a purr, she settled on his lap, swinging her shapely legs to one side as she placed a slender hand on his chest. Her fingers played on his pectoral muscles as she looked at him.

"Shall I make you something to eat, then?" she asked.

"That sounds wonderful, baby," he said. "But first, tell me about your day."

Her smile grew wider as she leaned forward and kissed his cheek. "Of course." She thought for a moment, her left ear giving a cute twitch as her gaze drifted to the left. "Well," she began. "I did some... hunting."

James chuckled. "Hunting? More mice?"

He smiled and reached up to kiss her, running his hands across her smooth arms. She shivered slightly under his touch and leaned into him a little more.

"Not exactly, baby," she replied.

James nodded. "Okay. Tell me more."

Sara gave another smile. "Well, we get pests in the cellar sometimes. Mice, sure, but other things as well."

"Other things?" James asked, still running his hand over her forearm. "This is starting to sound mysterious…"

His words drew a small laugh from his cute cat girl.

"Don't worry, honey," she said. "They're just bugs."

"Bugs?"

She shrugged. "Well, for as far as I know."

James raised a hand. "All right, all right," he said. "It's good we're having this talk, because I've had a few questions about this place — including the cellar — for a while now. So what you say we fix dinner together, have a nice bite, and then we settle down by the fire. You can tell me all about this."

Sara nodded, her tail giving a playful swish. "Sounds perfect!"

Chapter 18

They prepared dinner together, although James was more occupied with teasing Sara. She giggled at his attention, obviously doing her best to distract him with her blessed body.

But in the end, they prepared some spaghetti with a meaty sauce of tomatoes and herbs from Corinne's farm. There was plenty of it, and the meal was delicious and filling.

As it turned out, they were both ravenous, attacking the meal with vigor. By the end of dinner, they were both satisfied.

James settled back on the couch with a contented sigh before turning his eyes to Sara, who sat on the floor as per usual, her tail swishing as she rubbed her stomach.

"Delicious," she purred. "If I do say so myself."

James laughed. "Come on," he said. "Let's go do the dishes, and then we can chill."

"Leave them," Sara said, her big yellow eyes on him. "I'll do them tomorrow. For now, we should relax."

Music to his ears, of course. "You sure?" he asked.

She nodded. "Hm-hm," she said. "I have time to spare tomorrow."

James grinned. "Well, I'm not going to pass on that…"

Sara giggled. "I didn't think you would," she said.

Then, she got on her hands and knees and crawled over to him, her big yellow eyes studying him with that mischievous light that always seemed to burn in her gaze. With a deft hop, she ended up on his lap, nesting against him and resting his cheek against his chest.

"Hmm," he hummed. "This is nice."

She sighed. "I love it when we do things together,"

she said. "But there are days when I love it even more if we just hang out like this."

"Absolutely," James agreed.

They sat like that for a while, James scratching Sara behind her fuzzy ears as a low purr rose from her throat. The warmth from the fire kept out the cold of impending night as the world outside darkened.

It was perfectly cozy and comfortable, and James almost nodded off as they relaxed together, the light sounds of the forest their only company.

But his half-slumber was broken when Sara hopped to her feet to close the shutters on the windows. He blinked, stretched, and studied her, fascinated by how her midnight black hair swayed with every step as it cascaded down her slender back.

"So," she said as she turned back to him. "You have questions?"

He nodded as she headed into the kitchen to make them some tea. "I have a few, yeah," he said. "Did I tell you I had another ancestral memory today?"

She looked at him over her slender shoulder, excitement in her eyes. "No!" she said. "You didn't! That's great news."

James smiled. "It is," he admitted. "I learned a spell to clean and dry my clothes. Not sensational, but it was a compound spell."

She laughed. "Are you kidding, 'not sensational'? That's great news; I hate doing the laundry."

"Well, well," he began, giving her a naughty look. "You do look great when you're doing the laundry."

She grinned and wagged a finger at him. "Maybe," she said. "I bet I look even better when I'm *not* doing the laundry."

He laughed and rolled his shoulders as he watched her make tea.

"When the vision ended," he continued. "A... Well, a *deer* girl came out of the forest. We talked for a while, and she said her name was Hind. She seemed interested in my magic, but she was skittish. When she heard a noise, she hopped off."

Sara threw him a cryptic glance over her shoulder as she poured boiling water into the teapot.

"Hind, you say?" she murmured. "I don't know anyone by that name. But from the sound of it, she is a Fae like me — a spirit of the forest."

"And like Astra?" he asked.

"Hmm," Sara hummed. "Dragonkin aren't really Fae. They're magical... but not like me."

She and the Dragonkin did not get along — had even fought in the past. When James had asked for the reason behind their enmity, Astra had just shrugged, saying that their kind had a feud from centuries ago.

"When the deer girl left," James continued. "I believe I saw a pair of red eyes staring at me from between the trees."

Sara froze and turned around. "Red eyes?" she asked. "Are you sure?"

"Pretty much," he said. "They were gone in a flash. But I know what I saw."

"Hmm," she purred, her slender finger touching her lips as she contemplated his words.

"Any idea what they mean?" he asked, sitting up.

"Maybe," she said. "We've seen more of the creatures coming near Tour lately. Think about it: Kesha didn't use to come this close to civilization. And I never saw this deer girl before. And then we have Astra coming down from the Eltrathing Tree to spy on you..."

He laughed. "I'm not sure she's spying..."

She grinned. "Maybe. Maybe not. Anyway, that's more activity than we've seen around Tour in a long time. If you glean red eyes in the woods — well, maybe something is driving them toward us. It might be worth talking to Astra or this deer girl, Hind, when you next run into them again. Maybe Kesha knows more about what's going on! She lives deep in the forest as well."

"So this thing with red eyes is bad?"

"Not necessarily," Sara hummed as she put two teabags into the pot filled with piping hot water. "There are many things with red eyes — some of them bad, some of them good. It could be a Shifter... And some of the Fae have red eyes. Some High Mages are also known to have their eyes changed to a red hue after prolonged exposure to certain elements of magic." She rounded off her sentence with a shrug. "Could be very many things. Let's keep our eyes open."

"Sounds smart," James agreed.

Sara threw him a smile, then came over with the teapot and two pewter mugs. The two of them settled on the couch once more and enjoyed their tea, Sara humming softly as she sipped hers.

James took his time drinking his, letting the hot liquid ease his tired muscles and fill his belly with a pleasant warmth.

"Now," he said. "About the cabin."

She looked at him quizzically, her amber eyes sparkling in the firelight.

"I was considering the foundations earlier," he said. "And the cellar below it." He kept his eyes on her. "They are old, aren't they?"

She nodded. "It's hard to express their age in years,"

she said, her face taking a more serious expression than he was used to. "The cabin is ancient; older than the village of Tour, probably, although the village is old, too. I can't tell you its exact age, but it has to be centuries."

"So... Made by whom? The first settlers?"

She shook her head. "Older."

"Native Americans?"

She shook her head. "It wasn't..." She scratched her head and blinked, her left ear giving a twitch. "It's hard to explain. These places — the foundations of the cabin, the cellar, the location of Tour, not so much the village as it is now, but just... well, the nexus of energy that makes up the village — they exist in many places at once."

"What does that mean?" James asked.

"Think of Tour like... like a stairway," she said. "It cuts across many floors. And each floor is a plane of existence, like Earth. Tour is one of many nexuses of energy and power. It draws in magical creatures and those with the aptitude for High Magic. Didn't it call out to you? Didn't it seem like the place drew you in long before you even understood the mystical qualities of it?"

James nodded. "Yeah," he said, remembering his first

trip here with his father and how the land had seemed to call to him. "It did. That makes sense."

"I thought so," she said. "It has been like that for many centuries, since long before the first settlers came to these shores. And the foundations of the cabin have always been here, just as Tour has always drawn in people."

James considered this for a moment. "So, if I were to venture out into the woods, would I be able to cross into another place? Another dimension?"

Sara wagged her head, her left ear twitching. "It's not that simple," she said. "It takes considerable skill in High Magic to actually cross over into another place. I'm not aware of human High Mages who have done so — at least not during my life."

He regarded his mysterious cat girl for a moment, his hand on her shapely thigh. "Your life?" He asked. "So, this is maybe not the most polite thing to ask, but I feel it's relevant. How old are you, Sara?"

She laughed and gave him a playful poke. "Never ask a girl that!"

He chuckled along with her. "Sorry, sorry," he said. "But I can't help being curious. You know so much about all this magic business and about the history of this place. I get the idea you've been around for a while."

She smiled and leaned into him. "You can't really measure it in years. I've spent parts of my life dormant, other parts in cat form — almost completely feral and with few conscious thoughts. Other parts of my life, I have been like I am now." She thought for a moment, trailing a finger along his chest. "I really don't know, James."

"But you've seen all these things in person? All these things that you're describing — the village and its many inhabitants, the building of the foundation of the cabin?"

She looked up at him, her yellow eyes alive in the firelight. "You know what, James? I'm not actually sure. I have memories, but I couldn't tell you if they were actually mine or if they were passed to me in some way. I suppose I have always been around in some form... That is the nature of the Fae. But I do not remember everything."

It was fascinating and mysterious. To think that Tour was some kind of pocket dimension that stretched across multiple planes of existence, and that Sara had roamed here for so long in one way or another.

The nature of magic was simple when it was practical and allowed James to cast spells that eased his daily life, but there was this mysterious and enchanting side to it as well.

Whole worlds lay hidden behind a veil of magic.

Waiting to be discovered.

"When I first came to Tour," James said. "I had a vision. I was working for Lucy, chopping down trees at Rovary's Lot, when I encountered a ring of standing stones."

She nodded, rubbing her cheek against his chest. "I know," she said. "I called out to you then."

He smiled, scratching her behind her ear, winning another purr from her. "I expected that was you. But what was the vision that I saw?"

"It was an ancestral memory of sorts," she said. "There used to be a member of your house — the House of Harkness — whom I served as a familiar. This was a different life, different me, and the bond was far from as intimate as ours is today. But he lived here, in Tour, although I cannot recollect where."

"What happened to him?"

"He had to flee. That is what you saw in the vision. There was a... well, a dark time in the history of Tour. It was centuries ago, when humans mistrusted magic and persecuted those who practiced it."

James nodded. He remembered feeling fear and haste

in the vision.

"I never saw him again after that day," she said. "But when I sensed your presence, I understood you were of his blood — of his Bloodline. I was still dormant when I first sensed you, and all I could do to guide you was to send you that vision and have you seek me out."

"And I did," he said. "You guided me. And brought me to the cellar."

She snuggled up against him. "And I couldn't be happier."

He grinned and nodded. "Me, too," he said. "So, the cellar... It's magical, too?"

She nodded. "I don't completely understand its nature, and I have very little knowledge of it. All I know is that it goes down — deeper. I've never been very far down it, but I venture down a level or two from time to time to hunt."

She shuddered. "But if you go down far enough, there are these big spiders. They don't come up — and that's a good thing. But I don't want to see those things. They creep me out."

"Hmm," James hummed. "Do you think they are a threat?"

"No," she said. "They're not. I don't suspect they're evil or anything. They just sit down there — like normal spiders. But they're so big. It's yucky."

He laughed. "You know," he said. "I wouldn't have imagined a formidable cat girl like yourself to be scared of a few spiders."

She grinned and poked him in the chest. "Wait until you see them," she said. "You'll change your mind soon enough."

James nodded, taking another sip of his tea. "So, how does this cellar connect to the other planes of existence? Are they even connected? Do they share something in common? Is the cabin itself part of this place?"

She laughed, patting him on the side. "Whoa, there!" she said. "You're asking things I don't know! Maybe these are things for you to find out in the future, hmm?"

He chuckled and nodded. "You might be right about that," he said.

After that, they fell silent for a while, each of them occupied with their own thoughts.

For James, it was all very exciting. He loved the idea of exploring this magical new world. But he was going to take things easy. So long as there was no threat to him or his loved ones, he was going to savor every moment of his new life — from building the cabin to exploring the woods to venturing down into the cellar.

"Hey!" Sara said suddenly, perking up and fixing

him with her big yellow eyes.

"What is it?" James asked.

"Didn't you just say that you learned a new spell? One that cleaned and dried clothes?"

James nodded. "Yeah?"

She clapped her hands and gave an excited yelp. "Show me!" She said. "You can do the dishes! See if it works on them!"

"Hey," James said. "That's a great idea."

He gave her a pat on her round butt as she hopped up from his lap.

"Let's go try!"

Chapter 19

As it turned out, James's new spell worked perfectly on the dishes as well.

Sara watched in awe as James raised his hands, focused his intent, and spoke the mystical incantation he had learned from his ancestral vision.

In moments, his spell drew water from a big jug he and Sara kept under the kitchen counter, thoroughly and deeply cleansing the dishes before drying them. When the spell was completed, the dishes were clean, dry, and in a neat pile.

"That's amazing!" Sara purred as she hopped over to inspect the dishes.

She lifted a few of the plates, checking them to make sure they were clean to her standards, then gave a satisfied nod.

"Well done, my love," she purred, kissing him on the lips before turning back to the counter to put the clean dishes away.

James felt pretty good about himself as he stood there. In the grand scheme of things, being able to do your dishes as easy as snapping your fingers might not be revolutionary, but it was still true magic. And it would only get better from here.

"Do you think it works on everything?" Sara asked as she bent over to put some plates in a cabinet. Her short, pink dress hitched up as she bent forward, giving him a perfect view of her round butt and the cute lacy panties that she wore.

The sight quickened James's blood.

"Everything?" he asked, his voice a little strained. "What do you mean, everything?"

She giggled and glanced back at him. "I don't know,

James! I mean, I know you can do magic to wash the dishes and your clothes, but what about other things? Can you clean the entire house? What about your car? Our bed sheets?"

"I don't know," James said. "I haven't tried."

She looked at him for a moment, a wicked grin on her face. "Why not?" she purred. "Come on, let's give it a try."

Mirrored her grin and nodded. "Sure," he said. "Let's see what the limits are of this new spell of mine..."

James and Sara soon learned that James's new Cleaning spell was good for a lot of things.

An hour of experimenting proved that, while he couldn't clean the entire cabin at once, the spell served perfectly to clean parts of it. It worked on the floor, but only within the boundaries of the cabin's separate rooms.

James believed this wasn't due to some inherent limitation of magic, but rather related to his own way of thinking. When focusing his intent and trying to envision the cabin clean, he found that his mind needed to focus on a 'single thing'. Trying to picture the entire cabin clean all at once caused the spell to falter.

An interesting lesson, James thought.

He hadn't encountered any limits to High Magic so far, and this was the first time a spell of his actually failed. It was good to explore the boundaries.

In short order, and under the admiring and excited squeals of Sara, James cleaned the entire cabin to a high standard. In fact, the place almost appeared as new.

They then went outside into the darkness to use the spell to clean his car. As with the cabin, he required separate castings to clean different parts of the car. One for the outside, one for the interior, one for the trunk, and so on. But he was pleased to discover that he could clean all the surfaces of the vehicle with relative ease.

"This is really amazing!" Sara exclaimed, clapping her hands as she walked along the side of the vehicle, inspecting every inch for cleanliness. And it was clean. The only problem was the rust spots, the scratches, and the dents.

James gave a satisfied nod. He was getting tired now, though. Prolonged use of magic combined with a long day of work began taking its toll.

When she finished inspecting his car, Sara whirled around and threw James a bold look.

"Satisfied?" he asked, popping his shoulders.

Her yellow eyes roamed over him, and she licked her lips. "Partly," she said.

He chuckled as he studied her in her tight, short pink dress. "What's that supposed to mean?" he asked.

She bit her full lower lip as she regarded him for a moment from under heavily lidded eyes. "Well," she began. "All we've cleaned now is stuff... But the question is, does it work on people?"

With that, she grabbed the hem of her dress with both hands and pulled the garment off over her head, revealing that delicious, voluptuous body that James could just drown in for days.

She didn't wear a bra, so her big breasts bounced free, and she was left only in her cute pair of lace panties and her high heels, matching the think of her dress.

All thought of sleep vacated James's mind at once as he saw that bounty of delicious, ivory flesh before him. Blood flowed down, and his cock stiffened.

"Try me," she purred, spreading her hands to reveal her beautiful body to him.

James found his breath speeding up, his heart pounding, and he chuckled. "I'm not sure I can focus with you like this," he said, then cleared his throat. "Besides, I need a source of water nearby."

She grinned and threw him a naughty look before raising her hand and beckoning him over with a single finger. "Follow me to the creek, then," she said.

Heart pounding in his throat, James followed Sara deeper into the dark woods.

Chapter 20

Sara led them down to the creek where he had washed his clothes earlier.

As she moved with superhuman grace and beauty, her body was a dance floor for the moonlight as it threw shadows and light to highlight her perfect curves. And all the while, her fluffy tail swished with playful anticipation, poking out over the waistband of her lace panties.

James could do nothing but follow her, his mind already alive with images of Sara on her knees before him.

She stopped at the creek, turned, and watched him from hazy yellow eyes. Behind her was the boundless mystery of the forest. He had the scent of the pines in his nostrils, and his connection to the ancient earth rang as deep and profound as it could.

He felt at one with the world, as if he and Sara were woodland spirits playing under the forest canopy at the dawn of time.

She spread her hands once more, posing for him as she cocked her head.

"Here?" he asked.

She nodded. "Try it," she said as she hooked her thumbs behind the waistline of her panties and lowered them to the forest floor, her heeled feet stepping out of the garment with feline grace.

James took a deep breath, savoring the crisp forced air, as he tried to clear his mind of dirty images.

Then, focusing his intent on Sara's beautiful body, he began imagining her fully clean and bathed — soft, fragrant, and warm, as if she had just stepped out of a hot tub.

When the familiar sharp pang formed at the back of his skull, he raised his hands and spoke ancient words of power:

"*Vansmetta tod reinigt.*

"*Furanderinghe, herstellinghe. Wasser.*

"*Vansmetta tod reinigt.*

"*Danoock, vannatta tod droock.*

"*Furanderinghe, herstellinghe. Vurra.*

"*Vannatta tod droock.*"

For a moment that seemed to last an eternity, nothing happened. Then Sara, who stood with her arms raised, giggled.

"Oh, by the Elements," she exclaimed. "Wow, this feels... This feels great!"

Her body became wet — dripping, even — as James's spell drew water from the creek behind her. She gave a sigh of delight, squirming as she surrendered to the spell sensation. And a moment later, just like that, James's magic dried her beautiful body, leaving her squeaky clean, her hair shining with renewed luster in the bright moonlight.

Damn, James thought. *It works.*

"I feel cleaner than ever before!" Sara said. "It's amazing! I mean, I knew I was clean, but this is something else entirely! It's almost like every pore of my body is purged!"

She laughed and spun around with the grace of a ballerina, her curvy hips rolling, her pert ass jiggling enticingly.

James grinned as he straightened himself, letting go of the focus of his magic. "This is perfect," he said. "I wonder if I can use it on myself."

Sara laughed and gave an enthusiastic shrug that made her breasts bounce. "Try!" She exclaimed. "High Magic is all about trying, James."

She was right, of course. There was no reason not to try, so James undressed with little ceremony.

He pulled his shirt off over his head, discarded it, and kneeled to untie his shoelaces and remove his boots and socks. After that and under Sara's appreciative gaze, he reached for his pants and pulled them down, kicking them away.

It was not like it mattered if they got dirty.

He lowered and stepped out of his boxers, standing naked as the day he was born. Now even more so than minutes ago, he sensed his connection to the surrounding forest. Standing naked in the moonlight like the first children of man, full of wonder and questions, unashamed of their bodies or their desires.

He looked at Sara and saw the same primal desire

reflected in her eyes. He smiled at that.

"All right," he said. "Let's see what happens."

He held his hands out, palms up, and closed his eyes, picturing his entire body clean and fresh, the sweat and grime of the hard day's work washed away.

As the power of mana in his core strengthened from his intent, he once again spoke the ancient words, noting how their surroundings — the ancient, primeval forest — seem to lend even more power to them.

Sara was right; the feeling was amazing.

Fresh, but not icy cold, the water cleaned him in a way that no bath or soap ever had before. Indeed, it was as if every pore of his body was cleansed, leaving him pure and perfect as he had never been before. It was a delicious feeling, but it was fleeting. The big advantage of a bath or shower was that it took a while.

This was a matter of moments.

When James opened his eyes, Sara had taken a few steps toward him. The pale light of a big moon danced on her beautiful face as she looked him over, feline curiosity in her eyes.

"So clean," she squealed excitedly as she inspected him.

James chuckled. "Yes," he said, nodding. "Except for here..." He rubbed a spot just above his eyebrow. "It seems the spell isn't perfect."

"Whaaat?" Sara purred, stepping forward and rising to her tippy toes to inspect the spot he was rubbing, bringing her lips within less than an inch of his.

"Gotcha!" he exclaimed before placing his lips on hers as he snaked his arms around her waist.

Sara gave a surprised yelp, then giggled into his kiss as she surrendered to his embrace. She pushed her delicious body up against his, her soft breasts poking against his chest, her nipples firm and in need of his attention.

With a groan, he surrendered to the delights of feeling up her clean and soft body as she pulled herself loose from their kiss and fixed her hazy eyes on him.

"You tricked me," she purred teasingly before running her soft tongue over his cheek.

James grinned and nipped at her, eliciting another giggle from her as she wriggled against him playfully.

"You fell for my ruse all too willingly," he said, fixing her with his stare as his hands roamed over her limber back, dipping to that round ass that regularly haunted his dreams.

She gasped when he grabbed one butt cheek and squeezed it firmly before moving up to her neck and kissing her softly and lovingly. Her arms went around him, pulling him tight to her soft body.

"Oh, James," she crooned as he kissed her neck, breathing in percent. There was a hint of wildness to her, despite the magical cleansing he had just given her.

It drove him wild. It always did.

"Will you make love to me here?" she asked, her voice soft and vulnerable in a way it rarely was. "Please? Do it right now, please?"

James couldn't resist the siren call of that sweet voice, the lure of those succulent curves.

His cock hardened immediately as he moved down to kiss her again. His hands roamed over her body, touching and caressing her everywhere.

She was so responsive, so eager, so ready.

"Please, James?" she purred again.

He nodded, fastening her in his embrace as his body responded to hers.

Then, he leaned in for a kiss…

Chapter 21

"Hmm," Sara sighed as James licked her lips and nibbled on them before diving deep into her mouth.

His hands went exploring now, caressing that pliant and soft skin, squeezing the ample flesh of her delicious curves. He pushed against her, his hard cock poking against her soft stomach with profound need.

"I want you," he murmured, running his hands down

her sides to her hips and back up to her big and firm tits. "I want you every moment of every day."

"Hmm, James," she purred. "I'm all yours. Every day. Whenever you want me."

He growled deep as his hands roved down to cup her glorious globes, kneading them, pinching her nipples between two fingers to give them a gentle twist that made her yelp.

Sara moaned, her body arching and pushing back against him as his hands explored her perfect curves with a lusty passion. And when his hand dipped between them, trailing down the smooth slope of her flat stomach and over her mons pubis to graze the cute little triangle of black pubic hair, she shuddered with pleasure.

Then, with all fatigue drained from his muscles, he swooped her up, carrying her as if she were his bride toward the edge of the babbling brook where a lone tree waited for them.

She clung to him as he carried her, her arms around his neck, her lips showering him in soft but needy kisses. When they reached the tree, he lowered her softly and gently, placing her on her feet.

"Turn around," he said, his voice soft but full of lustful command. "Lean against the tree."

Her yellow eyes, blazing with excitement, fixed on him for a moment before she bit her lip and complied, turning to show him that perfect hourglass figure.

His eyes were drawn at once to where her back tapered to her round backside, her tail swishing with excitement.

With a grunt of approval, he placed his hand on the small of her back and let it trail down the curvature of her ass. She moaned with delight as his hand left goosebumps on its journey toward her inner thigh.

On instinct, she spread her legs, throwing him another inviting glance over her shoulder.

She wanted him; he knew that. And James was helpless against that great, hungry fire in her eyes.

She mewled with delight as his hand cupped her wet and warm pussy. She trembled with anticipation as his fingers slid between her slick folds to stroke her. As his index finger teased her pretty little clit, she threw back her head and moaned with rapture, her body shuddering in ecstasy at his touch.

"Yes, James," she hummed. "That's it…"

She was perfect like that, her body tense as she surrendered to her pleasure, her face flushed with excitement, her breath coming hard and fast as she writhed in the grip of his ministrations.

And she was so clean, so fresh. He just wanted to bury his face in her.

A lustful groan escaped him as he slipped one of his fingers into her. He could sense her heat and wetness, and it made his dick rage with need.

But not just yet...

"Oh!" she exclaimed as his finger curled to tease her G-spot, sending jolts of pure pleasure through her body.

But only for a moment...

He drew his finger back, grinning.

"James!" She wriggled her body, trying to guide his finger back to where it had been a moment ago.

A slight, teasing chuckle escaped him, and he leaned forward to press his body against hers, his hard dick poking against her plump butt cheek as he brought his lips close to her ear.

"Let me lick you," he whispered.

"L-lick me?" she moaned, half delirious with desire.

"Here," he grunted, bringing his finger up to tease her tight pucker. "Let me taste your sweetness."

She gasped and threw him a wide-eyed look over her shoulder.

"Y-yes," she moaned, the eagerness and speed of her reply almost catching her by surprise. Her tail curled around his leg, the tip brushing his swollen and cum-filled balls for a moment, making it hard to resist plowing into her right there and then.

"Oh, yes, James…" she crooned, writhing with desire. "Please do it!"

He kissed her on the back of her neck, making her purr with sweet satisfaction. And from there, his lips trailed down and down, tickling between her shoulder blades to her slender lower back and around her fluffy tail until he came to her perfect and round butt cheeks.

By then, Sara was wiggling and squirming with delight, her hands gripping the tree trunk fiercely as halting moans escaped her mouth. Her tail was a blur of movement behind her, writhing wildly, wrapping around him, enthralled by this new experience.

James kissed the round curves of her butt cheek, nuzzling and licking them as he explored the smooth curve inward. He placed one hand on each of her cheeks, then parted them slightly, revealing her beautiful pink rosebud.

"Oh!" she cried out softly, biting her lip in anticipation as her forehead leaned against the tree.

James ran his tongue along the inside of her soft butt, and Sara shuddered, sending ripples down those ample cheeks. Softly, his tongue made his way to that beautiful flower, and when it finally connected, Sara shivered with joy.

With a soft moan, she pushed her hips back in an invitation to explore further. James obliged, his tongue curling and probing her tight passage, giving her deep pleasure.

One of his hands dipped down to tease her dripping wet pussy again. The sensation was exquisite, her delicate flesh so soft and warm, her juices flowing freely to coat his finger as he slipped it into her tight tunnel.

Sara arched her back, moaning with delight, her ass pressing back against him as James ate it out.

When James pushed two fingers into that tight hole, she cried out in ecstasy, her eyes rolling back into her head at the sheer bliss of it all. He pulled back, then tease the edges of her pucker with the tip of his tongue in a way that made her body tense up.

She couldn't handle it.

Out of nowhere, her body began quivering as her orgasm crept up on her.

"Oh, by the Elements!" she cried out. "James! Fuck! I'm coming."

He surrendered to it, licking around her tight little flower as he pummeled her pussy with two fingers, curling them slightly to stimulate her G spot in a way that made her knees weak. Sara clutched to the tree against which she had been leaning, and James was sure that she would've fallen if it hadn't been for that mighty tree trunk.

"Ohhh," she cried out, her body releasing the pressure. "Ohhhhhh! Oh, fuck!"

She shuddered and shook, her body wracked with spasms of pleasure as she rode her own release. And when James felt her come down from her high, he withdrew both his fingers from her depths, leaving her empty.

He didn't give her a moment to recover. His mind swimming in an ocean of need, he rose to his feet.

His cock was throbbing with need, and he grabbed it now, slapping it against her round butt cheek hard enough to send a wave down it.

She knew exactly what was coming. She pushed back her hips, offering him access as she looked at him over her shoulder, cheeks flushed from her pleasure.

"Take me, James," she whispered. "I want to feel you inside me."

James's mind was swimming as he rubbed his cock

down Sara's butt crack, slick with his spit and her own juices he'd spread there with his fingers.

She was so sensitive there from her orgasm, she moaned with tortured delight as he touched her. Her thick legs trembled as he grabbed a handful of her black locks, pushed her against the tree, and lined his cock up with her tight little pucker.

"Mmph," she whimpered. "Fuck me!"

Then, with a grunt and a thrust, he pushed his cock into her rosebud. Her ass was tight, and he had to push gently to enter her, winning another yelp from the delicious cat girl. But she opened up to him fast enough as he plowed deep, driven by his primal need to fill this beautiful woman.

"Oh, by the Elements," she moaned as he filled her ass up with his long, thick shaft. "Like that! Fuck my ass, James!"

He happily obliged, pulling back so far that his cock almost popped out of her pucker before plowing into her again. Their skin slapped together, sending ripples along her delicious ass as she moaned under the violence of his love.

He fucked her ass harder and faster until they were both gasping for air, until sweat dripped down their bodies, and their muffled gasps and moans echoed through the forest.

The delight of their coupling was deep and delicious. Out here in the wild woods, they were like animals rutting, surrendering to their base needs and desires. He leaned forward as he thrust into her, kissing her neck, and in a primal instinct, Sara turned her head and snapped at him, almost biting as she flashed her canines.

It was so hot, he growled deeply and rammed into her again, pushing her up against the tree as she reached around and placed a hot hand on his back, her nails leaving a trace as they ran across it.

The slight pang of pain only excited James more, and he pushed her against the tree, grabbing her arm and folding it back above her ass as he leaned back to watch his cock piston in and out of her asshole, his every thrust making her delicious body jiggle.

"Fuck!" she moaned. "That's it, James! Hold me, hold me tight like that! By the Elements, I love it!"

He was unable to speak, so overtaken by lust as he plowed into her again, fascinated by the slapping skin and the rippling flesh. His orgasm rose from his very toes, his balls in need of emptying inside his beautiful companion.

"Oh, James!" she called out. "Cum for me... Don't

stop! Cum in my ass!"

He groaned, tried to push his own orgasm away, to postpone it, but when she gave a jiggle with her ass, her pucker clenching on his cock and milking him, he couldn't take it anymore.

James roared with delight, letting his pleasure wash over him even as the cute cat girl trembled and shook and moaned. He thrust deep, pushing thick ropes of cum into her warm and welcoming pucker.

Sara whimpered with delight as she felt his cream fill her up. He pulled back and pushed again, filling her more and more — so much that some of it was already spilling down to her trembling legs.

And even then he did not stop ramming into her as she moaned and mewled under the torturous pleasure of his orgasm until the strength fled from his body.

When he finally came to a stop, James leaned against Sara, panting as he pressed his chest against hers, placing soft kisses on her back and neck.

"Oh, James," she moaned, her voice trembling. "That... That was so extremely hot." She smiled at him over her shoulder, then leaned the back of her head against his heaving chest.

James sighed and muttered agreement, incapable of stringing together too many words at the moment. He held Sara tight, his arm snaking around her waist, her hand resting on her soft stomach.

They stood like that for a while, enjoying the enchantment of the forest at the side of this moonlight-dappled creek as they basked in the afterglow of their orgasms.

At length, they untangled, and Sara turned around to hug James.

With a broad smile on his lips, he unfolded his shirt at the base of the tree so they could sit on it together and enjoy the moonlit night a little longer. Sara nestled in his lap, pressing her warm and soft body against his.

It was perfect like this.

"This tree will always be special to me now," Sara whispered in his ear, her fingers playing on his chest. "I will always remember it as a place where you showed me pleasures that I hadn't even dreamed of."

He smiled, caressing her shapely thigh as he glanced over his shoulder at the ancient tree, the warden of the forest. "I don't think it would mind if we left it a little keepsake of this special moment, do you?"

She giggled as she looked up at the tree, then shook her hand. "No," she said. "It wouldn't mind. Us Fae can sense such things."

James grinned and nodded, then reached for his

pants without trying to upset Sara's weight on his lap. "Watch this," he said as he pulled the garment in and reached into the pocket with his free hand.

Curious, Sara hopped up from his lap as James's hand emerged from his pocket with a small foldable pocketknife.

When she realized what he had planned to do, she gave an excited mewl and covered her mouth with her hands. "Oh, James," she purred. "That's a beautiful idea."

Sitting on his knees, James carved their names in the tree, then carved a heart around them. When he was done, he leaned back, Sara hanging from his arm, and inspected his handiwork.

He gave a satisfied nod. "There," he said. "A special memory for just the two of us."

"It's between us and the tree," Sara purred, giving him a kiss on his cheek.

James laughed and looked up at the tree. It was vibrant, alive, perhaps even more so than before. But maybe that was just a trick of the eye.

"Yeah," he agreed before pulling her close.

"Between us and the tree."

Chapter 22

James and Sara strolled back through the moonlit forest, hand in hand. They stopped on occasion to share a kiss or hold each other as they let their eyes feast on some beautiful vista that the nightly forest offered.

As such, it took them a while until they returned to the cabin.

But for some reason, James was not done with the

night just yet. They stood on the porch together, and Sara gave a lazy yawn as she wrapped his arms around his neck and placed a kiss on his cheek.

"Tired?" James asked, a smile on his lips.

She nodded and gave a nibble on his earlobe.

"Why don't you head inside and get ready for bed?" He asked as he took a deep whiff of the fresh forest air. "I think I'm going to stay outside a minute longer and enjoyed the stars."

She chuckled and gave him a bump with her hips. "All right," she said. "But don't be too long…"

James laughed and gave her a slap on her shapely bum before she hopped inside, giving him a last look over her shoulder as she kicked the door shut with her heel.

Then James turned to the forest and went down the steps that led up to the porch.

Soft forest soil gave way under his boots, and the crisp air of pine trees grew stronger. He stood in front of his cabin and looked up at the grand display of the Milky Way — colorful swaths of stars, alive with the mysterious purple shimmer of nebulae.

They were so clear out here, far from the city and close to nature's heart.

A night like this reminded him why he loved being

alone out here in the wilderness.

Well, not *alone* alone…

He smiled at the idea of having found love so quickly and perfectly in Tour. He would've expected that moving to a small town like this wouldn't have worked any miracles for his love life.

In fact, he had expected the contrary.

It just goes to show how life can surprise you, James thought.

And now, he had *two* girlfriends — Sara and Lucy. And he expected — and hoped — that Corinne and he would hit it off on their date as well. After all, they had already shared much intimacy and had gotten to know each other fairly well over the past few days.

He was interested. She was interested.

So why not?

He closed his eyes and took another deep breath.

And as he stood there, eyes shut, relishing in the delights of the forest, he heard a gentle rustle. It could've been a forest creature — a bird in the branches, a curious squirrel coming to see what all the fuss was about.

But somehow, James knew it was more than that.

He opened his eyes.

About twenty feet away, her silhouette drawn

sharply against the massive trunk of a pine tree, stood Kesha.

She had one hand on the massive tree as she stood half-crouched, ready to bolt at the first sign of trouble. Her fox ears stood upright, and her three tails billowed behind her, the tufts of white at their ends easily visible in the moonlight.

She had come back.

She was cautious, wary, ready to run…

But she had come back.

James smiled and carefully took a step toward the shy fox girl.

She flinched, but she didn't run.

James took care not to approach her to swiftly, inclining his head to her.

"Hey, Kesha."

The fox girl did not respond at once, and James waited patiently, wondering if perhaps she hadn't heard what he'd said.

Finally, a thin smile graced her full lips. "Hello, James Beckett," she said, the wind carrying her soft voice to him.

"I'm happy to see you again," James said. "And on a beautiful night like this…"

She nodded, some of the weariness slipping from her stance. "It *is* a beautiful night," she said.

Curious, she peeked past him at the cabin. Then her eyes drifted to the materials he had gathered for his construction project.

"You've been busy," she said when her multicolored gaze returned to him.

He took a casual step forward and scratched the back of his neck.

"Yeah," he said. "I like having things to do. I'm expanding the bedroom and adding a kitchen an workshop to my cabin."

"Expand?" she asked. "Expand for what?"

"Well," he said. "It's a little small. Not that I need a palace or anything, but I would like to have a little room for…"

She cocked her head, her cute fox ears bobbing along with the movement. "For what?" she asked.

He studied her for a moment and folded his arms. "I can tell you," he said. "But if *I* tell you things about *me*, will *you* tell me things about *you*?"

She bit her lip, her body coiling a little again. "L-like

what?"

"Well," James said, not put off by the increased caution in her stance. "The last time we talked, you ran off the moment I was distracted. And I still have some questions about you… about the forest. I'd love to talk, but conversations aren't a one-way street."

"One-way street?"

He chuckled.

It was easy to forget that she had lived in the wilderness for years. Before that, she had lived in Tour. She probably didn't even know how to drive, let alone the basic rules of traffic.

"It's a figure of speech," James said. "It means that we can talk, but I won't be the one doing all the talking. I'm curious about you too, Kesha. I'd like to know more about you."

She thought about that for a moment before nodding, her curious gaze roaming over him.

"Okay," she said. "It won't be a one-way street. It will be *two* one-way streets."

He laughed and shook his head. "Close enough." He then looked over his shoulder at the porch of his cabin.

He took his time, giving her plenty of opportunities to run away if she were so inclined.

Because if she was going to bolt, she'd best do it now.

But when he turned his head, she was still there.

"Why don't you come out here?" he said. "We can sit on the porch together. I can get you a drink if you like?"

She considered this for a breath, then nodded.

Slowly, tentatively, Kesha took a single step closer to James. She kept her distance at first, keeping both her hands firmly planted on the bark of the nearby tree as she stepped between the firs and pines.

As James watched, a small smile came to her lips as she peered at him.

"Easy does it," he said, struggling to suppress a chuckle at the almost exaggerated care the fox girl was taking in her approach to him.

Then, the fox girl took a deep breath and stepped out from the tree line, bridging the final few feet between them.

And when she came close, she came very close.

Her scent — wild and of the forest — enveloped him as she came to a stop a little over a foot away from him. Her big, heterochromatic eyes roamed over him with bright curiosity, and she cocked her head slightly as if to ask what would happen next.

"Come sit," James said, gesturing at the stairs that led up to the porch of the cabin. "Do you want anything to drink?"

She shook her head, and she didn't move.

Slowly, James reached out and took her soft hand in his. She didn't protest; she only gave a furtive blink as she looked down at their hands now touching.

Then she smiled.

James led her to the steps and sat down first. Kesha sat down beside him, studying him still. They sat some distance apart, but not as much as strangers.

James shot her another smile, and she returned it — albeit somewhat shy.

Good, James thought. *Now we can finally have a conversation...*

"So," James began, letting his gaze drift to the starry sky above. "You asked me why I want to expand the cabin?"

Kesha nodded, a small smile playing on her lips.

"I want others to come live with me," James said. "Sara already lives with me, but we could use a little more room. And in time, I want others to join me as well."

Her fox ears straightened a bit. "Others?" she asked.

"Who?"

He grinned. "*Two* one-way streets, remember?"

She laughed — a beautiful sight — before nodding. "Yeah," she said. "You're right. Ask away."

"The last time we met," James said, fixing her with his gaze. "I tried to ask you why you had gone after Corinne's chickens. I would still like to understand why. I mean, you've been surviving out here in the woods for a long time, right? Why wait until now to go after the chickens?"

Her smile faded a little. "I don't like to talk about it," she said.

"Well, that's what you said the last time," James replied. "Look, I will not force you to talk about anything you don't want to talk about. But please understand, I can help you. If it's food that you need, I have plenty. Shelter…" He jerked a thumb at the cabin behind him. "I have some, and soon I will have plenty, too."

Kesha nodded, her expression softening a little as her shoulders slumped.

James gave her another warm smile. "I am not trying to dupe you or lure you into anything. I am not your enemy."

She was silent for a moment, her eyes drifting over

the canopy as she considered his words. He did not press on, instead choosing to relax and sit back, watch the stars, and let her come to her own conclusions.

If she didn't want his help, then that was fine.

If she did, he was right here.

"Well," she finally said. "I used to hunt rabbits and fish a little to the north of here. Lately, there is been... well, a *thing*..."

"A thing?" James asked when her voice trailed off.

She nodded. "Something with red eyes. Something that snarls. I don't know what it is, but I'm scared of it."

James nodded slowly, his mind drifting to the chance meeting he had had with Hind, the deer girl. She had left quickly, and James was sure that he had seen a pair of red eyes staring at them from the undergrowth.

"I think I've seen these red eyes," James said.

Kesha sat upright, her entire body coiling as if ready to run. "Really?" she muttered. "W-where? Are you sure?"

"Don't worry," James said, making a calming gesture. "It was some distance from here. I don't expect any pair of red eyes to visit my cabin at night."

She shivered, looking around at the trees with increased awareness, as if monsters might come shambling out from between them at any moment.

"Are you sure?" she asked.

He shrugged. "We might go inside. That would be safer."

She hesitated, still alert.

He watched her for a few moments, then followed her gaze as she looked at the tree line with fright.

At length, he spoke again. "What is this thing that you're so afraid of?" he asked.

She hesitated again before answering. "I don't know what it is," she said. "But the red eyes make me afraid. They watch me in a hungry way, and I do not trust them."

"When did you first see them?" James asked.

"Up north, the soil is a little firmer. It's where rabbits like to dig their holes, and I used to go there to hunt them. One evening, when I was chasing one of the little bunnies, I heard the thing snarl."

She shivered, then scooted over to him so that their legs touched. She gave him a big-eyed look. "I heard it before I saw it, James," she said. "And when I looked in the direction of the sound, I saw those big red eyes watching me. It felt like it was going to attack. I ran away and never came back. But the thing has followed me ever since. I've been... I've been moving farther south to the edge of civilization, giving away my territory, hoping it would be enough to appease this beast."

James nodded slowly. "But it hasn't been enough, has it?"

She shook her head. "I don't know what to do, James," she said. "There's nowhere else to go. Food around here is already scarce, and if I have to go farther south, people will see me."

James could understand why that would be a problem. People didn't know fox girls existed — nor cat girls or Dragonkin, for that matter.

It'd be a shit show for sure.

And it was clear that Kesha was very afraid of this threat. The fox girl was shivering right now, her eyes darting from left to right as if this red-eyed monstrosity might charge them at any moment.

James put his arm around her, and she gave him a wide-eyed look — a little furtive at first, but then she smiled and the shivering stopped.

"How about you stay here tonight?" James asked. "I mean nothing by it. You can sleep on the couch if you want. But I think it would do you good — just a night in a warm and safe place, away from this thing that has been hounding you."

She puckered her lips as she considered his words.

"You would do that for me?"

"Of course," James said. "I told you: I want to help you."

With that, the fox girl drew a deep breath and finally relaxed.

She scooted over a little closer to him and rested her furry head against his shoulder. The big fox ears tickled his neck, and the feeling was something that James could get used to. At the same time, a soft tail brushed his back.

"Thank you," Kesha said. "I think... I think it would be a good idea."

He grinned and gave her a playful poke. "And now you understand why I need a bigger cabin, right?"

At that, she laughed, the tension flowing from her as she looked up with a sparkle in her eyes.

"Come on," James said. "Let's head inside."

Chapter 23

James entered his cabin with Kesha in tow. The fox girl was still a little wary, but James had won enough of her trust to allow her to relax a little more.

"Welcome to my house," James said, giving her a smile over his shoulder.

She looked around, her big eyes curious as she took in the small living room with the kitchen, the fireplace, the couch, and the chair. Her eyes darted to the hallway that led to the bedroom as well.

"It's nice," she hummed. "Very cozy."

James nodded. "Normally, Sara would be bouncing all over the place, eager to question you. She's a curious one, as you probably know. But it looks like she's already gone to bed."

Kesha grinned. "Hmm, perhaps I'll see her some other time."

"I'm sure you will," James said, beckoning her to come in.

He parked Kesha on the couch and put the kettle on. Within a few minutes, he had a part of hot tea to share with her, and the fox girl gave him a thankful smile as he poured her a mug and handed it to her.

She was too cute, sitting on the couch with her knees drawn up, her dainty hands wrapped around the mug full of steaming goodness. As she sat there, her eyes darted all over the place — curious to a fault, the fox girl wanted to see it all.

Smiling, James sat down beside her.

"Better?" he asked.

She nodded. "It does feel nice," she whispered.

They sipped their hot drinks for a while, enjoying the quiet of the forest and the warm glow of the fireplace.

Then Kesha glanced at the door, her eyes narrowing slightly.

"Are you sure it's safe?" she asked.

He chuckled. "Yeah," he said. "Pretty much. I can lock the door, and if anything comes through the windows... Well, we'll hear it."

She relaxed a little, then leaned into him once more, her soft ears tickling his neck. "You're very kind, James," she said. "I've never had anyone be so nice to me before."

"I'm glad I can help you," James replied.

She took another sip from her mug, and her eyes drifted to his chest as they drank in silence for a moment. "I sense something special about you," she said. She raised a ginger eyebrow. "Why did you come to Tour?"

James considered her for a moment. His arm draped around her again — almost on its own. He wondered if he should share the details of what exactly was 'special' about him, or if he should keep it on the down-low.

But then again, James thought, *she is Lucy's daughter. She already knows High Magic exists because she is a Fae.*

No harm in telling her.

"I am a High Mage," James said. "Maybe that's what you're sensing? As for Tour..." He shrugged. "I already told you I came here because I inherited this cabin from my father. But I won't deny that I've felt a special pull to this place ever since I first came here."

She nodded, a smile making its way up to her eyes. "I knew it," she said. "It must be destiny. There used to be High Mages in Tour, but there haven't been any for a while. Your coming may set things right."

"Right?" James asked. "Are there things wrong?"

"Well," she said. "The red eyes, for instance. And the people of the town have been losing touch with us — with the forest and its spirits. More and more, they are leaving the village or turning more... bland. Look at mom, for instance," she continued, her expression turning a little wistful. "She's just running that store, selling stuff, and she never considers the world beyond the village. It's like she's frozen."

James considered Lucy, the lively and bouncy blonde shopkeeper, and he had to disagree with Kesha's assessment of her mother.

"She doesn't strike me as frozen at all," James said. "She's one of the most alive persons I've met in a long time — vibrant and intense are the words I would use to describe your mother."

She considered him for a moment. "Maybe she has already changed," Kesha finally said. "Because I don't remember her like that. But I haven't seen her for a long time."

James looked at her. "Would you like to see her?"

She pushed her lips into a thin line, considering his words for a moment before making eye contact again. "I know we agreed on this two-one-way-streets thing, James," she said. "But my relationship with my mother is a topic I rather wouldn't talk about. Not yet, at least."

"Fair," James said, and gave her soft shoulder a gentle rub.

She gave him a thankful smile before sipping from her mug again. "What do you think about my mother?" she asked after a few moments. "Do you believe she is happy?"

James frowned. "I'm not trying to broach the subject again, but since you asked, I think she is a little sad because of how things went between you two."

"Oh," Kesha said, her expression saddening.

"Don't worry too much about it," James said. "Whenever I'm with Lucy, she seems happy. The store might have her a little stressed right now, but it's nothing she can't manage. She is strong, savvy, and she has all the tools she needs to make a living."

"You know what I think?" Kesha said. "I think meeting you might have done her well. The woman you're describing is not the woman I remember."

"If so," James said. "Then I'm happy for it. She's sweet, with a good heart, and she deserves all the happiness she can get in life."

Kesha smiled and nodded, content with James's answer. After a moment, a deep yawn escaped her, and she covered her mouth as she stretched.

"Okay," James said with a chuckle. "I think it's high time for me to get you a blanket and let you sleep."

She gave him a tired grin. "Yeah," she said. "I don't know where it's coming from, but I'm suddenly exhausted."

James rose from the couch with a smile. "That's not uncommon; you've been out in the woods for a very long time, fighting for survival and sleeping rough. Any extended time of facing hardships will leave you tired the moment you enter a safe place. Let me get you some blankets."

James tiptoed into the bedroom, where the delicious shape of a sleeping Sara was outlined by the sheets. He took a few blankets from the cabinet and brought them back to the couch.

Kesha already lay curled up into a little ball on the couch, breathing heavily. Her eyes were closed.

Damn, James thought. *The poor thing must've been*

absolutely exhausted.

He kneeled beside the couch as he draped a blanket over her. She looked very cute sleeping like that, all curled up and snug like a little fox in its hole.

When he placed the last blanket over her, her multicolored eyes opened and looked at him lazily from under long lashes.

"Hmm," she moaned. "Thank you, James."

"You're more than welcome," James said.

She brought up a hand and placed it on his cheek as she gave another lazy moan and squirmed under the soft warmth of the blankets. In doing so, she pulled him a little closer.

James smiled at her and kissed her palm as she stroked his face.

"Hmm," she hummed as her lips parted.

Then her tongue flicked out playfully to touch his cheek.

James blinked, a little surprise, before he realized it must be a way for a fox girl to show her affection. And the sensation was nice; her tongue was soft and warm, and a shiver of delight passed through him as she giggled and gave him a kiss on his cheek.

"Sorry," she purred. "I'm not so good at restraining myself when I'm half-asleep."

James chuckled. "Oh, I don't mind," he said. "I like it, in fact."

"Hmm," she purred before placing a soft kiss on his cheek. "Good... I'd like to see more of you, James Beckett."

"Likewise," he said, stroking her soft hair and scratching behind her big fuzzy ear, winning another sigh of pleasure from her. "But you go to sleep now. You need it. I'm sure we'll talk more later."

She was already breathing heavily again as he rose. He gave her one last look — a fox girl curled up on his couch — before he tiptoed over to the bedroom.

Truth be told, he was pretty sure that she would be gone by morning. Kesha was like that — furtive, quick, and a little too shy to become the subject of Sara's relentless and curious questioning in the morning.

But that would be okay.

James was sure they would see more of each other.

Chapter 24

The next morning began cloudy — the first fully overcast sky since many days.

Still, the sunlight was more than bright enough to awaken James, eliciting only an annoyed grunt from Sara as she turned around and pulled the blanket over her head.

James chuckled, gave the cat girl a pat on her side,

and hopped out of bed to begin the day.

His mind was still reeling from the previous evening, its many delights, and his progress with Kesha.

But this day would bring its own exciting experiences: he had a date planned with Corinne. He wanted to be on his best with her, eager to bring the two of them closer, so he wanted to start out the day in the best possible way — with a wholesome breakfast and a big mug of coffee.

It didn't surprise him at all that Kesha was no longer sleeping on the couch. He had expected she would leave silently, but he did smile when he found a note on the low table.

'Thank you', it said in the handwriting of someone who obviously wrote very little.

She had drawn a paw-print under it, and James laughed at that. He pocketed the cute note, deciding to hold on to it as a keepsake of his progress with Kesha.

He would see more of her soon; of that, he had no doubt.

James prepared sandwiches for Sara and himself, using the last of the bread, cheese, and vegetables. They were almost completely out of food now, and James would have to drive down to Lucy's general store to get some more.

Not that he minded; seeing Lucy was always a treat.

Besides, he had agreed to meet Corinne at eleven, which meant he had plenty of time to do some shopping. He was happy that he had covered the cleared and leveled ground for his construction project with tarp, so he could easily leave the work for a day while he kicked back and relaxed.

He whistled a jaunty tune as he finished work on breakfast, then poured himself a mug of coffee. By the time he sat down on the couch, he heard Sara stir in the bedroom, and she came out a moment later, rubbing her eyes with both hands, dressed in an oversized T-shirt she had stolen from him.

He grinned and shot her a wink. "How are you doing?" he asked. "Sleep all right?"

Only half awake, she mewled something incoherent, then flopped on the couch beside him, resting her head on his lap. He scratched her behind her ear, enjoying her low purr as he ate his breakfast and drank his coffee.

After a few minutes, Sara livened up a little and rolled onto her back, staring up at him from his lap with big yellow eyes. She wasn't a morning person, and that was fine.

"What's the plan for today, baby?" she asked, her left

ear giving a twitch.

"I have a date with Corinne," James said around a mouthful of sandwich. "I'm picking her up at eleven, and I was thinking of getting some groceries before I meet up with her. We're practically out of everything."

"Ooh, Corinne," Sara purred. "Will you be bringing her back here?"

He grinned. "Not today, I don't think," he said. "I want to have a little private time with her — get to know her a little better before I involve you girls again." He gave Sara a playful poke.

She giggled and nodded. "That's probably smart," she said. "She might be a little shy."

James snorted. "I think there is something under the surface there, but we'll see. How about you?"

She stretched lazily. "Hmm, me? I'm going to sleep and be lazy all day."

He laughed. "Nothing else?"

"Hmm... nope. I'm just going to lie around here all day and do nothing." She gave a squeal as she squirmed with excitement at the prospect. "Well, maybe I'll lie around outside a little as well."

James chuckled. "Well, I guess I shouldn't be surprised, considering your feline nature." He gave her a teasing poke in her side that made her giggle.

"Some days are for running around; others for lying around," she said, a sage expression in her eyes.

James laughed before taking another swig of coffee.

They relaxed together for a few more minutes before James dressed up for his date with Corinne. He settled on a black button-down shirt and a casual pair of well-fitting jeans and neat, black shoes underneath.

But before he got dressed, he used his Cleaning spell on himself again, making sure that he was thoroughly clean and ready for his date with Corinne.

After assuring himself that he was looking sharp, he gave Sara — still lazing on the couch — a kiss on the cheek and headed out to his car.

The engine turned over on the fourth try, and James lowered the window to let in the balmy breeze and the fresh scent of pine trees as he drove down to Tour.

Chapter 25

James pulled into the quiet town of Tour. It was still early and only a few people were about.

By now, he noticed they cast him curious glances. His car had become something of a regular sight, and it wouldn't surprise James if people were starting to wonder who he was and why he was dropping by so often.

He was sure that, in time, he would meet most of them.

He parked his busted-up sedan in the lot next to Lucy's general store and turned off the engine. He got out, stretched in the sunlight, and looked around.

The sky overhead was still cloudy, but James noticed a swath of clear blue in the east. It looked like the wind was chasing off the cloudy layer and that, in an hour or so, the sun might break through and they would get another proper summer day.

With a smile on his lips, James walked to the entrance of the general store. The bell chimed as he pushed the creaky door open, and his gaze at once met that of Lucy.

The beautiful blonde was leaning on her counter with one arm, jotting down something in a notebook, as her eyes flashed up to look at him from under her long lashes.

She smiled and perked up. "Well," she exclaimed. "Mr. Beckett! And looking so sharp! Now, that's a pleasant surprise."

He laughed as he walked over to her, checking if there were no other patrons in the store at the moment. When he got to the counter, he leaned forward. She mirrored his movement and closed her beautiful eyes for a moment as their lips met for a short but intimate kiss.

When James drew back, he gave her a smile. "How have you been?" he asked.

Lucy grinned as she tucked a blonde lock behind her ear. "Busy. Busier than usual, actually."

"Are you feeling better?"

She gave a lopsided smile, one finger absently tracing the countertop.

"Hm-hm," she hummed. "Our time together helped. I was doing a lot better when you dropped me off at the store yesterday morning." She gave him a meaningful glance. "Tired, though…"

He laughed. "I'll tell you, I felt like a million dollars after I dropped you off. I did the rest of the work clearing and leveling the ground for my cabin expansions in one day!"

"Wow," she said, placing her slender hand on his forearm. "That's pretty impressive. I'd love to see the place when it's finished."

"Oh, you will," he said. "I don't need to tell you that you're always welcome at my place."

She smiled, and her fingers left goosebumps in their trail as they traced over his forearm. "That's good to know," she said. "Thank you."

She turned around to take some dry wares from the

shelves behind her and put them below the counter. As she worked, she threw him a glance over her shoulder.

"So what's next?" she asked. "I mean, after you finish expanding the cabin and building the workshop?"

He considered her words for a moment, only momentarily distracted by her limber movements — she was wearing a short skirt and her tight shirt with the faded print 'Lucy's Deals' on it.

"I don't want to get too crazy," he said. "But I think one of the important quality-of-life things that my cabin needs is electricity and running water. Hot water, too…"

Of course, he had his new spell to do the job that one needed hot water the most for, namely cleaning. But still, he loved a hot shower from time to time — the spell could not replace that relaxing sensation. And if he only wanted to rinse a cup or a plate, it would still be easier to do so under a tap rather than cast the entire spell.

"That sounds like a mighty operation," Lucy said, rousing him from his considerations. "Any idea how to go about it all?"

He looked over his shoulder, making sure there were no other customers, then leaned in a little closer.

"I think I want to try to find some kind of magical

substitute for those two things, you know? I would like to keep the cabin off the official electricity grid. There has to be some kind of way to use magic to generate power for appliances like a refrigerator or a coffee machine."

She nodded, a smile on her lips. "I'm pretty sure you're going to come up with something," she said. "You're smart... And very good with your hands, Mr. Beckett." She gave him a teasing poke in the ribs.

He chuckled. "Thanks. You're not so bad yourself."

Lucy's eyes sparkled with mischief. "Don't make me blush now, Mr. Beckett," she said, batting her eyelashes at him theatrically. "We both know how that will end..."

James grinned.

Lucy perked up. "Oh," she said. "By the way, I've been getting more than a few questions about you from my regulars. You haven't met most people in Tour, and some are getting mighty curious..."

"Uh, yeah," he said, hesitating for a moment. "I'm aware of that, but it would be a bit strange to go from house to house and introduce myself, wouldn't it?"

Lucy laughed, waving it away. "No, silly," she said. "That's not what I think you should do. I think the best way to go about introducing you to all the townsfolk would be to do something fun, like organize a barbecue or something, you know? We can have dinner and a few drinks. You can meet everyone."

He considered that for a moment before saying, "That sounds pretty good."

Lucy clapped her hands together excitedly.

James had to smile; the perky MILF was so bubbly and energetic that he couldn't help but feel happier whenever she was around.

"How about I set things up for you?" Lucy asked. "The people know me, and I know everyone in town. It would be easy for me to invite them all. Plus, I have all the necessary equipment — my uncle Rovary used to organize a barbecue at the end of summer for the entire town."

"Perfect!" James said. "And I can do a pretty mean burger, if I do say so myself."

"Yay!" she chirped, clapping her hands. "Then it's settled. The townsfolk will love you!"

It was a great idea. James was curious about the other townsfolk, especially since Sara's revelations about the town and its mystical nature. It only made sense that some people here had at least an affinity with High Magic.

Maybe I can learn things from them, he thought. *Or we*

can learn things together. *It would be interesting to see...*

The bell chimed behind him, announcing the entry of another customer. Lucy threw him a meaningful look, and he gave her another kiss before saying, "All right, I need to go grab some groceries. I have a date with Corinne later today, but I'll drop by again tomorrow. I'll be continuing the work on my construction project, and I'll need some supplies from your store."

She winked at him. "Oh, Corinne, hm? Tell her I said hi. I'd love to see her again soon."

"I expect you will," James said, a smile surfacing on his lips.

Lucy laughed and gave him a playful push. "I bet!" She then shooed him off. "Now go, get your stuff. I got other customers I need to help."

Laughing, he turned and headed into the store.

Most of the supplies James purchased were things that would keep well outside the fridge, but he threw a yearning look at the freshly cut strips of bacon, promising himself to prioritize a solution for refrigerating his food — magical or otherwise.

Still, he took a small carton of eggs. They were fresh — from Corinne's farm — not like the eggs one would purchase in the bigger chains in the city.

Those eggs were usually already a few weeks old at the time of purchase and couldn't be kept outside of the fridge for too long. These, however, were no more than one or two days old, which meant they would keep for another day or so. He and Sara could have them for breakfast tomorrow.

He also got cheese and sausages that kept well outside the fridge and a few pots of pasta sauce that were generous on the meat — just the way Sara liked it.

Then he got plenty of bread, vegetables, fruit, a bottle of wine for those romantic sunset nights, and some stuff to snack on, including crackers, a bag of crisps, and some jerky — he was pretty sure that Sara would love that.

When he got everything he needed, he paid at the counter, gave Lucy another kiss on her plump lips, and returned to his car.

It would soon be time to meet up with Corinne.

Chapter 26

James dropped the groceries off at the cabin. As promised, Sara still lazed on the couch — she had fallen asleep again, cuddled up in the oversized shirt.

Smiling at the sight of his cute cat girl napping, James placed the soft kiss on her cheek, stashed the groceries, and packed his stuff for a day at the lake in his duffel bag.

When he went outside to put the duffel bag in the trunk of his car, he noticed the clouds had already been driven off by the wind. The sun was now beating down on the forest, warming the earth and releasing the crisp scents of summer.

He took a deep breath before heading around to check on the work he had done yesterday.

The tarp he had used to cover the cleared and leveled ground was still in place and undisturbed. James gave a satisfied nod. He was eager to see Corinne and take her to the lake, but he was also looking forward to starting the actual work on his planned expansions and workshop. There was much to do.

He stepped into his car and drove down to Corinne's farm.

When he drove out of the ratty road that led to the cabin and onto Forrester Trail, he could already see the pretty redhead leaning against a fencepost of her farm.

God, James thought. *She looks beautiful…*

The sparkling image of summer, Corinne wore an airy white dress with a floral pattern. It danced about her slim and toned body as the breeze played with it, and her ginger locks were like flames billowing in the wind.

She saw him coming, and a bright smile marked her

beautiful face, making the sprinkling of freckles around her nose dance.

If ever there was a natural beauty, Corinne had to be her.

James's heart was thumping in his chest when he pulled up beside her. He turned off the engine and leaned over to roll down the window on the passenger side.

"Hey, cowboy!" she said, a teasing grin on her plump lips.

"Hey, yourself," he said. "You look beautiful."

She smiled, her eyes turning to the ground for a moment before she looked back at him from under long lashes. "Thank you," she said. "You look pretty snappy yourself too!"

He laughed, then pulled the grip of the door on the passenger side and gave it a firm push so it creaked open. "Not exactly a ride befitting of your beauty," he said, exaggerating the words to make it a little over-the-top. "But I'm afraid it will have to do."

She grinned as she pushed off from the fenceposts and walked over to the car, her beautiful hips swaying.

"A car is a car," she said. "I don't need fancy stuff; only *real* stuff." She turned to pick up the basket and cooler she had placed by the road.

"Well," James said. "Real is something I have plenty of." He nodded at the basket and cooler. "Let me get those." And he hopped out of the car.

But Corinne wasn't the type of dainty dame who would wait in the car while he loaded up the trunk. He liked that about her — her independence and her can-do attitude. She helped him put the food and drinks in the trunk, then went around to the passenger door as James took the driver's seat.

James admired her limber figure as she lowered herself into the passenger seat beside him.

She settled in, clicked her seatbelt in place, and looked at him. For a moment, her expression betrayed that she was excited about this — their date. "Let's roll out, cowboy," she said.

He laughed as he turned over the engine, put the car in drive, and pulled out.

With a beauty like her by his side, how could the day go wrong?

Chapter 27

The lake was on the south side of Tour, so their drive took James and Corinne down Main Street and past Rovary's Lot, where James had cut trees for a few days shortly after arriving in Tour.

As they drove, they spoke little, but the silence wasn't awkward.

Corinne had rolled down her window and leaned

back in her chair, letting the warm air caress her face. James could tell she was tired — she'd been working very hard to keep the farm running. She told him before that it was a challenge to do all the work by herself.

This is probably her first day off in a long time, he thought.

He resolved to make it a wonderful day for her; something to energize her for the days to come.

Finally, they came upon a narrow but tidy road that snaked into the woods, taking them through the forest to the south.

Their drive was scenic, especially with the sunlight shining through the trees and lighting up the path and dappling it with beams of sunlight.

"It's so pretty out here," Corinne said, the first words she'd spoken in a while.

"Hm-hm," James agreed. "And you know what the strange thing is? I've been here for a few days now, and I'm... Well, I'm not getting used to it, if you catch my drift? It never gets old."

An understanding light flashed in her pretty green eyes. "I know what ya mean, James," she said. "I've lived in Tour all my life, and the place still amazes me whenever I leave the house. There's nowhere else I'd rather be."

"You know," James said. "I think I'm beginning to feel that way too."

She placed her hand on his knee and gave a squeeze. "Good," she said.

There was a small lot before the trail hit the lake, but there were no other cars in sight. That made sense. Tour was small, and James imagined that only a few people came here from time to time.

Had a city been close, the cars would've lined up as far back as Main Street. But it looked like they had the place to themselves today.

James parked the car, and they got out.

Corinne stretched her limber body, giving James a moment to admire her willowy, almost sprightly, beauty.

She wasn't a Fae like Sara, but she certainly had something elfin about her. She could have easily featured in the painting of some classical master as a nymph or dryad from an ancient Greek myth, bathing languidly in a natural spring as her long, red hair cascaded down her slender shoulders.

James took the duffel bag from the trunk of the car, shouldered it, then took the basket with food and the cooler before walking up to Corinne.

She flashed him a smile and placed her hand on his

biceps. "I'm looking forward to this," she said. "It's been a while since I really relaxed."

He returned the smile and nodded for her to come along. "Let's make it a good one then," he said. "Come on. The lake is waiting."

As expected, they had the place to themselves.

Corinne let out a deep sigh as they entered the clearing around the lake. The cool breeze blew across their faces and brought with it the fresh scent of pine needles and clean water.

James took his bag off his shoulder and dropped it on the springy grass beside the cooler and the basket. Corinne crouched beside the basket and took out a blanket, spreading it on the ground in the same movement.

James smiled at that. Corinne had a way of doing things that were both practical yet elegant at the same time. He was glad he had met her — that they had met each other.

He sat down and took off his shoes before grabbing two sodas out of the cooler and handing one to Corinne as he settled down on the blanket beside.

She took the can and opened it with a fizzing sound. Then, she leaned back on her elbow, turned toward James as he sat cross-legged, peering out at the blue lake.

"That water looks really good," James said.

She laughed. "Well," she said. "It's a little early for lunch, so we could have a swim before we eat?"

He nodded. "I would like that. I even brought my swimming trunks!"

She grinned. "I'm already wearing my bikini."

He turned his eyes to her, and she lifted the hem of her summer dress, revealing a milky white thigh — thick and tasty — that led up to a cute, side-tied bikini bottom. It rode her shapely hips low and was the same color as her eyes — a vivid green.

James licked his lips and shook his head, chuckling. "Now you're just teasing me," he said.

She giggled and gave him a push before lowering her dress again. "I showed you mine," she teased. "Now you have to show me yours."

He laughed. "I have to change first. I didn't put it on this morning." He jerked a thumb at his duffel bag. "It's in there."

"Oh my," she said. "The cowboy has to change!"

There was a teasing edge to her voice and a naughty light flickering in her eyes as she watched him.

"But how will our gunslingin' hero go about that task without insulting the fine sensibilities of his lady companion? Will he change behind a tree, hopping around awkwardly as he rids himself of his breeches and changes into his trunks? Or will he just turn around and treat his fine lady friend to a full moon as he slips out of one and into the other?"

James grinned, leaning back on his elbows as he fixed her with his eyes. "You keep talking like that, and I'm going to toss you into the lake myself."

"Hmm," she purred. "I'd like to see you try."

James didn't reply. He lay back, a cryptic smile on his lips, letting her comment go.

But the moment she turned her eyes away, he shot to his feet with lightning speed. He hooked one arm under her knees, the other behind her back, and he lifted her up with a groan.

She yelped and kicked her legs, laughing as he lifted her up into the sky.

"No! James! No! Don't!"

She didn't weigh much, and she was a joy to hold in his arms.

But he would not hold her for long.

She laughed and kicked and tried to get loose as he carried her to the lake. When she realized she wasn't getting loose, she clung to him, throwing her arms around his neck as she laughed.

"I'm taking you with me!" she warned him.

The grin still on his lips, not in the least dissuaded. He waded into the water on his bare feet. The lake was of a pleasant temperature, having been warmed up all summer, but retained that unique freshness that you will only find out in the wild where people rarely come. He relished in how the water felt against his feet before wading in deeper.

By now, Corinne had burst out laughing, kicking her dainty legs as she draped in his arms. One of her slippers had flown off somewhere along the way.

"You're going in," James said, teasing.

"Then you're going with me!" she said, barely able to form coherent words through her laughter as she clung to his neck.

He waded deeper still, not caring that the legs of his pants were getting wet. It was a warm day, and it wouldn't be a problem. When he was up to his ankles in the water, he sped up.

"No! No! James!" Corinne laughed.

He threw her, laughing all the way.

But she hadn't been joking. Her grip on him was firm — she was a country girl, after all.

She clung to him with surprising strength, and James's eyes widened as he lost his balance, the fierce redhead clinging to him and burying her face in his neck. He almost recovered, with her still hanging from his neck, but she used her own weight for leverage.

For a moment, they hung in the balance — a tangle of limbs and laughter.

Then, with a splash, they both went in.

Chapter 28

James came up spitting water and laughing.

Corinne had given him a run for his money. He hadn't expected the limber and willowy redhead would be able to pull him along if he tried to throw her into the lake.

But she had some hidden strength.

She came up beside him, her beautiful hair now

colored a deeper red from being wet, and the sunlight shone in her bright emerald eyes, bringing them to life like mountain lagoons.

She was smiling.

So was he.

With a single stroke of his arms, he was with her. The smile on her beautiful lips, dripping with water, remained, but something smoky surfaced in her beautiful eyes as she watched him — something hazy, something of need.

He couldn't help himself. His arms found her narrow waist underwater, touched the soaked fabric of her summer dress still clinging to her body, and he pulled her in closer. She gave an amused mewl, and she wasn't complaining.

James knew he saw it right; she wanted him as badly as he wanted her.

His wet lips brushed hers, teasingly, and hers pouted slightly as they touched. Underwater, she raised her shapely legs and folded them around his waist, clinging to him as her slender arms wound themselves around his neck.

She laughed. Pure elation and joy, and it was an infectious laugh. James couldn't help but join her.

And at the end of that laughter, their lips met.

The sudden intensity of Corinne's kiss surprised James. Her grip on him tightened, and she pushed her entire body against his, both under and above the surface of the lake. She drew her arms back and held his cheeks as her tongue danced with his, soft moans rising in her throat.

Strands of wet hair cascaded down as she leaned into him, brushing his face, chest, and neck. The fresh and natural scent of Corinne danced about him, filling his nostrils and rousing his inner need.

When she pulled back from their kiss, her full lips pouting, there was a look almost of surprise in her bright green eyes. She loosened her embrace a little, and her cheeks crimsoned.

"Uh, I'm sorry," she muttered.

"Sorry?" he murmured, his voice husky with desire. "Sorry for what?"

She smiled. "That, uh, kiss was a little intense. I didn't mean to come on so... well, so *strong*."

He grinned, his hand still on her waist. "I didn't mind it in the least bit, let me assure you of that. In fact, whenever you feel like coming on so strong, go straight for it."

She laughed and bit the corner of her lower lip as she leaned into him again, her body pressing against his underwater.

"Good," she just said before resting a cheek on his shoulder.

They stood like that for a while, her in his arms, their upper bodies above the surface of the lake. Warm sunlight came down from the sky — clear by now — and spread on their skin the warmth of summer. By the way he held her and she held him, James knew Corinne was looking for much more than just a lover, and that she hoped to find all of that in him.

She would.

Deep within, feelings blossomed for Corinne. In fact, they had been blossoming ever since he first ran into the beautiful redhead on his way to the cabin for the first time. James was happy that she returned those feelings, and that she got along with Lucy and Sara. In his heart, hope grew that — together — they might be a family.

He closed his eyes, banning all thought and just enjoying Corinne — her touch, her weight, her scent — as she held him tight.

"I think I'm getting a little hungry," Corinne said after a

while, her voice muffled by her face being buried in James's neck.

He laughed softly at that. "Well, I think we should eat something. Did you have breakfast?"

"Barely," she groaned. "I spent all morning tending crops and taking care of the chickens."

"That fox girl been coming around again?"

"Nuh-uh," she mumbled against his neck, sending a delicious little tremor down his spine. "But they're still jumpy."

He grinned. "Well, I can't blame them for that." He reached down with one hand and gave her a pat on her round bottom. "Come on," he said. "We'll get out of the water, dry up in the sun, and grab a bite to eat."

"Hmm," she moaned. "I don't want to let go yet. One more minute."

He happily obliged, holding her a little longer before she finally heaved a sigh and said, "Let's go grab some food."

They waded out of the lake, hand in hand. They were both thoroughly drenched. Corinne's summer dress had been white and of a light fabric to begin with, so the water rendered it nearly transparent, revealing the cute bikini underneath.

She caught him looking and stuck out her tongue

teasingly.

They made it to the blanket, and James began undressing, ridding himself of his button-down shirt and slacks until he was down to his boxers. Corinne blushed a little as she studied him for a moment.

Since he wouldn't go back into the water right now, he just flopped down on the blanket and lay on his back, watching Corinne as she pulled off her dress, revealing her ivory body.

The fabric fell away from her shoulders and pooled at her feet. Her breasts were full and perky, capped with small nipples that had hardened slightly in the cool air, poking against her bikini top. Her flat stomach was smooth and firm, and James had to fight back an erection as he saw how the cute bikini bottoms clung to her plump pussy.

She flashed him a smile as she raised her hand, an elastic hair tie between her teeth, and he watched with delight as she gathered her wet red locks and tied them into a cute bun before sitting down on the blanket beside him.

"All right," she said. "Let's eat."

Corinne reached into the basket and took out a sandwich. She handed it to him, and he accepted it with thanks.

"All fresh," Corinne said, pride on her beautiful, freckled face. "Well, at least the produce is. The baloney is from Lucy's store, obviously. I'm not a rancher. But I bake the bread myself."

He bit down. It was delicious. Few things could match a freshly baked bread, and James could tell by the taste that Corinne had gone out of her way to make sure that they had a delicious lunch together. He really appreciated that, and it told him that today was important to her.

Corinne took a sandwich for herself, and they ate in silence for a few minutes, just enjoying the day.

The birds chirped merrily, and the breeze was pleasant. The weather was warm and sunny, perfect for a picnic, and they were alone. It was good to be outside, eating sandwiches in the shade.

James glanced over at Corinne and smiled. She was gazing up at the sky, her head tilted a bit. Her eyes sparkled in the sunlight, and he wondered if she was thinking the same thing he was, that they had the rest of the day ahead of them. He felt like he could spend every waking second with this woman, and it would never be enough.

She turned her face to him, her green eyes twinkling. She smiled and licked her lips.

"Enjoying the sandwiches, cowboy?" she asked.

"Oh, yeah," he answered, grinning. "You are an amazing baker."

"Why, thank you," she said. She giggled and leaned toward him, kissing his cheek. "I have a feeling this is going to be a perfect day."

He laughed. "A perfect day? You bet."

They finished their sandwiches and relaxed on the blanket. Corinne was quick to roll onto her side and snuggle up against him, and he wrapped his arms around her, pulling her close as the two of them relaxed.

Her body was still wet from their little dip in the lake as she nestled against him. She brought up one of her shapely legs to drape it over his, her thigh brushing the wet leg of his boxers.

They lay like that for a while, drying up in the sun with their stomachs nice and full. After a few minutes, Corinne began breathing a little heavier, and James smiled when he realized that the beautiful redhead had fallen asleep in his arms.

It was peaceful — and endearing sign of complete trust.

She was right; this was going to be a perfect day.

After about ten minutes of drying up in the sun, Corinne stretched lazily and gave a cute moan.

"Uh," she hummed. "I fell asleep?"

James chuckled. "Yeah. Just for a few minutes."

She rolled onto her back and covered her face with her hand. "Ugh, I'm sorry."

"Don't be," he said. "I liked it. I wouldn't mind if you slept against me more often."

She rolled onto her side again, her big green eyes contemplating him as a smile crept up her lips.

"Ya mean that?" she asked.

He grinned and nodded. "Cross my heart."

Her smile broadened. "Then I guess I'll keep falling asleep on you."

She pushed against him, her skin hot from the sun, and her thigh brushed his, arousing the flame within.

He groaned softly as she rubbed against him.

"Hey, uh," she said. "Do ya mind if I ask you something?"

James looked at her curiously. "Sure," he said. "What's up?"

She swallowed hard before blurting out, "Did you... did you enjoy what we did? Y'know, the other day?"

He looked at her and grinned. "I have no idea what you're talking about," he said, teasing her a little.

She laughed and rolled her eyes. "Ugh, are ya gonna make me say it?"

"I'm gonna make you say it."

"Fine," she huffed and sat up suddenly, making her full chest bounce a little. "Did you enjoy me... touching myself while you were playing with Lucy and Sara?"

He grinned. "Of course," he said. "Why wouldn't I? You were worried about that?"

Corinne shook her head, hesitated, then nodded. "Maybe a little... I... It was very hot, but I never did anything like that before. I'm just..." She gave a nervous chuckle. "I'm new to all of this." She fixed him with her eyes, cheeks positively crimson.

He propped up on his elbows. "Wait?" he muttered, an eyebrow perked. "Are you saying...?"

She nodded.

"No way..."

She laughed, the tension escaping her a little.

"Well, there are no men around here, are there?" she said, gesturing wildly as if she had expected there to be many here. "I lived here all my life. My dad never took me anywhere. We didn't have the time."

She bit the corner of her lip and shrugged. "It just... It never happened." She sighed. "Is it bad? Please don't tell me ya think it's bad!"

He shook her head, sat up straight, and embraced her. "Of course not," he said. "Corinne, I like you for who you are. I think it's sweet you're telling me."

She surrendered to his embrace, and a little shudder passed through her. "Really?" she asked.

"Yeah," he said.

He kissed the top of her head, and she sighed in relief. He held her tightly and let her relax against him.

"It's... It's why I was hesitant to actually join in," she said. "I was kinda scared that everyone would think I was weird."

"Sara and Lucy would never think that. And neither would I, but I understand if you want to take things slowly. It makes perfect sense."

She sighed again. "I can't tell you how happy I am to get this off my chest."

He chuckled, embracing her a little more tightly. "Me too," he said.

He stroked the side of her wet hair with his hand. "I like you the way you are, and I think it's beautiful that you wanted to share this with me. So don't worry. We can do whatever feels right for us. Okay?"

She smiled and nodded. "Okay. Thank you."

She pulled away, her hair tousled, and her cheeks flushed.

James got up and took her hand. "Come on," he said, tugging her toward the lake. "Let's go for another swim."

She giggled and followed after him as they headed down to the water. "Wait," she said suddenly. "You're still in your boxers!"

He laughed and shrugged as he half-turned toward her. "They're wet, anyway."

She bit her lip as her sparkling eyes dipped to the snake in his boxers. "I reckon that's true," she said.

James grinned and beckoned her along. "Come on."

Chapter 29

James and Corinne ran into the lake together, water splashing everywhere.

The cool water was refreshing, and they splashed each other playfully as they waded deeper. Once their footing was gone, they swam out to the middle of the lake together. James caught Corinne's hand in his own and pulled her close as they floated in the deep water.

The surface was calm and peaceful, and James could see the ripples across it as Corinne and he kicked water, floating in the heart of it all.

Out here, the lake was warm and inviting, and James felt himself relaxing more and more as they drifted together. They were alone, just them, a pair of lovers enjoying the summer day.

James wrapped his arms around the redhead, pulling her close and pressing their bodies against one another.

She gave him her radiant smile. She had such a pretty face; he couldn't believe he had been lucky enough to find someone so lovely.

Her lips were soft, warm, and tasted like candy as he kissed her deeply, his hands exploring her body underwater.

The anxiety she had displayed earlier when making her confession flowed from her as she surrendered to his kiss with a moan. Her lips parted to his, and she wrapped her arms around his neck to pull him closer. She pressed against him, and her stiff nipples poked against his chest as she kissed him passionately.

His cock stiffened, and it poked against her as she wrapped her legs around him. Her cheeks flushed, but she didn't stop, instead giving him a teasing grind.

"Hmm," she moaned as she kissed his neck. "It feels

nice."

He grunted, his hands now dipping to cup those two full butt cheeks that had been smiling at him all day.

"You drive me crazy, Corinne," he whispered. "You've been driving me crazy ever since I first saw you at the farm."

"Oh, James," she moaned. "If you only knew what I was thinking right now..."

"What?" he breathed. "Tell me, Corinne. Tell me what you're thinking. You know I'd love to hear it."

She nipped at his earlobe before whispering, "I want you to be the one," she said. "I want to do it with you, James. And you alone."

His breath halted for a moment, his heart pounding. "Now?" he asked. "Here?

She chuckled, arching her back a little and pressing her tits against his chest. "N-not yet... But..." She bit her lip and gave him a challenging look. "I want... I want to be naked with you. I want to *see* you. And I want you to see me."

She ground her pelvis against his stiff cock again, making sure he understood what she was talking about. "And touch you." She giggled.

He nodded, a light moan escaping him at her teasing. His eyes took in their surrounding and found a little sheltered corner of the lake where the water lapped against large rocks with overhanging trees.

She followed his stare and nodded, her cheeks flushed, excitement in her expression.

"Yes," she hummed. "Let's go over there."

James swam after Corinne, his heart pounding in his chest, his gaze fixed on her limber body as she seemed to glide through the water.

In the sheltered corner of the lake where she was leading him, the water played gently with the rocks and the canopy of overhanging trees provided some shadow.

Corinne rose from the water when she reached the shore, her fiery locks dripping as she turned to watch him.

She looked delicious like that, in her green bikini. Goosebumps ran playful trails over her pretty body, and the cold of the lake had left her nipples straining against her top.

She watched him come with a smile and shivered in the cutest way.

Like her, James emerged dripping and wrapped her in his arms, holding her tight against his bare chest.

Her scent filled his head as she pressed her face against his shoulder, letting out soft whimpers as they kissed and touched each other.

"You smell delicious," he said, kissing her neck.

"Oh, James," she muttered, pulling back to look up at him. Her green eyes were bright and full of life and lust. "I love being so close to you. I love touching you."

He smiled down at her, his arm going around her waist. "Me too."

As they hugged, their hands roamed across one another with mounting hunger, sharing the heat between them. There were no barriers; nothing but desire.

Their lips met again, and her fingers threaded his hair. He pulled her closer, tangling his tongue with hers, and then he stood, lifting her into his arms. She wrapped her legs around him as she hummed her pleasure.

The water glistened on her body as she loosened herself from their kiss and leaned back in his arms, affording him a view of her smooth and delicious body.

She had the perfect hourglass figure — large but firm breasts and sweeping hips and thighs, combined with a narrow waist and a flat stomach, kept toned and smooth by long days of working the land.

"You are beautiful," James mused as he studied her body.

Corinne's cheeks flushed, and she bit her lip as she glanced down to where her pelvis pushed against the firm rod outlined in his boxers. Her emerald gaze shot back up to meet his, and her cheeks flushed as she raised a hand behind her back — to the cord of her bikini top.

She hesitated. "Do you... I... Do you want to see me?"

"More than anything," he said, without even thinking.

Her cheeks colored a deeper crimson, and her eyes dipped again as she gave a single tug at the cord that kept her bikini top in place.

James's breath skipped, excitement blazing in his veins

"Here we go," she hummed, looking at him with burning cheeks.

Chapter 30

Still clinging to James, Corinne brought up a single hand to lower the bikini top as it came off — bashful as she revealed herself to him.

His eyes swept over her lovely breasts, her pink nipples hard and erect as they pointed slightly up.

"Beautiful," he whispered.

An excited moan escaped Corinne as James raised a

single hand — the other still holding her tight against him. He tenderly touched one of her breasts, trailing his fingers softly along its curvature.

His finger journeyed outward until he finally took her breast in his palm. His fingers brushed the erect nipple, winning another sigh of delight from Corinne.

By now, she was softly gyrating against him, and he could feel the plump lips of her womanhood against his rod despite the bikini bottom and boxers between them. A fiery need to bend her over against the rock and have his way with her blossomed in his mind, but he pushed it away, wanting to be gentle with her.

Her big green eyes took up his entire world as she fixed them on him. "This is so nice," she whispered.

"Hmm," he agreed, still caressing her soft breast. "There's something else I want to do to you."

She bit the corner of her lower lip. "What's that?"

"I want to kiss you down there," he said, need rising in his chest. "I want to taste you."

She giggled, flashing a look over his shoulder, then looking back at him. "Yes," she whispered. "Please."

He grinned, then shifted her to his left hip before placing both hands on her round butt cheeks. With practiced ease, he lifted her onto a lower outcropping of a rock by the waterline in their secluded little corner.

The rock peeked just over the water, and Corinne leaned back, a little insecure as she spread her legs for him.

He could see her tender pussy lips outlined by the bikini, and his eyes drifted to where the garment was tied — a simple knot riding low on her hips. He made eye contact with her.

"Can I?" he asked.

She nodded vigorously, then took his hand and placed it on the simple knot.

He pulled at the thong, and Corinne's bikini bottoms fell away to reveal her cute pussy, pink and glistening, with a trimmed triangle of ginger pubic hair.

She spread her tasty thighs a little wider for him, her bikini bottom still clinging to her left leg.

"So pretty," James hummed as she studied her naked form before him.

She blushed, and a little tremor pass through her body. James understood from her expression that she didn't really know what to say. Unlike Lucy or Sara, Corinne was inexperienced and probably more than a little insecure.

And so he took his time.

James snaked one arm around her slender waist, pulling her up against him as he kissed her once more.

Their lips touched, and the freckled redhead pushed herself up against him with a lustful moan as she surrendered to the pleasure of their kiss.

As they explored each other's mouths with their tongues and lips, James let his right hand play with and explore her smooth and limber leg, trailing a finger across its surface or softly kneading the thicker flesh of her tasty thighs.

Her lusty moans told him she wanted more, and so — as they kissed — he slipped his hand to the inside of her thighs. It was warm and soft, and James's mind reeled with the idea of burying his face between those two thighs.

Driven by his own need and by hers, he let his hand slip higher and higher.

Corinne sighed into their kiss as he felt her slick pussy against his palm, her juices already flowing.

"Hmm, James," she hummed. "God, James! That's so nice…"

They kissed as he continued to tease her, rubbing her mound and prickling her sensitive lips with his deft fingers. Corinne gasped and twitched as she rubbed herself against his hand, the wetness of her arousal soaking his fingers.

With a growl, James finally released her mouth and

kissed the slope of her neck — down, down, down.

She let her head hang back, her wet, ginger locks swaying as she surrendered to the hard kisses trailing from her neck, to her breasts, to her soft stomach, and finally to the sweet mound of pubic hair on her mons pubis.

"Oh, James," she moaned. "Please… I want it. I want it to be you, James… Only you."

With a grunt of desire, he wedged his hands under her round butt cheeks and pulled her in.

She gave a little yelp as she almost lost balance, then giggled as she lay half on her back, propped up on her shoulders on the rock, with her legs spread to him.

He began with a teasing lick along her slick lips. Every muscle in Corinne's body tensed, then relaxed, and a sigh of pleasure escaped her.

"Oh my God, James," she murmured. "That's so good."

"Just you wait," he said, husky desire lining his voice.

She leaned back with a groan of surrender as he ran his tongue along her soft womanhood once more, parting her folds with it to glimpse her cute little nub — glistening and pink.

She was ready for it. He could tell.

He lapped at her pussy, tasting her sweetness while

he teased her labia with his tongue. His hand slid up between her thighs, finding her clit and massaging it lightly from above with his thumb as he continued licking her.

"Mmm," she cooed, her hips writhing beneath his tongue as he flicked at her tender bud.

He discerned from her reactions that she was getting close, but he wasn't going to rush her, not with this.

Oh no.

He was going to take his time and enjoy every moment of her first orgasm with him.

She began to tremble. He knew it wouldn't take her long before she would be coming all over his tongue.

"Hmm, James... It's... God, I think..."

"That's it," he murmured. "Surrender to it. I want you to come, Corinne."

"Hnng, James... God!"

He lapped faster, his tongue now focusing on her swollen little clit, his hand moving down to push into her slick pussy and curve up, seeking her g-spot. When he found it, her body tensed — even the butt cheek he still cupped with his left hand tightened as Corinne prepared for her delicious release.

"James!" she yelped, his name a cry of pleasure as her pussy clamped down on his fingers. "I'm coming!"

As she came, her pussy squeezed and spasmed under his attention. He lapped faster, giving her no mercy as he kept his face buried between her thick thighs and sucked at her pussy. Her body went rigid, and James smiled inwardly with satisfaction as her orgasm surged through her. Slight moans escaped her lips as she quavered and squirmed.

When she finally settled, her breathing ragged, he gently removed his hand from her pussy and gave one more teasing lick at her clit, winning a moan from the glowing redhead and sending another delicious shiver through her body that left her ample curves rippling.

As he adjusted his rock-hard cock in his boxers, he rose to study her as she lay there, wrecked by her orgasm. Her bikini bottoms still hung from her trembling leg.

"You're so beautiful," he breathed.

She looked at him with hunger, all bashfulness now gone. "I want to see you, James," she purred. "I want to touch it."

Those words alone made his cock jolt in its swim trunks.

She was ready for him.

James hooked his fingers behind the elastic waistband of his boxers and lowered them. His cocks sprang free, firm and ready.

Corinne's eyes widened as she gazed upon his engorged rod in wonderment.

"Wow," she hummed as she propped herself up on her elbows a little. Her eyes raised to his. "Can I... Can I touch it?"

James smiled. "Yeah, of course."

She extended her hand slowly, and a grunt of lust escaped James as she wrapped a gentle palm around his shaft. She bit her lips as she fondled it, exploring the full length, and when she touched his sensitive tip, a shiver passed through him.

"Does that feel good?" she asked, looking up at him with big, green eyes.

"Yeah," he grunted. "Nice and soft like that."

"And if I do this?" she asked, stroking him.

She lay there like a sex goddess, propped up on one elbow on the rock, her legs still spread, bikini bottom clinging to one thigh, breasts jiggling from the firm pump, naughty green eyes on him...

"Hrrm," he groaned. "That feels so good."

James watched as she stroked his hard cock. She had a steady hand and seemed to have an instinct for how far to go without being too rough or fast.

"Like this?" she purred.

"Ah," he sighed. "That's good... Really good."

Her eyes sparkled with delight as she worked his cock. As she did so, she inched toward him until she sat on the edge of the rock. Her wet and ready pussy drew James's eyes in, and she noticed it as she studied him from under her long eyelashes.

He wanted little more than to enter her and have her wet warmth milk his cock. And by the looks of things, she wanted it too.

She bit her lip, and she gave his firm rod another pump. "I... I kinda want to feel..." She shook her head. "It's risky..." She looked up at him. "Maybe if I just... rub it on me a little?"

The idea made James's cock buck in her hands, and he nodded vigorously, moving closer and bending his knees a little, so that his firm weapon aligned with her slick womanhood.

Corinne mewled with pleasure as she placed the tip of his cockhead against her pussy. A shiver ran through her as James slid himself down her hot slit.

The sensation was heavenly for both of them, and they remained like that for a moment as their bodies adjusted to the novel sensation of experiencing each other this intimately.

Then, he withdrew his cock and pressed it back against her pussy — only to repeat the process again and again, sliding down her hot slit and pressing teasingly against her tight entrance, but not slipping in.

"Ahhn, James," she moaned, moving her hips to stimulate him, giving him a delicious pussyjob with her lips. "I love it. I love your big cock."

James grunted, and a big bead of precum formed on his tip, dripping down to her flat stomach as he slid up and down between her lips again.

"It's so hard," she purred, big green eyes on his glistening tip for a moment before she looked up at him.

"Can't we... I really want to feel what it's like inside me... Just... uhn... Just for a moment."

James groaned with desire as he slid down again, his tip pressing against that wet and warm opening...

Ready for him.

"Ahnn," Corinne moaned, throwing her head back. "Just... Just a little." She brought her hand down, placed it on his thick shaft, and pushed, increasing the pressure on her tight hole.

"Fuck," James groaned, and surrendered.

He let her silky heat engulf his tip. She was so very tight and so very hot as she lay there, mewling with pleasure as he took her womanhood. It took every ounce of willpower at his disposal to not push through and plow as deep into her as she could take him.

"God, oh my God," she whimpered, her body arching as he took her. "Just... Ahnn, a little more."

He grunted with delight as he let her pull him in a little deeper. Her walls squeezed his throbbing member, and he sensed his balls draw up as his cock swelled within her.

"Just... Ah... just do... Uhn, do me... For a little bit."

That was it. James surrendered to his lust, pushing deeper into this delicious redhead as he grabbed her thick thighs for leverage.

A spasm shot through her, making her arch her back, as he claimed her womanhood for himself. She had one hand on his chest to control how deep he plunged into her, and he let her guide him and set the pace.

With every thrust, she let him go deeper.

The sensation was ecstasy itself. Their combined juices making her smooth and tender as he plunged into her, his cock filling her, stretching her tightness.

"Oh God!" she cried out in pleasure, and James grinned with delight as he pushed in with renewed vigor. She writhed beneath him as he fucked her.

Her pussy clenched tightly, squeezing his cock, milking it as he plunged into her over and over again. James let himself go as his lust overtook him. She clenched around him as he pounded into her, his balls drawing up as he pistoned into her pussy.

"Oh God, oh God, oh God!" she gasped.

It was heaven for James. He fell into her, lost in the moment, in her. Her pussy gripped his cock with such delicacy, and he loved the sensation as she impaled herself upon him. With every thrust, their skin slapped together wetly, sending delicious waves through Corinne's body, making her breasts bounce and her thighs jiggle.

"Fuck," he groaned, his pleasure almost sneaking up on him. "Corinne... I'm... I need to pull out."

"No!" she purred, wrapping her legs around him. "Don't stop now! I'm... I'm coming. I want to feel it inside of me."

His balls tightened when he heard that dirty request, and her pussy clenched on him as a second orgasm swept through her. "F-fuck," he grunted. "Are you..."

"Yes!" she cried out, arching her back as her delight

swept her away. "Cum in me, James!"

There was no resisting this. James groaned with fiery lust as he pumped into Corinne again and released a thick rope of cum, giving the redhead the risky creampie she so desired.

"Oh yes," she moaned, digging her fingers in her thick red locks. "Fill me up, James!"

He pumped again, spurting deep inside her, emptying his balls into her hot depths as she moaned with pleasure.

"Ahnnn," she cried out, gasping as he filled her to the brim with his seed. "Oh God, that feels so good!"

He gave another deep push before he finished with a sigh. At the same time, her spasming at her own orgasm eased, and Corinne let out a deep, satisfied moan.

With a grin on his lips, James pulled out and collapsed onto the rock beside her, his cock slipping free of her slick pussy, leaving her juices coating his shaft.

"That was perfect," he grunted.

"Hmm," she moaned, nestling against him. "I had expected it to be good... But not *this* good. Can we please do this every day?"

He chuckled as he wrapped an arm around her and pulled her in. "Music to my ears."

She laughed, stroking his chest with her soft hand as they lay together on that rock, basking in the afternoon warmth and listening to the gentle lapping of the lake. It was a perfect moment, and James surrendered to the lazy relaxation that followed a good bout of sex.

They lay on the rock together, naked and in a tangle of limbs.

As they relaxed and recovered, James even dozed off once — not for more than a few minutes but waking up in Corinne's arms as she gently stroked his chest and played with his hair was something he could get used to.

At length, Corinne spoke again. "So, uh," she began. "Do ya think the others don't mind? I mean, Lucy and Sara."

"No," James said. "They've both been clear with me when it comes to their feelings about sharing me." James turned his head to look at her sideways, admiring for a moment how beautiful the sunlight made her emerald-green eyes.

"And they like you, Corinne," he added. "They love having you as a part of our..." His voice trailed off as his mind sought the perfect word.

"Family?" Corinne suggested.

He nodded. That sounded about right.

"Yeah," he said. "Family."

Corinne smiled. "Are you sure?"

"Yeah," he said. He was sure. They'd discussed it, agreed on it, and the girls were eager to move forward.

Corinne reached across him, stroking the side of his face with her delicate fingertips, and James couldn't help but smile. He kissed her fingers, grazing them along his cheek.

Then, in a sudden movement, she rolled over and straddled him, facing away from him, and sat up on his chest. He laughed, enjoying that her light weight pinned him down. His cock twitched when she gyrated on him.

"Well, in that case," she said. "I think I need a little more practice..."

Chapter 31

The sun was on its way down when James and Corinne untangled.

After having sex on the rock, they had returned to the blanket, ate and drank, then continued where they had left off.

As they lay there afterward, James asked if she wanted to return to the cabin with him. She wanted to, but she had some work waiting for her at the farm; crops needed tending and animals needed fodder.

She seemed a little sad about it.

"I'll come by again," James said. "And soon, too. I still want to help you around the farm once I finish work on the cabin."

Corinne nodded and gave him a soft smile. "I'd really appreciate that," she said.

Then she glanced at the sky. "We really should be going! I need to finish my work while I still have daylight."

James nodded. He really wanted to help Corinne — not only to make her a little less burdened but also to free up her time. She had a day off today — a nice little Sunday to enjoy with him. But it was impossible for her to do absolutely nothing for a full day. A farm — especially one with a few animals — simply didn't allow it.

"All right," he said. "I think I should be able to finish my project somewhere in the course of this week. What do you say if I come by on Wednesday to check up on you, and we can start making a plan for what we'd like to do to make life a little easier for you? "

Her eyes widened. "You would do that?" she asked. "That's so sweet! Yeah, perfect. I could use help with the harvest!"

"Sure," James said as he stood up and began putting his clothes back on.

She studied him with a smile on her full lips as she lay there in her bikini, while he looked at her as he buttoned up his slacks.

He grinned. "What are you looking at?"

She laughed. "A very handsome and very sweet man," she said. "Ya know what, Mr. James Beckett? I'm a lucky girl to have run into you."

James smiled, extending his hand to her. "Believe me," he said. "*I* am the lucky one."

Corinne took his hand with a broad grin and began dressing as well, slipping her dress back on, which had dried in the sun while they lazed about, swam, and made love.

Once dressed, they walked back to James's car, holding hands.

As James drove them back, it was already dark enough under the canopy that he had to turn on his lights. He couldn't help but notice that his right front light didn't come on.

This car is on its way to the graveyard, he thought. *I need to get a new one — or some other mode of transportation.*

"Bit of an oldie, ain't it?" Corinne said, ginger

eyebrow perked.

James laughed. "Yeah," he said. "It's your typical thousand-dollar car. It's had so many problems, and I had to sink so much in it that I wonder if I wouldn't of been better off if I'd spent a little more at the beginning."

"Yeah," she said. "My dad was really good with cars, but that is one thing I did not inherit. I'm good with plants, and I'm good with animals — cars?" She shook her head. "Not so much."

James grinned. "Well," he said. "I'm actually hoping that my magic might serve me here and present a solution. I mean, I love driving; I wouldn't want to give it up. But if there is some way High Magic can repair my car or provide a temporary alternative…" He shrugged. "Well, we'll just have to see."

"Ooh," she teased. "How about a flying carpet? Or maybe a broomstick?"

"I'll give you a broomstick," he said.

She laughed and slapped him on the wrist. "James!"

He shot her a crooked grin. "Tease and get teased, my fiery little redhead," he said. "Lesson one of being with James Beckett."

Smiling, she shook her head. "You're going to be a handful," she murmured.

"And you'll be two."

She laughed again, and he joined in.

Soon enough, Corinne's farm dawned along the side of the road. He pulled over next to the fence where he had picked her up this morning.

Corinne remained seated beside him and shot him a happy look.

"Thanks for today, James," she said. "I really enjoyed myself. In fact, I haven't enjoyed myself this much in a long time. This was the perfect Sunday."

He smiled. "I had a great time, too, Corinne."

Corinne reached over, squeezing his thigh. "And what we did was... very special to me."

"It was special to me, too," he said and smiled. "I expect that I'll be thinking about it for a while still."

She chuckled. "I sure hope so, cowboy," she said, then leaned in.

He met her halfway, and they shared a deep and passionate kiss there on the side of the road as the sun slowly lowered itself in the west. It was easy to forget time with Corinne, and James was tempted to just go with her now, so that he could help her, and they could share the rest of the night together.

But there would be more time for that.

They released their embrace, and James left the car,

walked over to her side, and opened the door for her. She gave him another kiss on the lips, a tight hug, and a wave before she set off toward the farmhouse. James watched her leave, drinking in the way the waning daylight played with her perfect body when she turned around for a final wave before she headed inside.

With a satisfied sigh, James got back in his car and drove the rest of the way to the cabin.

His expectations had been correct; it was indeed a perfect day...

Chapter 32

James hadn't had a weekend like this in a long time. He drove home with a big smile on his lips, parked his old sedan in front of the cabin, and went inside.

Sara was exactly where he had left her: lazing on the couch. When he entered, she blinked and stretched lazily, purring from the back of her throat as she watched him.

"How was your day?" She asked. "Everything good with the pretty little redhead?"

James laughed. "Yeah," he said. "We had fun."

With surprising speed for someone who had been sleeping a moment ago, she hopped to her knees on the couch, her left ear twitching once as her tail gave a playful switch.

"*Fun* fun?"

He grinned and nodded. "*Fun* fun," he confirmed.

"Ooh," she crooned. "So I guess we will see more of Corinne, then?"

"I sure hope so," James said as he walked over to give her a kiss on her forehead, scratching her behind her ear as he did so.

She shut her eyes and purred a little, before looking back up at him with her big yellow eyes. "So do I," she said. "I like her."

"I promised I would help her out at the farm this Wednesday," James said. "But I'm still going to try to finish work on the cabin this week. What do you think? Four days? Will that be enough?"

She brought a slender finger to her lips for a moment. "Well," she replied. "With the help of your High Magic, you should come a long way."

He nodded, considering the work he would need to

do in order to complete the bedroom, kitchen, and workshop. Cutting more trees for timber would be pretty hard, but once he had enough, he might use his Board Crafting spell to make the timber into boards and varnish them.

The varnish would take about twenty-four hours to dry, so it would be perfect if he finished work on the boards on Tuesday, then head down to Corinne's farm on Wednesday. He could do the actual building on Thursday and Friday, maybe bleed a bit into Saturday if he needed the extra time.

It should all work out.

Sara came up behind him as he stood at the kitchen counter and wrapped her arms around his waist from behind, leaning her head against his back.

"It's sweet of you to help Corinne at her farm," she said. "I suspect Corinne has been in need of a good man — someone who is not just a good lover, but also a good friend — for a long time."

James smiled, placing his hand over hers, intertwined on his stomach. "I hope so too," he said. "You know, in time, I would like it if we were all together."

"Together?" she asked.

"Yeah," he said. "In one house. I mean, I know the cabin is too small — at least the way it is now. But I want to make it bigger and more comfortable. Wouldn't it be great if we all just lived here, together all the time?"

"Hm-hm," Sara hummed. "That sounds perfect."

He nodded. "I'll have to talk to the others as well," he said. "But I hope they might like it, too. I suspect Lucy and Corinne are tired of living alone, and it's not like they couldn't commute to the farm or the general store from here, right? It's only a short drive."

"Yeah," Sara said. "If you can finish the bedroom, kitchen, and workshop, I bet you can expand the cabin even more!" She kissed his neck. "You could build us a sauna, hmm? And all kinds of nice, comfortable places to sleep and relax? There would be no way Lucy and Corinne would turn down an offer to live here if you made it all like that."

He laughed, patting her on her soft hands. "You'd like that, wouldn't you?" he asked. "A place where you can be lazy all day long."

She chuckled. "Well," she said. "I don't want to be lazy *all* day long..." As she spoke, one of her hands drifted down to his groin as her tail curled around his leg.

With a smile, he turned around and took her up in his arms. "No?" he asked. "Are you planning on certain activities?"

"Maybe," she crooned, her voice trailing off as her gaze dipped to take him in.

He laughed, then pressed her to him, his precious cat girl, and gave her a deep kiss.

Within moments, they were stumbling their way to the couch next to the fireplace, ready to continue a perfect lazy Sunday of making love, relaxing by the fire, and eating good food.

Chapter 33

James dedicated the next day completely to chopping wood for his cabin. He already had some lumber ready after clearing and leveling the terrain for his construction project. However, most of it was fit only for use as firewood.

He began his day by sorting out the pile of lumber until he'd set apart everything he could use to craft into boards or use for the log walls. When that was done, he shouldered the axe he had bought from Lucy at the general store and headed into the woods.

Since James had fallen completely in love with the woods around Tour, he planned to cut lumber in a pattern that left the serenity and peace of the forest as intact as possible.

He wouldn't clear all the trees in a single location, leaving a waste of stumps. Instead, he was going to chop down a tree here and there, leaving the general forest largely intact.

It involved extra work, of course; he would spend more time walking around and moving the lumber from one place to the other.

But he'd had an idea to make the process a little easier, and it had something to do with his spell to summon his Grimoire.

It had to be possible to use a similar spell to bring other objects to him. He would try to search his ancestral memories for a teleportation or transportation spell that would allow him to bring the lumber to the building site in the blink of an eye. If that failed, he would have to move it by hand.

With a merry tune in his mind and whistling, James began the work.

It was good to be chopping lumber again — he had spent his first few days in Tour chopping wood for Lucy at Rovary's Lot, and he enjoyed the peaceful and satisfying feeling the honest work instilled in him.

When James had finally chopped down a few sturdy trees that would make for good boards, he began his experiment to find a teleportation spell.

Leaving the logs where he limbed them, he walked back to the cabin, his axe resting on his shoulder.

Once there, he sat down in the shade and focused on his construction site.

With his Summon Grimoire spell, he needed to visualize the book in his hands. He expected that the intent required for any teleportation or transportation spell was similar — he would have to visualize what he wanted to transport and the location he wanted to transport it to.

James took a deep breath, then set to it.

He visualized the stack of lumber in front of him, neatly piled and ready for use. Slowly but surely, strength began to simmer at the very foundation of his soul. It was that familiar sensation of his mana, pulsing out from his core to fuel his magic. The feeling grew stronger and stronger until it transitioned from a surge of power to a slightly painful pang at the back of his head.

That was the moment to turn it inward.

He relinquished the visualization and at once began the search of his ancestral memories, visualizing those who went before him and who achieved similar effects, moving things from one place to another by the power of High Magic alone.

This time, the vision came swiftly. He felt the sands of time closing in, and memories of those who lived before him came to him now out of the mists of time.

Chapter 34

When James opened his eyes, he stood in a narrow corridor with a vaulted ceiling. The walls were made from sand-colored bricks, and except for the flickering light of a torch, it was dark around him.

Something — a feeling — told him he was behind thick layers of stone and earth, within a mighty bulwark.

A sudden noise made him turn around. It was a scream — the type of scream made in agony and death's grip. A metal clattering followed it, and more voices rang out in fury.

A man came into view.

He ran, and he wore some kind of quilted garment. A metal cap rested on his head, with a long nose guard and a firm brim above the eyes.

Despite that, James did not struggle to recognize the blazing green of those eyes and the long locks of dark hair that came out from under the skullcap.

Here came one of his ancestors, and by the sword at his side and his primitive armor, James expected this vision came from medieval times.

As the man came running toward James, he stepped aside — realizing a moment later that the man would pass through him as if he were a ghost.

Voices rang out behind him. They spoke in a foreign language; something that resembled — or even was — Arabic.

And they sounded furious.

But James would not wait around. He quickly turned on his feet and ran after his ancestor. The man scooped a torch from the wall as he passed by, running with all the speed he could muster.

James followed him. Down the dark corridor they went, with a raging mob giving chase.

Ahead, an arched wooden door loomed. The man entered through it, slammed it shut behind him, and bolted it. Luckily, James could step right through.

He came into a room, illuminated only by the torch held by his ancestor. It was a vaulted room, almost seven feet high, which made it a little higher than the corridor. There hung a musty and earthen smell, and there was no window except for a small horizontal slat near the ceiling, although it let in no light.

It was night outside.

But voices drifted into the room — more of the Arabic-sounding language. Some barked orders in anger; others complied or made reports.

But whoever they were, James's ancestor paid no attention to them. He threw the door behind him a single look before turning toward the center of the room. And as the ones who had been giving chase came to the bolted-down door and began ramming it, James is ancestor spread his arms and focused.

He said nothing as each attack on the door reverberated in the small room. But after a few seconds, James's ancestor opened his eyes and spoke words of magic.

"Vanealders tod heer.

"Brengang, bestansvlack. Rhuimte.

"Vanealders tod heer."

It was the exact same spell as the Summon Grimoire Spell. But as the objects that his ancestor had summoned began to appear, James understood the extra step he had to take.

Three small kegs manifested in front of James's ancestor, each with a fuse sticking out of them.

And each was marked with a sign for one of the Eleven Elements of Magic: the sign for Space.

So that's the trick, James thought. *You need to mark them.*

It made sense; the Grimoire itself bore such marks. It also fascinated James to learn that High Magic was not only about intent and the spoken word. Apparently, signs and symbols played a part in its practice as well. He wanted to learn more about that in the days to come.

The banging on the door intensified, and James's ancestor threw a hurried look over his shoulder before stepping forward.

With a quick word of magic — the spell very familiar to James — a small flame sprang forth from the man's fingertips. He lit one of the fuses, then stepped back and spoke another spell:

"Vanheer tod terugganga.

"Brengang, bestansvlack. Rhuimte.

"Vanheer tod terugganga."

And as the fuse sparked, the flame crawling its way to the small kegs, James's ancestor simply disappeared from the room, the space he had stood a moment ago now filled with nothing but air.

That's a neat trick, James thought.

And just as the door broke down to reveal angry faces and curved blades, the spark hit the keg, and the world around James exploded in fiery destruction, the very room coming down on them as the men screamed their last words.

Before James faded away to return to his own time, he heard the clamor of battle and cries of victory ringing from outside. Beyond the billowing smoke and dust, an army approached, its footmen dressed in white tabards bearing a red cross.

On they came, unto the breach his ancestor had made in the walls of this fortress.

Then, he faded away from this time to return to his own.

Chapter 35

James drifted back to his own world, the words of his ancestor still echoing in his mind.

It took him a moment to recover from the dream and to realize where he was — standing outside his cabin. But when he regained his composure, he summoned his Grimoire and penned down the new spells he had acquired from his vision.

When that was done, James headed back out to the stack of logs he had felled. Luckily, he had purchased woodcarving tools from Lucy's general store.

But before he'd try it by hand, he focused on the logs with arcane intent, trying to visualize the result and search his ancestral memories   for some kind of spell that might aid the process here.

He tried for several minutes, but nothing came to him out of the mists of time.

A shame, James thought. *I suppose I'll have to do this the old-fashioned way...*

He got to work carving the symbol of the Element of Space in each of the logs he had felled.

His first few tries were fairly awkward and took him a long time; James possessed little skill in carving wood, and the symbol contained a few squiggly lines that were difficult to get right. However, James pushed away any impatience and took the time needed to do the job right.

After an hour or two, he had carved the symbol — or at least, something he expected was close enough to the symbol — in each of the logs.

Satisfied with his work, James cast his new spell right then and there. He did not want to walk back to the cabin, only to discover that the symbols he carved into the logs did not suffice for the purposes of the spell.

As his ancestor had done in the vision, he closed his eyes and raised his hands as he visualized the stack of logs in front of him. And sure enough, after he spoke the words of power, the entire stack of lumber manifested in the location he visualized.

Perfect, he thought.

He left the logs where they lay and returned to the cabin, only to cast the spell again. He did notice that this particular spell strained him more than the simpler ones, such as his Word of Boiling spell, his Summon Grimoire spell, and his Fire spell. He wondered if the strain of this spell on his mana would be less if he were trying to transport fewer items.

It was something to experiment with in the future.

Again, the spell was successful, and the neat pile of logs now appeared in the exact location where he wanted them.

After a short break, James got to work felling more logs. He used the same method as before to teleport the logs to the cabin, visualizing them in his mind and speaking the words of power to make them transcend space.

As the day neared its end, the pile of logs next to his building site grew to an impressive number.

James smiled, knowing that the day's work had been productive. He also knew that tomorrow was going to be another busy one.

When James returned to his cabin, Sara was already there. The beautiful cat girl had donned her silly apron again and was busy preparing a meal for them.

Using the fresh ingredients that he had procured from Lucy's general store, she had made for them a fresh garden salad with fruit and bread. For meat, she served the sausage with cheese — cold but delicious.

James peeked over her shoulder and gave her a pat on the bottom as he watched her work. "You know," he said. "For a carnivore, you sure do prepare a lot of meals with fruits and vegetables."

She gave him a grin over her shoulder. "Well, it's important for us to have plenty of fruits and veggies. Besides, I love cooking, especially since it gives me an excuse to be in control of what we are eating."

She raised a spatula, almost tapping him in the chest with it. "There are places where I like to *give up* control, and there are places where I like to *be* in control."

James laughed and nodded. "I think I understand what you're getting at, baby."

She gave him a meaningful smile, then a playful push. "Go!" she said. "Go have a seat. Let me do the work. You did plenty for today."

James didn't argue. He sat down at the low table in the living room, lounging on the couch as he watched Sara finish cooking.

When she was done, she served the salad, bread, and cheese.

She joined him at the table, and they enjoyed their food. It was tasty and balanced with plenty of herbs; James admired Sara's cooking skills. He had expected her — a cat girl wild enough to catch mice in the cellar — to prefer her food raw and bloodied, but she was actually quite civilized when it came to food preparation.

James ate slowly, savoring the taste of the various flavors in every bite, accentuated by Sara's selection of fresh herbs.

"This is great!" he said. "I'm not normally a salad guy, but I'm enjoying this."

She winked at him from her position next to him on the couch. "So, does this mean you're a salad guy *now*?"

James laughed, then picked up his glass of water. He

took a sip, then shook his head. "Nothing can beat a steak."

Sara grinned. "I can prepare a good steak," she said.

"So can I," James said. "I'll make you one once we have some kind of system for refrigeration set up right now. If I were to go out and buy steaks, they would just spoil."

Sara looked thoughtful, then nodded. "That would be nice. Do you think you might find some good meat somewhere?"

James shrugged. "Well, I've seen some at Lucy's general store. We'll just have to try it."

He didn't know of any ranches nearby — Corinne only grew crops and herbs at her farm, although she did keep a few chickens for the eggs and probably for the meat as well.

Back in the city, James used to order his steaks online from a local ranch that delivered meet straight from the ranch to the table. If all else failed, he might try to get them to make deliveries to Tour as well.

His chain of thought was broken when Sara put her plate back on the table and leaned against him. He draped an arm over the back of the couch and scratched her behind her ear as he finished his meal. She purred pleasantly, and her body relaxed against his.

"So," he began. "What have you been up to today?"

"Oh, I went into the cellar to do a bit of exploring." She looked up at him with her big yellow eyes, and her left ear gave a twitch. "You know, ever since you claimed the cabin and I became your familiar, I've had this feeling like the cellar is... well, opening up."

James perked an eyebrow. "Opening up?" he asked. "What does that mean?"

Sara licked her lips. "I don't really know. It's hard to explain. Ever since I started living here, it feels like there's this sort of... energy in the air around me. I told you before that Tour is a kind of nexus, right?"

He nodded. "Yeah," he said. "You did."

"I suspect the cellar below the cabin might actually be part of that nexus," she said.

He frowned. "So, wait," he said. "Let me get this straight. You think that the cellar might connect to these other magical worlds you mentioned before?"

She wagged her head — something in between nodding and shaking. "I'm not sure," she said, and her tail gave an excited swish. "But it might be worth exploring it together."

"Is it dangerous?" he asked.

"I don't believe the creatures that live there are hostile," she said. "I've told you about the spiders. They never made the slightest threat toward me. Besides, most creatures that are drawn to High Magic are not violent. There is the occasional squabble or clash, but it is rarely very dangerous, let alone lethal. Still, we would be wise to prepare."

James nodded thoughtfully. He was willing to explore whatever lay beneath the cellar, but he was not going to rush into anything.

Even if the creatures that dwelled in the cellar were not hostile, traveling under the earth presented risks of its own. High Magic could play a part there — if he could master some kind of spell that would keep Sara and him safe...

He remembered the vision he had had earlier about an ancestor on a ship — the vision that had taught him the Fire spell. The woman on the ship had had some kind of shield active that protected her when the ship was tossed on the waves and she fell.

I'll need something like that, James thought. *That would keep us safe.*

"This might be an adventure for later," James said. "I want to finish my construction project first and take the time to experiment with High Magic to see if it can help us if we decide to go deeper into the cellar."

She nodded vigorously. "Yes," she agreed. "We

shouldn't go in unless we're sure that we're safe. Like I said, most creatures that practice High Magic or are in some way entwined with it are not violent, but it never hurts to be prepared."

He nodded, leaning back on the couch.

It sounded like an interesting adventure. Who knew what they would discover? If Tour was indeed a kind of nexus and his cellar was in some way part of it, then traveling down into the deeper levels might give access to magical realms or other places of interest. Who knows what he could learn there?

Sara nestled closer to him, drawing his attention, and all thoughts of adventure drifted away as he studied the cat girl's enticing curves. She gave him a meaningful look from under long lashes.

He grinned.

Tonight, there was only one adventure he was undertaking...

Chapter 36

The next day, James awakened well rested, with Sara still slumbering beside him under the sheets.

By now, he understood well enough that she liked to sleep in.

He gave her a kiss on her soft cheek and scratched her behind her ear — something that made her purr even in her sleep — before heading out.

He had eggs and fried some jerky as a substitute for bacon. He washed the delicious breakfast down with a pot of coffee and slipped into his work clothes, trying to keep quiet for Sara's sake.

However, by the time he got dressed, she was already up. They shared a quick kiss before James went out into the fresh air, the day's warmth already swelling.

Yet another day of hard work ahead of him.

After giving his stack of felled logs a satisfied look, James got to work with his Board Crafting spell. He had learned the spell and the words from a vision in which an old woman — another ancestor — made repairs to her house.

James first summoned his Grimoire to make sure he remembered the words right. When he was satisfied that he knew them well enough, he did as the woman from his vision. He shut his eyes and focused his intent on the pile of lumber, visualizing it processed into a neat stack of sawn boards, varnished and ready.

Then, he spoke the magical words:

"Vanhoudt tod plancka.

"Bawerckinghe, maacken. Kraft.

"Vanhoudt tod plancka."

Magic pulsed in his veins, radiating outward from his core as it coupled with his intent to manifest the effects of the Board Crafting spell, which would take the green wood to fashion it into seasoned boards. And when James opened his eyes, he found he had control over the logs. The movements to do so came naturally to him, as if he had always known them.

When he raised a hand, the log he targeted would float up, and when he made a simple cut with his hand in the air, an unseen force stripped the log, removing the bark and branches before stacking them in a neat pile on the ground.

Finally, with another cut of his hand, the same unseen power sawed the timber into boards. A broad sweep of his hand covered the newly crafted board with a coat of varnish, drained it directly from the large pot he had bought from Lucy's general store.

Then, with a gentle gesture, the boards were set down to dry.

It was extremely satisfying.

James had a big grin on his lips after he finished work on the first log. Given, it would take him a while to do the entire stack of logs, but it was so much faster than doing it all by hand and so much more gratifying than to just purchase the boards from a DIY store.

And there was something very fulfilling about directing all this labor with mere gestures, almost like he was conducting an orchestra, making everything come together in a smooth symphony.

Still smiling, he continued his work. Log by log, he processed, cutting boards, varnishing them, and making them ready for their use in the workshop's construction.

In a bout of creativity, he tried to use the drying element of his Cleaning spell to dry the varnish on one of the boards. Unfortunately, that made the layer of varnish brittle and cracked. Apparently, the magical process for drying bodies or items didn't work on the varnish.

As he worked, he amassed a big pile of wood chips, branches, bark, and other refuse he would be able to use as tinder or fuel for his fires.

But as he had expected, the spell was very draining as well. He had to take more breaks than when he was felling the trees in the first place, and he noticed an increased hunger and thirst, leading him to believe that his use of mana somehow required more fuel for his body.

But he had plenty of food, and Sara was around as well to prepare it for him while he took a breather.

All in all, it turned into a fine day of work, with precious moments of relaxation and joy. By the looks of things, he would finish his work as planned.

As the light diminished, James finished processing the last log. The sun was on its way to dip below the horizon, painting the sky red, and Sara was standing in the cabin's doorway, leaning against the doorjamb as she looked at the finished product.

"Wow, James," she murmured. "You've done a lot of work in a single day."

He nodded happily. "I did," he agreed. "But I still have quite a bit left to do."

"I can see that," she said. "But it's good that you're taking your time."

"Yeah," he agreed. "And all these boards can dry tomorrow, while I'm at Corinne's farm and..."

Sara perked up suddenly, moving from a relaxed position leaning against the doorjamb to a half-crouching position. She raised her hands in a way that emphasized the sharp nails protruding from them.

Her yellow eyes focused on the tree line in a way that made James swivel around.

There, at the edge of the clearing in which the cabin stood, a lone figure sat in the branches of a high tree.

The female figure was squatting on toned legs, white- and blue-feathered wings folded on her back as her blue hair snapped in the wind. She was a beautiful feminine creature, and the scales covering her shoulders and arms and legs and the dragon tail only added to her regal beauty.

"Astra!" Sara hissed.

The cat girl and the Dragonkin did not get along — in fact, they had fought in the past.

Astra bared her white teeth, her dragon tail swooping once as her purple eyes fixed on Sara.

James took a step forward, standing between his cat girl and Astra as he raised his hands. "All right," he said. "Let's try to remain calm, please."

Neither spoke, but they did not attack each other either.

James turned on his heels to face Astra and nodded at her. "Good to see you again, Astra," he said, choosing his words carefully. "What brings you to our cabin today?"

Her purple eyes shifted from Sara to James, and she licked her plump lips in a mischievous way.

The last time they had seen each other, Astra had tried to seduce James in order to learn his magical secrets. He knew she was cunning and thirsty for knowledge, but he did not believe that the Dragonkin was evil or malicious.

In the end, she had tried nothing violent. She had even accepted his invitation to get to know each other better.

"You told me I was welcome at your home, Mage," Astra said. "And so, I decided to come visit."

Sara gave a disapproving hiss. "You told her she was welcome here?"

James made a calming gesture as he looked over his shoulder at his cat girl.

"You said it yourself, Sara," he said. "The creatures that are drawn to High Magic are not evil, and I do not believe that Astra is a threat. I believe she can teach *me* things, and I can teach *her* things."

Astra straightened her back, her wings unfolding as she shot a proud look at Sara.

"Your Mage is right, Fae woman," she said, her tone imperious. "Perhaps you should make your way into the house while us practitioners of High Magic speak of things you are unlikely to understand."

Sara took a step forward, claws at the ready, but James made a calming gesture before turning back toward Astra.

"Don't talk to her like that," he said. "Sara knows

much about High Magic, and she knows much about this place. And I will not tolerate anyone disrespecting her. Do you understand?"

Astra cocked her head as she considered his words for a moment.

"I said you are welcome here," James continued. "And you are. But if you intend to disrespect Sara — who lives here as well — your welcome ends now. What's it going to be?"

Astra rose a little on her branch, a predatory light in her eyes as she kept her head cocked in a most birdlike manner.

But ultimately, she gave a single nod.

"Very well," she said. "I will speak no ill words, so long as none are aimed at me."

James nodded, then looked over her shoulder at Sara, who still stood in her battle ready stance.

"Sara?" he asked. "Is that satisfactory to you?"

She licked her plump lips, her yellow eyes staring daggers at the Dragonkin. But in the end, she nodded once. "All right," she said. "If she behaves, I'll behave."

"Good," James said. He turned back to Astra. "Now that the rules of been laid down, would you like to come in?"

She narrowed her eyes for a moment before she

hopped down from her branch, spreading her wings for a single beat to soften her descent.

When her taloned feet touched the ground, she gave James a single nod.

"Lead the way, Mage," she said.

Chapter 37

Sara remained wary of Astra. The cat girl leaned against the kitchen counter with her round behind, keeping her yellow eyes on the Dragonkin at all times.

And Astra, as it turned out, didn't like to sit on couches or chairs. Instead, she settled into a squat beside the table, eyeing the house with suspicion — as if it might come to life and attack her.

This is going to take some skill and diplomacy, James thought as he studied the two wondrous and beautiful creatures that obviously struggled with each other.

"Very strange," Astra muttered as she studied the fixtures and fittings of the cabin.

James looked at her. "Strange?" He asked. "What's strange about this?"

She turned her purple eyes to him. "Everything," she said, looking up at the ceiling. "You live in this place? It feels... constricting. Very small?"

James shrugged. "It keeps out the cold and the rain," he said. "But I suspect you and I have different requirements of the places where we live. I mean, you said you live in a tree, right?"

She shot him a proud glance. "Yes," she said. "The Eltrathing Tree is my home."

"I hope I get to see it one day," James said.

She nodded at that, the hint of a smile appearing in the corner of her mouth.

"Perhaps you will," she said. "But we will need to find a way for you to fly before you can go up to where my kind actually live."

"Or climb..." Sara said, studying her long nails before flashing Astra a yellow-eyed look.

"None may climb the Eltrathing Tree," Astra said,

returning Sara's gaze with equal boldness. "You understand this well, Fae."

Sara gave a mischievous grin. "Just as you understand the Fae care little for rules."

James couldn't suppress a smile as he raised a hand.

"Now, now, ladies," he said. "Let's keep it civil. We're not here to lecture each other on rules." He smiled at Astra.

Both women nodded, although the fire remained alive in their eyes.

They are actually quite alike, James thought. *Fiery, willful, and wild. Maybe that's why they clash?*

Astra fixed her purple eyes on him. "Last time we spoke, Mage," she began. "I asked you to teach me some of your spells. You wanted to get to know me first. Have we now done this?" She cocked her head. "Are we now known to one another?"

He laughed at that. Even Sara chuckled. But the innocence in Astra's eyes told him clearly enough that she wasn't joking; the Dragonkin simply had no idea how to be less direct and focused — no idea how to relax.

She perked a blue eyebrow as they both laughed, a little hostility returning to her stance.

"What?" she demanded.

"We're not making fun of you," James said, making a calming gesture. "And yes, we *are* getting to know each other. But it's a process."

"Fine," she said, curiosity still in her gaze. "What more would you like to know about me?"

"Well," James said. "If you ask me that way, I have like a million questions. But let's start at the beginning: how did you learn High Magic in the first place?"

"It is an innate talent of my kind," she said. "All dragons are masters of magic, and their descendants — the Dragonkin — have inherited this trait."

James nodded. "If that's so," he said. "Then why do you want to learn spells from me? Can't you call upon your ancestral memories to learn them, like I can?"

Astra shook her head. "There are certain rules that apply to the dragons and their kin. While we are born with the aptitude for High Magic, our kind was wronged many thousands of years ago by an ancient goddess. She wrongfully stole from us the power to access our ancestral memories or to learn magic from each other. Luckily, she lacked the power to take away our natural aptitude for High Magic. But we have been forced to learn our spells through unconventional means ever since."

Sara shook her head. "That power was not stolen,"

she said. "It was taken away as a punishment for the arrogance of the dragons."

"And what would you know of it?" Astra snapped. "Were you there, Fae?"

"Were you?" Sara bristled.

"No," Astra admitted.

"So all we have is hearsay," James said. "So let's not fight over it, all right?" He nodded at Astra to continue.

"As I said, I must learn my spells from others. I cannot learn them from ancestral memories, and I cannot learn them from my own kind. So, when I first sensed you, a new Mage, out here, I wanted to learn from you what I could."

"That makes sense," James said as he leaned back on the couch. "Now," he continued, looking between Sara and Astra. "Why are you two fighting? What's the reason?"

The two beautiful women exchanged looks, although they were less hostile than before.

Sara spoke first. "Her kind looks down on the Fae. I don't like that."

"It is known that the Fae are just descendants of animals that were infused with High Magic. They are a byproduct."

Sara clenched her jaws and glared at Astra. "We were

created by a goddess," she said. "We were not some kind of accident!"

Astra shrugged. "So you say."

James blinked and frowned. "What would it even matter? You are all here now, today. You're obviously both smart and skilled. What would it matter if you were the result of some kind of natural process influenced by magic or the conscious creation of some kind of supreme being?"

Both were silent, their eyes fixed on one another.

"Look," James said. "I may be an outsider, but the solution seems obvious to me." James looked first at Sara. "You shouldn't put any value in what others think about your kind; their opinions do not influence who you are. They do not change your strengths and what's beautiful about you. Letting it in can only create weakness."

James then shifted his gaze to Astra. "And you shouldn't be so dismissive of others because of perceived ancestry. The only thing you get in return is anger, and the only thing it does is signal your own insecurities about your weaknesses."

"Insecurities?" Astra muttered. "What insecurities?"

"Your inability to learn magic through ancestral memories, for one," James said, holding her gaze firm with his. "I've only known you for a few minutes, Astra, but I can tell you with certainty that you are insecure about your ability as a High Mage because you can't learn High Magic like most of us do. Now, go ahead and tell me if I'm wrong." He sat back, studying her.

"This is outrageous," Astra muttered.

"But is it wrong?"

Behind him, Sara chuckled, but James silenced her with a gesture.

"We're not poking fun at you, Astra," he said.

She licked her lips, her eyes darting between James and Sara. "Is this 'getting to know each other' supposed to be so unpleasant?" she snapped.

James smiled at that. "Most of the time, getting to know new people is pleasant. But we all have things — perceived weaknesses — that we are sensitive about."

"Very well, Mage," she said. "Now that you know something I am insecure about, why don't you tell me something that *you* are insecure or sensitive about?"

That was actually a good question.

James noticed that Sara perked up as well. Hostility disappeared from her yellow eyes, and they turned large and curious as they turned to him.

Before answering, he thought for a moment. He

wanted to be truthful with Astra and with Sara; he believed in honesty, especially with people he cared about.

"My relationship with my father," he finally said. "He passed away recently. In fact, I inherited this cabin from him. Our relationship has always been difficult, and he always gave me the idea that he didn't approve of my choices in life."

Astra nodded slowly. "Our elders may often hurt us with their expectations."

"Is it the same with Dragonkin?" James asked.

"We have elders," Astra said. "Mine have gone away a long time ago, flying to new worlds as our kind are wont to do. They cared little for their nests in this world, and I am the only one of my direct siblings who has survived."

This time, Sara stepped forward and spoke. "Survived?" she asked. "What happened to the others?"

Astra's expression turned a little sad. "They were hunted over the years. By humans who distrust supernatural races, but also by creatures from other magical realms seeking power over dragons. Many believe such power can be attained through us, the Dragonkin. As a consequence, most of my kind live in hiding now."

"I'm sorry," Sara muttered. "I had no idea."

Astra waved it away. "It is not your fault, Fae," she said. "The history of the Dragonkin is an ancient one, and it is fraught with ill deeds of the dragon, human, and everything in between."

James smiled, happy at the progress. The hostility seemed to have faded a little, making place for something that might one day be the foundation of mutual understanding.

"Well," James said after a while, leaning back on the couch. "I'd be happy to teach you some of my spells, Astra. I'm afraid I don't know too many yet, but you can have a look at my Grimoire if you want."

She smiled at that — a genuine, soft smile that brought a sparkling beauty to her face.

"Thank you, Mage," she said, inclining her head. "In return, I would like to offer you something of my own."

James raised her hand and smiled. "You don't have to do that, Astra," he said.

When last they had spoken, Astra had offered 'favors' in return for knowledge of magic. But James had made it clear that he would never trade for affection. If he was interested, he would win it by being himself and not barter it for magical knowledge.

Astra smiled. "I do not mean that," she said. "That

was an ill-advised attempt to bribe you. How about in return, I teach you a secret of my own? Do you know the power of the Sigils representing the Eleven Elements of Magic?"

"Ooh," Sara purred. "That sounds interesting..."

It did indeed.

James sat up, one eyebrow raised. "No," he said. "I can't say that I know much about that."

Astra leaned forward, a crooked smile on her lips. "Well then," she said. "Listen well and watch closely, Mage."

Chapter 38

James and Sara sat enraptured, leaning forward as Astra demonstrated her arcane art.

With a long fingernail — it extended into a claw at her will — the beautiful Dragonkin woman carved something in a block of firewood James had given her.

"Now," she said. "As you know, the Eleven Elements of Magic are Time, Space, Fire, Lightning, Force, Water,

Air, Life, Death, Blood, and Earth."

James nodded.

"And every spell that exists is linked to one or more of those Elements. By carving the relevant Sigils into an object, we provide that object with an anchor for our magic."

James flashed a look at Sara. "I believe I did that for my Teleportation spell," he said. "The spell only worked on objects after I carved the Sigil of Space into their surface."

Sara looked at him with big, admiring eyes and gave a quick nod. "It sounds like the same principle…"

Astra nodded at her. "It is," she said. "Magic comes from within us, but we can channel it through anchors that have we have prepared in the proper manner. Doing so allows us to create a magical effect that might linger on after the casting of the spell, depending how much of our mana we infuse in the object."

"Enchanting," James muttered. "You're talking about enchanting objects, aren't you?"

Astra smiled. "I suppose one could call it that, yes."

Excitement flushed through James. "But that's great!" he exclaimed, glancing at Sara.

"Just imagine," he continued. "I could make my magical effects last longer — a permanent fire, a longer-lasting boiling effect. Hell, maybe I could simply cast a long-lasting Board Crafting spell and go do something else while my magic does the work for me!"

Astra chuckled, placing one hand on James's forearm. Her touch was warm and soft as she fixed her purple eyes on him.

"There are many possibilities indeed," the Dragonkin affirmed. "But let us not get ahead of ourselves. We must learn things one at a time, no?"

James grinned and nodded, her touch firing him up a little. She was beautiful, toned and fit, but with luscious curves. And she showed a dexterity and agility that... well, it was promising.

"Watch," Astra said as she continued her work carving a Sigil into the firewood. "This is the Sigil of Life."

James observed, fascinated, as she finished her work on the Sigil.

When she was done, she looked at James first and then at Sara. There was excitement in her eyes now, and James was getting to see a whole new side to the Dragonkin, whom he had considered so standoffish.

"Now for the magic," Astra said.

She rose to her feet and headed over to the basket with firewood to get another piece. She placed it on the table beside the other, so that there now laid two pieces of firewood — one with the Sigil of Life carved in its surface and the other plain.

Then, in rapid succession, Astra cast the same spell twice.

She did so while squatting next to the table, placing a hand on the piece of firewood she was casting the spell on as she focused on that piece of firewood, gathering her mana, and finally spoke the magical words of power.

"*Vantoda tod lefand.*

"*Herreasing, plantan. Lefan.*

"*Vantoda tod lefand.*"

A moment later, a branch sprouted from the dead piece of wood. Little leaves popped up, growing like they would on a time lapse recording of a growing tree. It was beautiful to see the trappings of life work so fast and so visibly. An excited meow escaped Sara as she obviously found the process as captivating as James did.

When she was done, Astra looked up at James and Sara. "Now," she said. "My spell is over. This is all the life that I gave to this dead piece of wood. It won't be enough to let it take root and form the foundations of a new tree. In less than a day, this little branch will have died."

She seemed genuinely sad for that, and she stroked the leaves with a slender finger, nail retracted, as she spoke.

Then, her eyes lit up with a new liveliness as she turned them to James. "But with the Sigil," she began. "Now, with the Sigil, I achieve much more."

She then turned to the second piece of firewood — the one she had carved the Sigil of Life in. Once again, she cast her spell, and once again, a small branch sprouted from the dead piece of wood and began growing, with tiny leaves unfolding at its end.

But when Astra completed her spell, the effect did not end. It slowed down, but it continued, with little branches popping out all along the surface of the piece of firewood. Some of them bore leaves, while others were more root like, burrowing and twisting as if they sought earth and water.

"See?" Astra said, watching the little piece of firewood come to life with love in her eyes.

"Because of the Sigil of Life, the spell will continue," she said. "I've cast it so that it will last for at least a few hours. If we were now to place this piece of firewood outside, its roots would dig into the earth and drink. From this piece of dead wood, new life will blossom."

"Amazing," James muttered.

Beside him, Sara nodded in agreement, her eyes wide.

Astra shot them both a happy look. "This is one thing I enjoy," she said. "Life blossoming and prospering." She chuckled. "Come, we shall plant it outside."

Together, the three of them went outside under the darkening sky. They found a beautiful little place at the edge of the clearing where they dug a shallow hole for Astra to plant her tree in. When she placed the piece of firewood in it, they all observed as the little roots burrowed into the earth.

The beginnings of a new tree.

After planting the tree together, the air between James, Sara, and Astra had been cleared.

Astra joined them back inside the cabin, explaining to James the intricacies of carving Sigils on the surfaces of objects. She didn't know too much about it — only that it didn't work on everything, and that some things lay beyond her abilities. She couldn't say whether that was because she lacked power or because there were absolute impossibilities in play.

Either way, James listened with fascination as Astra taught him the secret skill of Sigil-carving.

His mind was ablaze with the possibilities of this new art.

It was exactly what he had been looking for in order to get some of the creature comforts at the cabin set up. For instance, if he could master a spell that harnessed the power of cold, he would be able to create a refrigerator. He would only need to recast the spell from time to time to make sure that it didn't run out.

Astra also taught him how to regulate the amount of mana he poured into the Sigil when casting the spell. When focusing intent prior to casting a spell and speaking the magic words, he had a moment to draw from his power and regulate the intensity of a spell. It was an intuitive and instinctive aspect, channeled mainly through intent and willpower. In that phase, he would have to focus his intent on the duration of the effect as well.

"In time," Astra said. "Regulating your mana in this way will come as natural to you as deciding how deep a breath you will take. It just takes practice."

They continued until deep in the evening, with James and Astra focused on the art of Sigil-carving, while Sara prepared them a meal, looking on with great interest.

When James felt like he understood the art well enough, he had in the process learned Astra's Revive Plant spell as well. In return, he offered Astra a look at his Grimoire.

To James, that was a more than fair trade for the highly valuable skill she just taught him.

Astra read in the magical book for at least an hour with great interest while James helped Sara prepare them a meal. After Astra had learned what she wanted from his Grimoire, they ate together, and conversation drifted to lighter topics.

Astra told of her favorite pastime, and it delighted James to learn she had this in common with Sara. Both the cat girl and the Dragonkin loved hunting — mainly small prey like rodents or birds — and they ended up exchanging advice on hunting grounds and strategies.

As night approached, the conversation came to a natural lull, and Astra rose from her crouching position at the table.

"I must go soon," she said, and she seemed a little disappointed about it. "But perhaps we may meet again some other time?" She gave them both a smile, and her eyes danced in the firelight.

James smiled back. "Of course," he said. He looked

over at Sara, who was watching him with amusement.

"Sara," James said. "What do you think? Do you want to meet up with Astra again sometime?"

Sara grinned and nodded. "I would love to."

James looked at Astra, who appeared a little nervous now. It was actually kind of endearing.

"Well then," James said. "You're more than welcome to come visit again."

"Good," Astra said. "It was an enjoyable night."

With those words, she rose fully, and James took another moment to admire her limber figure and perfect curves. She dressed in little more than a loincloth and a halter top made of leather. Her colorful scales shimmered in the firelight.

James believed there was a profound interest in her purple eyes as she studied him for a moment.

She was not lying; she would be back.

And James found that a pleasant idea.

"Come on," he said. "Let me walk you to the door, then."

Sara stayed on the couch, watching them go with a slight smile on her full lips.

James opened the door to Astra and gestured outside. It was fully dark now, with only the starlight dancing in the sky. As always, it was beautiful out here in the woods. With no light pollution from the cities or the highways, nature was free to give its most lustrous show. And out here in the great wild, it was easy to accept that magic existed, to accept that he was speaking to a descendant of dragons, and to accept that there was more to the universe than Earth.

Astra turned on the threshold and regarded him for a moment. "Thank you for your hospitality, Mage," she said. "And to your companion as well. It seems I was… mistaken about her."

"And she about you," James said. "Let the bad blood be forgotten."

She gave a solemn nod, standing there like a proud, mythical being of legend as she studied him for a second longer. "Agreed," she said. "Until we meet again, Mage."

James inclined his head. "Fly safely."

She laughed, then turned.

With three steps she was off the porch, then she hopped in the air, spreading her wings with supernatural grace, catching the wind under them as she beat them. With great speed, she flew up, her Dragon tail billowing behind her, and disappeared over the treetops.

James watched her go with admiration in his heart.

She was an interesting one, for sure.

With a smile, he turned around and went back inside, closing the door behind him. Inside, the sardonic, yellow-eyed gaze of Sara awaited him, and he grinned at the sight.

"What are you looking at?" he asked.

Her expression broke, and she chuckled, shaking her head. "How many women will be enough for James Beckett, I wonder?" she mused.

He laughed as he walked over to her and flopped down on the couch, placing his head in her lap. She began stroking his hair at once, looking down at him lovingly.

"Not that I mind," she added.

"Not even Astra?" James asked as he surrendered to her gentle caressing.

She worked her head, and her left ear gave its signature twitch. "Hmm," she hummed. "I am not sure yet..."

James grinned. "Well," he said. "I'm not in a hurry. And I don't think Astra is, either. Think about it. I wouldn't want to involve anyone you don't feel good about." His eyes drifted to the door through which Astra just exited.

"But you *do* like her," Sara purred. It was not a

question.

"I do," James said. "And maybe there's more I can learn from her and more to teach her. It could be a useful alliance... and an enjoyable one."

Sara chuckled. "So long as you don't expect me to go live in a tree..."

He laughed along with her and gave her a squeeze in her shapely thigh, winning a cute yelp from her.

"I'll show you a tree," he joked as he gave her a playful poke.

She laughed, and he joined in. Soon enough, the cabin was alive with their laughter and conversation.

Chapter 39

James rose early the next day, enjoying a light breakfast before he went out to inspect the boards he had crafted yesterday. When he found everything in order, he took his car and drove down to Corinne's farm.

He was an early riser, and he was beginning to notice that the mornings were already a little colder than they had been when he first came to Tour.

Summer would last a while longer, but its end was drawing near.

And before fall began, he wanted to have the cabin in order.

With Astra's Sigil-carving technique, however, things were looking up. He had no doubt that he could come up with a way to use the Sigils to provide his cabin with a steady source of warmth. A single continual Fire spell would be able to function as a small space heater, and all he would have to do was recast the spell whenever it threatened to expire.

In addition, he had plenty of firewood on hand so that they could light a fire if they wanted to.

A magical source of heating is great and all, he thought. *But nothing beats an actual wood fire.*

His mind was still dwelling on the fall when he turned onto Forrester Trail, leaving the rutted road that led to the cabin behind him.

Ahead lay Corinne's barn, and James pulled up next to the fence. This time, Corinne wasn't waiting for him, but he knew his way around. After parking, he walked up the tree-lined path leading to the old farmhouse.

He knocked on the door, and Corinne opened shortly thereafter.

"Well, hey there, cowboy," she said, shooting him a

broad smile. "I'm happy to see ya!"

"Likewise," he said, stepping in to give her a kiss.

She grinned, her cheek slightly flushing as she wrapped her arms around him and kissed him back. James had missed those full lips and the soft and tender kisses of the redhead.

He drew back from their embrace and studied her for a moment. She wore a tight white tank top with a pair of Daisy Dukes underneath. Her cowboy boots finished the look. She'd done up her lush, ginger hair into two pigtails, and the effect was just too cute on the freckled, green-eyed redhead.

"If you're looking like this," James said, studying her with rising fire in his blood. "We're not going to get a lot of work done on the farm."

She laughed and playfully slapped his shoulder. "Come on in," she said. "I made coffee, but maybe you need a big glass of water to cool down."

He grinned and followed her inside.

He had been in the farmhouse before; it was a place in need of some renovation and repair. Corinne had been clear about the history of the place — it had been in her family for generations. But she was the last of her family to still live here, and she was all alone to boot.

The place needed the care of more than one person,

especially if you counted the farm and as grounds.

Corinne and James sat down at the old table in the kitchen. The wooden chair creaked when James placed his weight on it.

But the coffee was good. Corinne knew how to brew a mean cup, and he enjoyed it profoundly as she rummaged around the kitchen, fixing up a few light snack to go with the coffee.

When she was done, she sat down beside him and shot him a broad smile, making her freckles dance on her face.

"So," he began. "What's the plan for today, Corinne?"

She folded her hands on the table before her. "Well," she said. "I've been thinking about what I need help with, and…" She hesitated for a moment, her eyes drifting to the checkerboard tablecloth. "Well, I have to admit, it's not the most sensational job."

He laughed. "Out with it!"

She grinned. "I need some help to pick the potatoes? Most are ready to be harvested now."

"Sure!" he said. "Sounds like honest work."

She sighed with relief. "Good," she said. "I'm happy that you're up for it. I will help out for most of the morning, but after lunch I'd like to go into the house and do some work here, ya know? I really need to clean up."

"That sounds perfect," James said. "Look, if you want me to, I can stay all day?"

She bit her lip as her eyes widened. "Really?" She said. "That's great! I'll cook for ya and... well, you can stay the night if you want to. I'd actually like that... a lot."

He reached out and placed his hands over hers with a smile. "I'd love to," he said. "It sounds great. We'll work our asses off, and then will kick back, eat some nice food, and relax."

She clapped her hands enthusiastically. "Yes, please!" she said. "It's been way too long since I've had fun around here."

He grinned and downed his coffee, then took a chocolate chip cookie from the platter she had placed on the table. "I'll have this one on the way out," he said. "Let's get started!"

Chapter 40

As James and Corinne headed out into the fields together, Corinne explained to James that potatoes were ready to be harvested once the top foliage had dried.

"For early potatoes," she said. "It's best to wait until the flowers are gone. But then we're talking June or July. These potatoes are my main crop. And in that case, my dad taught me it's best to wait until all the leaves and stems are yellow or brown. Like this."

She gestured at a stretch of land where neat rows of potatoes had been planted, their foliage turning yellow or brown, as she had indicated.

"Over there," Corinne said. "Is my second main crop." She pointed at several more of those neat rows of potatoes in an adjacent field. Although they were yellowing at the tops, they were still green at the base.

"I planted those later," she said. "It's a necessity when you don't have a lot of staff to make sure that you don't have to harvest your entire potato crop in one go. That it be too much work, and I would lose some of the harvest."

Next, she showed him how to dig up the tubers using a spading fork. No doubt the large agricultural companies had machinery to do this work, but Corinne still relied on good old-fashioned elbow grease.

"Most of the farmers around these parts are small families like mine was," she explained as she dug up the big potatoes with considerable skill and care, then handing James the fork to let him try.

"And we don't really compete with the agricultural giants," she continued, watching him work. "With the population of Tour being so sparse, it doesn't really pay for them to invest in this type of small town. We simply don't buy enough in bulk."

James nodded, turning the earth with the garden fork. It took him some time to find a way to do it that was comfortable and still allowed him plenty of leverage to do the work correctly.

But with Corinne's pointers and experience, he was quick to pick it up.

The trick was really to turn the earth in a way that didn't damage the tubers themselves.

"If you damage them too much," Corinne explained. "They will rot in storage."

"Storage?" James asked, rubbing his forehead. "They're not going directly to market?"

Corinne shook her head as she took over the garden fork, placed it at the edge of one of the plants, and gently lifted it out of the earth, revealing a bundle of mature potatoes.

"No," she said. "The early harvests — the ones from June and July — go straight to market; they don't keep for long. But these are the main crop. You let them ripen in the earth longer than the early crop. And you don't take them out until the skin is like this."

She picked up one of the big potatoes and rubbed her thumb over the skin. "Look here," she said. "The skin is thick and firmly attached to the flesh. Ya see? When you take potatoes like these and store them at about forty-five to sixty degrees for, say, two weeks, they will cure and keep for a longer time."

James nodded as she handed him the garden fork again. He mimicked her movements, pushing the prongs into the thick soil at the edge of one of the potato plans, then lifting the whole thing out of the soil. He watched with satisfaction as the big potatoes dangled from the roots of the plant.

"So you sell these to Lucy after they are cured?" he asked.

"Yup," she said. "When we had bigger harvests, we used to sell them to a couple of other towns as well. But I don't have the manpower to plant more than this." She threw him a hopeful, green-eyed look. "But maybe that will change in the future."

He grinned. "I plan to be around for some time," he said. "I can help you. But I would like to find some kind of spell to make this process a little easier."

She looked at him with surprise and a touch of wonder. "That sounds great," she said. "I think that could help a lot. I ain't gonna pretend I won't appreciate your help."

He smiled and nodded. "It'd be good practice for me to find some proper spells to help you out."

"You're a lifesaver," she said. "Why don't you finish his row, and I'll check on the next?"

He nodded. "Sure," he said. "No problem."

She grinned and gave him a hug before moving away to check on some of her other crops. James did as she had showed him and kept harvesting potatoes, leaving the yield on the ground to be picked up later.

It was pleasant work — hard but rewarding. To see the soil yield fresh produce that would feed the people of Tour — and probably end up on his own table — had a certain appeal that James had not experienced before.

And so, he worked with satisfaction, whistling a tune to himself as the earth yielded its treasures to him and the sun crawled across the sky, smiling down on his neck and shoulders.

As James worked, part of him wondered if there would not be a spell accessible to him that ease the job. But then again, doing the work by hand was enjoyable. He got to know the land and the work, and the focus required for the physical labor allowed him to relax mentally.

Busy hands, quiet mind, after all.

After a few hours, Corinne came to check on him. She grinned broadly and clapped her hands. "Wow!" she exclaimed. "You're really good at this."

"Thanks," James replied with a smile. "It's actually a lot of fun!"

She laughed and stepped forward to put her arms around his waist. Her hands went under his shirt and caressed his stomach.

With a smile, he stabbed the garden fork into the earth and placed his hands over hers as they stood in the sunlight together, swaying lightly. She kissed his neck as a soft breeze picked up and played through their hair, cooling the sweat on their brows.

"You know," Corinne said. "I could get used to having you around here."

He smiled, giving her hand a squeeze. "Me too," he said. "This is pretty much perfect."

Her lips found his, kissing him softly at first, then with growing passion.

"Hmm," she then hummed, drawing back. "Let's not get carried away, cowboy. We still have some work to do."

"Of course," he agreed, pulling off his shirt, letting the warm, summer air cool the sweat on his chest and abs.

She bit her lip as she let her emerald eyes wander over his physique. "No fair!" she exclaimed.

He laughed. "What? It's hot."

"It sure is," she crooned, giving him a playful poke. "I'll make us lunch in a few minutes, okay? After that, I got some stuff to do around the house, but I'll be back to check on you."

"Sure," he said. "Let's take it easy."

She winked at him before she sauntered over back to her own stretch of the fields, ready to continue our work.

He watched her go with a smile on his lips. She was a good woman, and he enjoyed her company, and it was very nice to know that the feeling was mutual.

Corinne and James ate lunch together on a blanket in the field — a little picnic just for the two of them.

Corinne had prepared sandwiches and a light fruit salad to go with them. It was a reinvigorating meal, and it combined with Corinne's home-brewed coffee to revitalize James for the day to come.

As James took another bite from his sandwich, Corinne threw him a sideways glance. She lay on her side on the blanket, propped up on her elbow, and she had kicked her cowboy boots off, revealing her dainty feet.

"I wasn't kidding, you know?" she said after a brief silence.

James looked at her. "Kidding about what?" he asked.

She pressed her lips into a thin line as she considered her next words, then took the plunge.

"About having you here." She sat up, a sudden worry spreading on her pretty face. "I mean, I don't want to intimidate ya, but... Well, I ain't gonna lie. I like you, James. Today, being with you like this... I reckon it's perfect."

"And I wasn't kidding when I said I agreed," James said. "But my place is at the cabin for now. There is some kind of connection between me and that place — something I need to explore before I move on."

She nodded. "Well, I understand that. Still, I would like us to spend more time together, y'know?"

He reached out to take up her hand. "Come stay with me," he said. "A few days a week."

Her green eyes brightened. "You mean that?"

"Absolutely," James said. "I want to have you around. All the time, if it were possible."

She gave him a slow smile and leaned in to kiss him.

James kissed her back, running his fingers over the

curve of her cheek, then down to her neck. He pulled back and stared deeply into her emerald eyes.

"I like you," he said. "It's as simple as that. From the moment I saw you coming out of that barn."

She laughed, sincerely and deeply, until tears formed in her eyes. "Yeah," she finally said when she recovered. "I remember that. I looked like absolute shit."

"Hot shit," James corrected her.

She grinned and gave him a playful push.

"I'm not even joking," James continued. "You look better in a dirty shirt and old overalls than any girl flaunting around the city in expensive clothes and makeup. You are beautiful on your own, just the way you are."

She sighed and leaned into him, at a loss for words.

"And I want you here with me," James continued. "To share my life, my home, everything."

She nodded. "Yes," she said. "I would like that."

James smiled at the joy that spread across her face. It was the expression of a woman who had been waiting for someone like him for so long.

"But what about the others?" she asked. "What about Lucy? And what about Sara?"

"How I feel about *them* doesn't change how I feel

about *you*," he said. "In time, I would want all of us to be together. You can bet I will ask Lucy the same thing in time — to come join me at the cabin."

She laughed. "That might get very crowded."

He grinned. "Crowded in a good way," he joked. "But yeah, I would need to expand the place to make sure there's plenty of room for all of us."

"And what about the farmhouse?" she asked.

"We'll see about the farmhouse when the time comes," he said. "It's been in your family for so long, we could try to restore it to its former glory. Hell, we might even make it into a bed-and-breakfast or something. I bet people would love staying in a rustic country house like that."

She thought for a moment, bringing a slender finger to her lips. "Hmm," she hummed. "You know, that's not such a bad idea."

"I have my moments," James said.

She laughed. "You certainly do."

With a smile, James looked up at the sky before turning back to Corinne. "You know," he said. "I'm glad we had this talk."

She smiled, her cheeks flushing a little, which made her look lovely in the sunlight.

"I had to get it off my chest," she said. "I've been

thinking about you a lot, James. And not just since we had our date at the lake, but before that as well. It feels..." She shook her head. "It feels like it's fate. Weird, huh?"

He shrugged his shoulders. "Ever since I came to Tour, I learned that most things I believed about the world are either not true or way too limited. I wouldn't be surprised if there is actually something like fate that draws people together. And if so, I think fate wrote you and me in the stars."

She blushed and nestled against him, placing a soft kiss on his bare shoulder.

James smiled and kissed her on the top of her head, smelling the sun on her beautiful red hair. Then he threw another look at the sky.

"All right," he said. "I think lunchtime is long past. What do you say we get back to it?"

She grinned and nodded. "Yeah," she said. "If you can get back to the harvest, that would be great. I have some work to do around the house, which I wouldn't of gotten around to if you hadn't been so nice to come and help me here today." She placed another kiss on his arm. "I'm really happy that you did."

"So am I," James said. Then he gave her a pat on her rump as he rose to his feet. "All right, back to work."

Chapter 41

The hard work helped pass the day quickly. At the end of the afternoon, James surveyed his handiwork with satisfaction: he had picked clean every row of potatoes that had been ready to harvest, leaving neat piles of the tubers along the rows.

He got to work gathering them all — one wheelbarrow at a time — and moving them to the barn where they could cure for a week or two. The task took him what remained of the daylight.

When the last load was laid out in the barn, James went outside and narrowed his eyes at the sun on its way west. It promised to be a beautiful sunset, and James was looking forward to enjoying it with Corinne.

A smile broke across his face as he thought of her, and he began walking toward her farmhouse. As he approached, he saw the front door open and Corinne emerge, still dressed in her Daisy Dukes and her tank top. She waved at him.

"How'd it go, cowboy?" she asked once he got closer.

"Pretty good," he said. "I got all the potatoes that were ready to harvest and laid them out in the barn in a single layer so they can cure."

She grinned and flashed him a thumbs-up. "Perfect! You go relax. I will make us dinner."

James didn't need to hear that twice. He gave her a kiss on her soft cheek, then headed into the farmhouse. Throughout the day, the house had remained nice and cool, and it was a delight to relax at the kitchen table while Corinne bustled about in the kitchen.

Like her, he could get used to this.

He watched her from his chair, admiring her toned figure in the skimpy farmgirl attire.

"So," he said. "What's for dinner tonight?"

She smiled at him over her shoulder. "Homemade baked fries, cowboy," she said. "And I got us a couple of steaks from Lucy's general store. I reckon that and some veg straight from the farm should keep ya happy, huh?"

His stomach growled. "That sounds perfect," he said.

"Good," she said with a chuckle. "And you'll find I make a mean steak, too. My dad taught me, and if there was anything that man was picky about, it was his meat."

"Sounds like my kinda guy," James said, folding his hands behind his head and stretching his long legs under the table.

She smiled softly. "I suspect you two would've gotten along perfectly."

She had told him her father had passed away three years ago, leaving her in charge of the farm. She had hinted his death had been sudden and unexpected, and judging by how often she mentioned him, James reckoned they were close.

"Do you miss him?" James asked.

She gave a wistful smile. "Every day. He was a good man, the kind who looks out for his own." She glanced at him over her shoulder. "I'm sure many people would've called him a simple man. Maybe even dumb. But to me, he was a hero. And I want nothing else than to be here and to do this. I love farming. I like that it's close to the earth. I like that it provides sustenance, and I like that it requires a lot of care and love."

"And you're good at it," James said. "You're good at it because you love it."

She turned around and faced him, leaning against the counter with crossed arms.

"Yes. Exactly. Thanks for saying that. You know, sometimes I wonder if I'm doing wrong by just staying here." She chuckled and shook her head. "I wonder if I'm not clinging to the past, and if it wouldn't be better for me to just move on. Go to the city. Get a job there."

"Are you kidding?" James said. "You would become just like everybody else. You're great the way you are. I love everything about you."

She blushed. "Thank you." She walked over and bent down to kiss him on the lips. "You have no idea how much that means to me."

His heart swelled at the words. "The only thing we need to do is make this place a little more lively. And we will start on that soon enough."

Corinne looked up at him and smiled. "Really? That makes me feel a lot better."

They continued talking like that for a while, with Corinne explaining that her father — and she — were part of a family that had owned the farmhouse here in Tour for the past four generations. Corinne was the fifth generation.

They had originally come from Mullaghmore in Ireland, descendants of a seventh son who stood to inherit nothing and journeyed to the United States to find his own path.

Considering Corinne's freckled, pale skin and lively red hair, her Irish roots did not surprise James in the least. He could easily picture her walking down the rolling beaches of County Sligo with flowers in her hair, her soul alive with the primal beauty of the people of that beautiful corner of Irish land.

She also told him that the only other siblings that remained were brothers and sisters of her father. But they had all moved out of Tour, leaving the farmhouse in the care of her father as they traded the rustic life for the hustle and bustle of the city.

They spoke very little, although Corinne had done her best to keep in touch.

"They probably think I'm simple or something," Corinne said. "And even if they don't, what's there to discuss? Their lives are so different from mine, and they care about such different things from what I care about..." She gave a shrug. "We would have nothing in common."

"Well," James said. "If that's what they think, then I suppose *they* are the simple ones."

She laughed. "Maybe," she said.

"Look," James said. "Don't worry so much about what they think. You have to trust that people know to make the right choices for themselves. If they left Tour and moved to the city to submerge themselves in whatever they hoped the city might offer, then that was their decision. All you have to do is choose what's right for *you*." He sat back and studied her for a moment. "And I suspect you know what's right for you."

"You are," she said, throwing him a wink.

He laughed. "Well, that too. But I'm talking about staying here — at the farm, doing the work your father did. Does it feel right?"

She considered his question for a moment before she nodded. "Yes," she said.

"Then there's your answer," James said. "And what does it matter what other people think of you if you're doing what feels right?"

She smiled, leaning back against the kitchen counter for a moment as the vegetables behind her boiled and the fries simmered in the pan.

"You know what?" she said. "You're right."

He grinned and nodded. "It's something I only recently figured out. I used to worry about what my family thought — about what my father thought especially. But a while ago, I met with my family members to discuss the inheritance, and you know what? I found I didn't care one bit about what they thought of me, even though I was sure they were calling me crazy in their minds for not caring about any of my father's money. They can have it all. I'll make my own fortune. I'll carve out my own way."

She smiled. "I admire that about you, James," she said. "I hope to be more like that one day."

"I think you will," he said.

She raised her spatula. "Now, if you don't mind, Mr. Beckett, I need a few minutes of total silence and peace while I dedicate my mind, my body, and my soul to the most important task of today."

He chuckled, raising an eyebrow. "And what's that?"

She grinned. "The steaks."

He laughed and relaxed in the chair as Corinne turned around to get to work on the steaks.

Corinne hadn't been bluffing; she made a steak that came close to perfection — if perfection even existed at all.

James was silent as they ate, a tribute to how delicious Corinne's cooking was. She understood exactly how to season the food, so it was neither too salty nor spicy or bland, and she used the perfect amount of herbs, so the meat was bursting with flavor. It was the kind of meal a man should want to enjoy every day.

Afterwards, they shared a bottle of wine from the cellar downstairs and sat in front of the fireplace, enjoying each other's company and relaxing. The mood was peaceful and pleasant, and they spoke of their hopes, dreams, and ambitions for a while before turning to different topics.

"So," Corinne said. "How are the magic studies coming along?"

"Pretty good, actually," James said. "I've been learning new spells and new skills to go with them." His eyes darted to the bowl of grapes Corinne had placed on the table for them to snack on. "Here, check this out."

He took a grape from the bowl and focused on it. As Corinne watched, he harnessed his intent, willing fresh roots to grow from the seeds within the grape.

And when that familiar sensation rose in the back of his mind — slightly painful — he opened his eyes and spoke the words as he maintained his intent.

"Vantoda tod lefand.

"Herreasing, plantan. Lefan.

"Vantoda tod lefand."

At once, the grapes stirred with light, with fresh roots — small and vulnerable still — poking out from the grape, seeking water to feed on.

Corinne's eyes widened. "Wow, James," she said. "That's amazing!"

He nodded. "I learned this spell from a Dragonkin woman."

Corinne raised a ginger eyebrow. "A... *Dragonkin*?" she asked. "Is that... Is that what I think it is?"

James chuckled. "Yeah," he said. "It's pretty much what it says on the cover. She's a descendant of dragons."

"And she... she lives around here?"

"In the woods," James said. "And there are more like

her — Dragonkin or Fae, just like the fox girl that used to have a taste for your chickens."

She chuckled at that and nodded. "It's so strange to imagine that there are all kinds of wondrous creatures practically living in my backyard. It kinda makes ya wonder."

"Wonder about what?" James asked.

She gave a slight smile as she picked up her wineglass and sat down on the couch beside him, resting her head against his shoulder. "Well," she began. "I reckon it makes me wonder if they are dangerous. I mean, I know there are dangerous things in the woods — wild animals and the likes. But the idea of intelligent, dangerous creatures... Now, that could be scary."

"As far as I know, they're all harmless," James said. "They pose no threat to us humans at all. I think the closest thing to dangerous that I ran into was the fox girl, because she was after your chickens. And she bolted like a scared doe the moment she saw me."

Corinne nodded. "Well, that's a relief."

He smiled and put his arm around her, but she grinned and recoiled a little. "I'm very smelly," she said. "I need to take a shower before I can properly cuddle."

James grinned and sniffed the air mockingly. "I don't exactly smell like flowers after a hard day's work either," he said. "Come to think of it, I wouldn't mind a shower either."

She bit her lips as her green eyes shot up to meet his. "Well, Mr. Beckett," she said. "I'm afraid that warm water in my humble abode is limited. I do have a boiler, but it shuts off after about half an hour."

James placed his hand on Corinne's bare thigh. "I guess that means we'll have to shower together to conserve warm water."

She pouted her lips, then covered her mouth in an overly theatrical fashion. "I guess it does," she said.

With a grin, James hopped up from the couch, then extended a hand to pull Corinne to her feet.

"Come on," he said. "I hope your shower is big enough for both of us."

James followed Corinne upstairs. The farmhouse had a small bathroom on the top floor, and the old tiles and simple showerhead told James it needed renovation.

Still, it was kept clean and comfortable, and the air

smelled fresh.

"Here we are, cowboy," Corinne said. "It's modest and simple, but it does the trick."

"It's perfect," James said, pulling the curtain aside. He stepped inside and turned on the faucet, adjusting the temperature so it was hot enough for a nice steaming shower.

When he looked over his shoulder, Corinne was already pulling off her tank top. She seemed a little self-conscious as her large breasts bounced free, the perky, pink nipples that crowned them already swollen and stiff.

A familiar surge of lust passed through James as he shot her an appreciative glance. "You're beautiful, Corinne," he said.

She grinned and threw the tank top at him before opening the buttons on her Daisy Dukes and wriggling out of them.

"You're not so bad yourself, cowboy," she said. "How's the shower?"

He held his hand under the flowing water and nodded. "Looks like it's warm."

"Then let's get to it," she said. "Unless you'd rather take a cold shower?"

James grinned at her and pulled off his shirt. Next, he

undid the belt and his jeans, shucked them off, and watched Corinne as she finished undressing.

She wriggled out of the tight Daisy Dukes, pulling her cute striped panties down along with them. The sight of her pretty pussy and the cute triangle of ginger pubic hair caused James's cocked to rise to firm attention, tenting the boxers he still had on.

Corinne shot him a naughty glance. "Are you going to keep those on?" she asked, nodding at his boxer shorts.

He laughed, lowered them, and kicked them away. "Nope," he said.

Corinne bit her lip as she studied his cock. "My, oh my," she hummed. "I'm not sure the two of us will fit in the shower when you're sporting that thing."

He laughed. "There are ways to make it smaller," he said, shooting her a wink.

She laughed as she kicked her Daisy Dukes with the panties still inside toward him. "Are you making indecent proposals, Mr. Beckett?" she asked.

"I'm only being practical," he said and laughed.

She grinned and shook her head, then stepped forward until she was in front of him and placed her hand on his chest.

"I think you need a good scrubbing," she said. "And I

might shrub that mouth of yours while I'm at it."

He grunted his approval at the sight of her toned naked body in front of him, then snaked an arm around her and gave her firm, round bottom a squeeze.

"You can certainly try," he said. "But I'm pretty sure that you're going to end up on your knees, and it'll be *your* mouth that's going to get scrubbed."

She bit her lip at the dirty talk, then gently pushed him — past the curtain until his feet touched the warm water pooling on the floor and he felt the warm trickle on his back.

She joined him, her hand still on his chest, and her full lips sought his for a fiery kiss.

"Turn around," she purred when she pulled back. "I'll wash you..."

Chapter 42

James hummed with delight as Corinne's slender but strong hands trailed his neck, lathering him up to wash away the grime and sweat of the day.

She worked her way down from his neck to his back, washing every inch of his skin as she occasionally kissed him or pushed her soft breasts up against him.

"Hmm," he groaned. "Here's another thing I would

like to do every day…"

She chuckled as she pushed her delicious body against him. Her soft thighs brushed his, sending a burst of desire to his already rock-hard cock. With her full breasts poking against his back, she wrapped an arm around his waist, making it dip lower until her fingers brushed the tip of his rod, making it twitch with need.

"Oh my," she purred teasingly. "He feels like he's up to no good…"

James chuckled as she teased his cock with her fingertips. "If you tease him like that," he said, "he certainly won't be."

Corinne laughed and rubbed herself against him again, then leaned in close to whisper in his ear. "Now that your back is clean, it's time for your front," she said.

James grinned and turned so he could watch her work, letting the hot water rinse off the soap on his back. His eyes were glued to the sight of her beautiful, toned body as she washed him. And as she worked, he grabbed the bottle of soap and squirted some over round, wet breasts.

She gave him a challenging look. He grinned as he placed both hands on her big tits and began spreading the soap.

Her eyes widened in surprise, and she giggled before leaning in for a passionate kiss. As their tongues danced in the shower, James reached down and began squeezing her breast with one hand, while his other hand slid down between her legs.

"Ahh!" she gasped when his fingers brushed her plump pussy lips, causing her to arch her hips forward as he rubbed it with slow, gentle strokes of his forefinger.

Her hand found his cock again as she took in air with a hiss. She caressed it gently, making it buck before she wrapped her slender hand around it and began tugging his shaft, the tip pressed against her toned stomach.

"Hmm," James groaned. "That's it..."

As they continued kissing, James moved his finger faster, sliding it over her clit, while he brought his other hand up to play with her swollen nipples, winning a mewl of pleasure from her.

It was delicious, sharing each other like this under the warm shower. Corinne's warm body was pressed against him, and he was touching her in all the right places, rubbing her where she needed it most.

His finger slipped inside of her, and Corinne moaned softly as he began to thrust it deeper inside her.

"James," Corinne moaned. "I... I want to come again. It felt so good... when you made me come."

The sound of her voice was music to James' ears. He wanted nothing more than to fuck her right here in the shower, but he would please her and make her come first.

He moved his finger in and out of her slowly, pressing it deep, then withdrawing it to rub her swollen little clit. Corinne sighed with pleasure as she looked up at him, a smile on her lips as she continued tugging on his cock.

"Ahn," she moaned when his finger touched her sensitive nub again. "That's... That's it, James."

She squeezed his swollen shaft and gave a moan of desire. "God, I want to... I want to feel it inside me again. I want you to fill me up."

With a groan of lust, James pushed Corinne up against the bathroom wall, her slender back against the tiles. She raised her long, lithe legs, letting him wrap his hands under her to lift her and pin her against the wall, her lower legs dangling over his arms.

"Yes," she moaned. "Do it like that!"

His only reply was a lustful groan as he lined his throbbing shaft up with her slick heat. Then, without a word, he pressed himself against her and entered her pussy.

She was tight, and she moaned with delight as he parted her walls and entered her womanhood, claiming it once more for his own. He went in inch by inch, keeping her pinned against the bathroom wall, her arms wrapped around him as she moaned her pleasure into his ears.

Then, he lowered her, impaling her on his cock by her own weight.

Corinne let out a sharp cry and threw her head back as he sank balls-deep into her.

"Ooohh! James," she purred, clutching him with all the strength in her body as he kept her pinned against the wall, pulled back, and thrust into her again. "That's it, James!"

He held himself still for a moment, savoring the sensation of being deep inside her, her body trembling around him. Then he started moving in earnest, pounding hard and fast into her with powerful thrusts that had her moaning with delight.

He grunted with every move, his body straining against hers as he fucked her in the shower.

Already, his pleasure heightened. And whenever he looked into Corinne's big, beautiful green eyes, his orgasm only drew nearer. She enjoyed his plowing with abandon, clinging to him like he was a buoy in the ocean, her body gathering itself as the height of her pleasure drew nearer and nearer.

Seeing her like this, her big breasts bouncing and her delicious body against his as the warm water of the shower trickled over his back was enough to make him come, but he didn't want to yet.

He groaned as he pulled out, his cock popping free from her ready and wet pussy. She gave him a look of surprise as he lowered her feet to the ground with a controlled movement and spun her around as if she was a ballroom dancer.

When she realized what he was going to do, she gave a yelp of delight in anticipation.

"Oh God, James," she moaned. "Yes! Please give it to me!"

With her back to him, he pushed her against the tile wall of the bathroom once more, pinning her in place as he lined up his shaft, dripping with both their juices, with her eager pussy. This time, he eased right in, and Corinne gave a deep moan of delight as he began thrusting.

At the same time, he wrapped his hand around her slender waist and dipped down until his fingers found her sensitive clit.

"Ahhn! Yes!" she cried out as he began rubbing her little nub, and she tightened in his embrace at once, leaning into his furious lovemaking and surrendering to his touch.

Soon, Corinne was riding the crest of an orgasm, moaning in ecstasy as she came on his cock, her body tightening and releasing as she shook with pleasure.

In the throes of her orgasm, her pussy clamped on his cock, milked it with a fiery need, and James was unable to contain himself any longer.

"Do it," she moaned, her voice hoarse from her own orgasm. "Cum inside me, James…"

With a grunt that transitioned into a growl of satisfaction, James came hard, pumping rope after rope of cum into her waiting womb, sending waves of pleasure coursing through him as he filled her with his seed.

Corinne gave a deep moan of satisfaction as he spurted the last of his warm seed inside of her, then leaned back, the back of her head against his chest, her arms reaching around as she turned her head to give him a kiss. His cock still deep inside her, he met her kiss with passion, pulling her close against him as they shared the final embers of their fiery lovemaking.

"Oh my Lord," she said softly when she finally broke

the kiss. "I love you, James. And I love loving you."

James smiled at the words and kissed her forehead.

"Hmm, that was great," he grunted, still feeling the warm water clatter on his back. "The perfect ending to another perfect day with you."

She giggled, then shook her ass a little. "I'll say," she purred.

Then, James let out a sharp hiss as the shower — which had been pleasantly warm a moment ago — suddenly turned cold as a mountain stream. Corinne yelped, then broke out laughing as she loosened herself from their embrace and hopped out of the shower to escape from the cold.

"Looks like the boiler ran out," James said, then joined her in her laughter.

But he didn't get out yet.

A cold shower was nothing he wasn't used to, and he wanted to rinse off after such an intense session of lovemaking.

From behind the shower curtain, Corinne shivered and laughed. "I can't believe you're staying in there!" she exclaimed.

He chuckled. "Just making sure I'm proper clean before I get in bed with you."

She giggled. "Well, you'll be squeaky clean after this.

How about I towel myself off and we'll head downstairs to relax by the fire and warm up before we go to bed?"

James nodded with a smile as he did his best to ignore the cold. "Sounds like heaven," he said. "I'll be down in a sec."

After he toweled himself down, James found Corinne already dozing off by the warm fire. They sat on the couch together — Corinne leaning against him as he watched the flames play and flicker. Soon enough, his fatigue overcame James as well, and he put out the fire and brought Corinne up to bed.

There, they experienced a brief revival of energies and made love a second time under the clean and fragrant sheets.

After that, Corinne nestled herself against James, and they fell asleep together.

Chapter 43

The next morning, James enjoyed a quick breakfast with Corinne before heading back to the cabin. He was eager to finish work on his expansion, and he was pleased to find that the boards he had prepared with his Board Crafting spell were now ready for use.

The next stage of construction was a little more difficult. He would use High Magic to cut the planks and beams to the size he needed them to be and set them in place, forming the framework for his expansions and workshop.

To that purpose, he would use the Woodcraft spell he learned when he had witnessed the old woman build a log wall from a pile of raw lumber.

The way he would use the spell differed slightly from what he had seen in the vision — he was not using raw logs, but rather seasoned boards.

Additionally, he would use the Woodcraft spell to build the log walls for the actual cabin expansion. After that, James would have to remove the old walls to open up the expansions. He expected the Woodcraft spell might work for that as well.

He would begin construction on the skeleton of the expansions and the workshop first, then put the boards and logs in place, and he expected he would have to do most of the hammering manually.

But cutting the planks in the right shape and placing them where needed would be achieved with High Magic, which would shave a lot of time off the entire process.

In fact, James thought, *I think I should be able to finish this in two days.*

Before he got started, he headed into the cabin to find

Sara.

The cat girl was nowhere in sight, but there were sure signs that she ate breakfast there before heading out for the day. Hopefully, she would drop by later today and check in on him. Even though he'd had loads of fun with Corinne, he still missed Sara.

After he had a mug of piping hot coffee, James went outside and got started.

He measured out several large beams that would form the framework of his project — the skeleton to which all the other boards or logs would be attached, and which would have to hold the entire structure together.

When he was confident that the beams were of the proper length and sturdiness, he arranged them all on a piece of tarp and moved to an excellent position to oversee his entire lot.

Satisfied with his vantage point, he took a deep breath and began casting his spell. He visualized the result he wanted; the framework of the expansions and the workshop as he had drawn them out.

Once he locked that mental image in his mind, he began focusing his intent on that result, drawing forth the mana from his core and sending it out down the channels of his body, willing the result into existence.

When the time was right, he raised his hands, opened his eyes and spoke the words he learned from the ancestral memory of the old woman:

"Vanhoudt tod kervthoudt.

"Bawerckinghe, maacken. Kraft.

"Vanhoudt tod kervthoudt.

"Danoock, vanealders tod meinenwil.

"Brengang, furanderinghe. Kraft.

"Vanealders tod meinenwil."

And as he had envisioned, the beams began moving into the proper positions, fitting into the holes he dug for them. They came together smoothly, fitting perfectly, and he made the requisite carvings in their corners, allowing them to lock together.

So fitted and put into place, the boards latched together to form the crude framework of James's expansion on the north side of the cabin — the kitchen and the lean-to workshop.

All right, he thought with no small sense of wonder. *That worked.*

Up next was the bedroom expansion on the west side. He used the same process and placed the beams where he needed them, applying High Magic to make the necessary carvings so it could all latch together.

It worked like a charm.

He let out a deep sigh of relief, chuckled to himself, and gave a nod. Up next was the actual physical labor.

He had a stepladder for this work, and he had done plenty of the type before: driving nails and self-tapping screws into the wood. Still, it took him a while until the frameworks were sturdy enough that he was satisfied.

He could only imagine how much work it would be if he focused himself on larger projects, and as he worked up a sweat in the morning sun, he agreed with himself that he would master more magic to aid him with construction once he would further expand the cabin.

Come afternoon, the framework stood.

James then headed back inside and took a break for lunch.

James was happy to find that Sara joined him for lunch after he took out his sandwiches to sit in the sun and relax.

She came from the tree line this time, dressed in a simple and loose-fitting shirt and a matching skirt — an outfit that would work well for anyone on the move or hunting.

And by the bloodstains on the collar of her shirt, James guessed that was exactly what she had been doing.

"James!" she purred happily at the sight of him, her yellow eyes growing large. "You're back!"

He grinned and nodded, and she came up to give him a warm hug and a kiss. She smelled wild — of the forest, and he was certain that she had been romping around, hunting things and having a good old, primal time.

"I'm happy to see you, too," he said. "What have you been up to? Hunting?"

She laughed and nodded. "You won't believe this, James," she said. "But I've actually met up with Astra, and we had a little hunt of our own. We made it into a competition..." She loosened herself from the embrace and stood a little straighter. "Naturally, I won."

He laughed. "I am not surprised at all."

She grinned and flopped down on the porch steps beside him, resting her head on his shoulder as her left ear gave its signature twitch.

"And you?" She asked. "How were things with Corinne?"

There was a teasing note to her voice that told him she had her expectations about how things would have been.

He laughed. "They were good. I helped out at the farm, and we ate dinner together."

She nudged him with her hips. "I bet that's not all that you ate."

He laughed and shook his head. "That mind of yours is permanently in the gutter, isn't it?"

She rolled her eyes playfully. "Don't act like you don't like it, James," she purred.

James smiled at that and kissed her on the temple. "I talked to her about staying with us at the cabin more often."

Sara tilted her head to one side. "Oh? What did she say?"

"She liked the idea," James said. "Only a few nights every week."

"So, things are serious?" Sara asked, her yellow eyes big as her tail gave a playful swish. "Good! I like her!"

Her gaze drifted to the frameworks James had reared. "And it looks like you've been hard at work?"

James nodded as he took a bite of his sandwich. "Yeah," he said around a mouthful. "I want to finish it tomorrow."

"Why tomorrow? Sara asked.

"Well," he began. "If Corinne is going to stay with us

from time to time, will need more room. I also want Lucy to drop by more often; with her in town, I see less of her than I would like." He shrugged. "Long story short: we need a bigger cabin."

Sara laughed and nodded. "Okay," she said. "I like that. Is there anything I can do to help?"

He thought for a moment. "No," he said at length. "I have it under control. But things might get trickier when I want to further expand the cabin. I will need more powerful magic in order to do the work well and quickly. Maybe you and I can sit down together for an hour or so and try to think how High Magic could help the construction project."

She nodded enthusiastically. "Sure!" she said. "I bet we could come up with a few ways to make life easier."

He smiled and gave her a pat on the thigh. "Good." He shot her a sideways glance. "So... how were things with Astra?"

Sara laughed and shook her head, her tail curling playfully.

"She is not as bad as I supposed she was. She's... Well, there is something arrogant about her; I won't lie about that. But I expect you were right; there is a good person — *Dragonkin*, I mean — underneath all of that. I expect that the more we see over, the more she'll be able to drop that mask."

James nodded. "I had the same idea about her."

Sara leaned in and placed a kiss on his cheek, then her eyes turned big as she considered something. She placed a finger to her lips. "But if she ever comes to live with us at the cabin," she mused, "you'll need to build her a roost or a nest or something."

James laughed. "Yeah," he said. "Maybe. I don't know how Dragonkin live, but I can imagine a woman like Astra will have her specific requirements when it comes to where she lives."

"Hm-hm," Sara agreed.

James squeezed Sara's knee. "But let's not think about that too much. For now, I have my eyes on Corinne and Lucy — and on you, of course. If we can expand the cabin just a little, we should be all right. More important are the creature comforts — hot water, refrigeration, heating for when fall begins... stuff like that."

Sara nodded. "Yes, we'll definitely need those."

"And we will have them," James said. "Anyway, I'd better get back to work." He rose and stretched.

She nodded and gave him a kiss on his cheeks. "I'll make you some coffee and a snack for later in the afternoon, okay?"

"You're an angel," he said as he blew her a kiss, then strode over to his construction site.

Chapter 44

James's estimate ended up being correct. He spent the rest of the day and the entire next day on his construction project, carefully placing planks and logs where he needed them with his High Magic.

Thanks to the meticulous perfection afforded by his magic, James could cut the logs and boards down to the perfect size and make them latch together. He then fastened them with wood glue, nails, and self-tapping screws.

He left openings in the walls for windows, although he had not yet come up with a way to make window frames.

For now, he would attach shutters to the outside. That way, he'd have fresh air and ventilation for the remaining days of summer. Once the fall began, he would shut them to keep the cold out.

The work was satisfying. Like most of the things he undertook since he came to Tour, there was something deeply rewarding about physical labor that resulted in something tangible.

This differed completely from order picking, sorting boxes, or handling customer calls — not that those things were not respectable or satisfying in their own right, but there was something innately rewarding about building things.

James enjoyed it. Not just the result, but the process as well — coming up with new ideas, making drawings to test their feasibility, troubleshooting designs, and finally putting his plan into action.

Although he needed to put in a little overtime on Thursday, by Friday mid afternoon, he surveyed his finished expansions with no small sense of satisfaction.

On the north and west sides of the cabin now rose two expansions with log walls and slanting roofs of sturdy boards. The wood was still pale and fresh compared to the more seasoned logs of the cabin itself, but time would solve that.

The workshop leaned against the expansion on the north side. It was a rectangular structure of planks neatly fitted and nailed together, with a continuation of the expansion's slanting roof overhead.

It would all need a little more work in the days to come, especially the roofs, which consisted of bare boards right now. He still needed to seal them and make them as waterproof as possible.

But he was not in a hurry to do that. He expected the rain spells of fall would not begin anytime soon.

Thoroughly happy with the result of his work so far, James finished the day with an extremely satisfying job: opening the walls to his expansions and laying the floors.

Normally hard work, this was a job almost wholly done with High Magic. His Board Crafting and Woodcraft spells allowed him to open up the walls to his new expansions, then cover the level floor with neatly fitted and seasoned boards.

It a way, putting in the floors was almost like playing

Tetris.

James had to laugh at that thought.

He finished up by putting matching baseboards in place and making sure any cracks were sealed to keep out the bugs — although an occasional bug was part of any life in the woods.

After that, he moved most of his tools into the workshop. Admittedly, he wouldn't be able to use the workshop until he had completed the workbench and done the last bit of work, but moving his tools to their new home gave him a sense of completion.

When he had finished moving the last of them, the sun was already on its way down.

Finally done, he thought as he surveyed the result of work.

He was tired but happy, and the light shimmering behind the shutters of the cabin looked very inviting. Sara would probably be home in a few minutes, and they would cook a delightful meal together.

With a satisfied nod, he turned toward the entrance of the cabin.

And that's when he saw the eyes.

They looked at him from the tree line — big, one blue, one green.

Kesha.

She had come back again.

James stood silent on the porch of his cabin, studying the skittish fox girl as she eyed him.

She was beautiful; her red hair fell past her shoulders and her light skin made her appear ethereal. She drew her lips into a smile as she studied him carefully with her beautiful eyes — one green, the other blue.

Her fox ears stood upright, and three fluffy tails bristled behind her. She wore a simple white T-shirt and a pair of khaki shorts underneath, almost as if she were out hiking.

"Looks like you finished it," she said, cocking her head slightly.

He smiled, happy that she had been the first to break the silence — happy that she had come back again. He had nothing else planned for the rest of the day except to move his tools into the workshop.

And that could wait another day.

He wanted to talk with her, and the way she looked at him promised she had made up her mind as well. She wanted to get to know him better, perhaps even be closer to him.

"Thanks. I worked hard on it. It took me forever to get all the wood together."

Kesha nodded and turned her gaze down to the finished project. "Forever?" she asked. "I think you did it fairly quickly."

James wriggled his fingers in the air and grinned. "Magic," he said.

She laughed, her posture relaxing. "You're not even joking, are you?"

He shook his head. "No," he said. "I learned a couple of new spells that were of great assistance. In fact, going forward, they will help me further expand the cabin and make it exactly the way I want it to be."

She stepped out from among the trees, her luscious hips swaying as she kept her heterochromatic eyes on him.

"So the cabin is getting more expansions," she asked. "Just like you said it would?"

"Hm-hm," he said. "Corinne is coming over to stay a few days a week."

She came to a stop, placed one hand on her hip as she regarded James's cozy home with a raised eyebrow.

James grinned and crossed his arms as he studied her. "Anything on your mind?" he asked.

She licked her lips as her gaze returned to him. "I liked staying here," she said.

"That so?" he said, a teasing note to his voice. "You were gone awfully quick."

She pouted. "I left you a thank-you note, didn't I?"

He chuckled. "Yeah," he said. "I'll admit it was cute."

She took a few more steps forward, her expression turning a little serious. "Uhm, James," she began. "I didn't mean to insult your hospitality. But I was... Well, you know... When you two would wake up... I was scared it would be awkward." She wrung her hands as she spoke, her eyes taking on a pleading note.

He waved it away. "Don't worry about it, Kesha," he said. "I'm only joking with you. You were more than welcome, and I didn't mind you leaving at all. In fact, I understand it perfectly fine."

The smile returned to her lips. "Good," she said. "I wasn't sure how things would go."

"Well, I don't want you to feel uncomfortable around me. I can tell you're a little nervous, which is totally understandable, but I hope I will be able to prove to you that I'm your friend."

"You already proved that," she said. Her eyes shot over to the cabin, now doubled in size, and there was a curious glow in them.

"You want to look inside?" James asked.

"Can I?" she asked. "I'd like to see the workshop!"

"Really?" James asked. "Well, sure. There's not a whole lot to see just yet, but go look around if you want to."

She gave an excited clap of her hands, then hopped over to the workshop.

James watched her go, moving with a wild grace that made her ample curves bounce in an enticing way, and she threw him a broad grin over her shoulder as she headed over to the workshop to sate her curiosity.

He was catching feelings for her; he was sure of that.

The pretty fox girl pushed all the right buttons with her curious but shy demeanor. And he loved the dash of wildness about her — something to make her personality spark all the brighter.

She stepped into the doorway and hesitated.

For a moment, there was only silence.

Then she looked over her shoulder, her multicolored eyes blazing with more than just curiosity.

"W-why don't you come in with me?" she asked. "You can, uh, show me around?"

His heart thumping in his chest, James nodded and followed.

Chapter 45

The workshop was small, still alive with the delicious scent of freshly shaped wood — that aroma of a new place, tinged with the clean air of the surrounding forest.

Kesha stood in front of him, her shapely back turned to him as she studied his handiwork with big eyes.

But this was about more than the workshop; James

was sure of that.

And where the fox girl had been skittish and tense before, she now did her best to show her enticing body in the most flattering of poses. She leaned forward, her head cocked, to study the woodwork, and as she did so she rose to her tiptoes, pushing up her perfect butt with the three fox tails waving above it.

He wouldn't mind feeling those brush his chest as he took her from behind…

James cleared his throat, trying to clear his mind as well.

After a few 'ohs' and 'ahs', Kesha turned around, her full lips slightly pouting as she studied him.

"You like it?" James asked.

She nodded vigorously before taking a step forward. She was in his personal space now, and he in hers, and he could sense the electricity sparking between them as she fixed her big eyes on him.

"I like it," she purred.

On a whim, James reached out and took up both her hands, raising them from where they hung at her side to his chest. "Good," he said.

A slight dash of crimson colored her cheeks. "James," she began, too soft or anyone else to hear. "I have been thinking… And I wanted to ask you something."

"Sure," he said, rubbing his thumbs over the back of her hands, savoring how soft she felt. "Ask me anything."

She swallowed as she gathered courage, looking at the ground for a moment before she reestablished eye contact.

"I wanted to ask you if I can... Well, if I can stay here with you a little longer. T-the last time, I felt really safe. I haven't slept as well as I did here in your house in... well, years. I don't think I really realized how tired I was. I mean, I love the wild — I love being out in the forest. And to an extent, I like being alone as well. But... it's been so lonely, and so cold. And I've been so scared. E-even if it's only for a little while, I would love to stay here."

He smiled down at her, still holding her hands. She was so sweet like this, looking up at him with her big, pleading eyes, her fox ears standing straight.

How could he say no to that?

Not that he wanted to...

"Of course," he said. "The offer still stands. You're more than welcome to stay with us. And I'm pretty sure that Sara wouldn't mind, either."

She perked up, her eyes brightening. "Really?" she asked. "Do you really think she wouldn't mind?"

He chuckled and shook his head. "Sara likes you," he said. "And she firmly believes in the philosophy 'the more, the merrier.'"

Kesha laughed and made an excited little hop that made her firm and perky breasts bounce along.

"Yay!" she purred. Then, without warning, she shot forward and threw her arms around James's neck, embracing him tight enough to make him gasp for air.

He smiled, closing his arms around her as he pulled her in.

The delicious scent of her — the spirit of the wild — made him heady, and her limber and lithe body under his hands added to the sensation until he felt like he was spinning.

"Thank you so much," she crooned in his ear. "I don't know how I can ever repay you for this."

"You don't have to," he said, his voice a little husky as his excitement grew. "Like I said, you're more than welcome."

She pulled back from the embrace, her face only an inch from his. "Thank you," she hummed again.

He nodded, lost in the green and blue depths of her eyes. "It's fine," he said, reaching out to brush a stray lock away. "I'm actually very happy that you asked."

"Oh?" she said, a teasing note to her voice. "Why is

that?"

James grinned and leaned forward, brushing his lips over hers. "You know why."

She mewled as she drew closer. Their lips touched, and he let her set the pace and playfulness of their kiss.

As they explored each other, their bodies pressed together, their lips and tongues intertwined, their hands began roaming each other's bodies.

James was delighted to have her fingers trailing his back, the tips of her nails lightly scratching his skin as she traced the muscles beneath. A grunt of pleasure escaped him as his own hands roamed down to cup her round butt, his fingers sinking into the soft flesh as he massaged it.

"Hmm, James," she hummed as she came loose from his fiery kiss for a moment. "This... This is so nice."

"I've wanted to do this for a while," James whispered, holding her close.

She bit her lower lip and gave a little whimper of surrender. Then, their lips parted as they came together once more, and James drew her into another deep kiss, tasting her sweetness and letting it wash over him.

She moaned, her lashes fluttering as she tilted her head back and let James take control.

He did just that, kissing her passionately with a

growing urgency. He pushed his tongue inside of her mouth, swirling his tongue around her own as he savored the touch of her soft and full lips.

She was hesitant at first, but soon she was mimicking his movements with eagerness and enthusiasm.

He held her close. Heat radiated from her body as he kissed her with all the passion and desire that had been burning inside of him since he first laid eyes on the fox girl.

When Kesha finally broke the kiss with a lustful moan, he was panting, alive with the need to delve deeper into her.

She giggled, and when he looked up at her, she was blushing a little pink.

"This is..." She gave an excited squeal. "I'm so happy!"

He laughed and swept her into his arms again, playfully pushing up against her limber body until her round butt was parked against one of the walls he had crafted with care.

As he pushed her up against the wall, Kesha gave a playful yip and nibbled at his ear as she pushed her delicious body up against him.

His hands roamed and explored the enchanting contrasts of her — toned and flat stomach, full and round ass. Unable to contain himself any longer, his hands moved up to cup her pretty breasts. They were not as large as Sara's or Lucy's, but they were still good handfuls, firm and with perky nipples to boot.

"Hmm," he groaned. "You are a delight."

She giggled as she slipped a hand between their bodies. On its way down, she grazed his defined abdominal muscles, and she gave a purr of delight. Finally, her dainty hand came to rest on the bulge in his cargo pants, and she gave a little squeeze that made James gasp for air.

"You know," she whispered, a teasing note to her voice. "I can see — and feel — another advantage to staying at your cabin…"

He grinned as he let one of his hands dip behind her and play with the soft fur of her fluffy tails.

"And what exactly did you want to do with that advantage?" he hummed.

She squeezed him again, then bit her lower lip. "Let me show you…"

With a playful push, Kesha created some distance

between her and James, loosening their embrace.

With deft hands, almost too quick for the eye to follow, she pulled her shirt over her head. Her perky tits bounced free — delicious and pink, with slightly darker nipples.

James's cock bucked in his pants at the sight of them, but she wasn't done yet.

Kesha popped the buttons of her shorts and wiggled out of them, no small feat considering her wide hips. She pulled her panties down at the same time, revealing a beautiful, pink pussy with a cute little landing strip of ginger pubic hair.

"You look absolutely delicious," James groaned.

She laughed, kicking up her panties and whirling them around her forefinger before throwing them at him.

"Now it's your turn," she purred.

Desire raging in his chest, James pulled his T-shirt over his head, discarding the garment in the workshop's corner. His boots, cargo pants, and boxers followed a moment later, and he revealed himself fully to Kesha, his firm cock almost pointing at her — eager to claim her and add her to his harem.

She touched her plump lower lip with her forefinger as she quirked an eyebrow at him. "One thing about us fox spirits, though," she purred.

"What's that?" James rasped.

"You have to catch us first."

And with that, she bolted past him, through the doorway, and out into the forest — almost faster than James had seen anyone run. Her laughter drifted to him on the wind as she hopped past the tree line.

"Oh no, you don't!" James said, laughing.

A moment later, he gave chase, following the limber and lithe fox girl through the forest.

Chapter 46

Kesha was fast.

But James had chased and caught her before. And this time, the need that drove him to catch up to her was even more visceral.

His eyes were on her pretty butt, bouncing with every leap and bound as she cleared the undergrowth, darted between tree trunks, or hopped over sprawling roots. She shot him a coy glance over her shoulder every once in a while, giggling and laughing as she led him on.

But the distance between them was shrinking.

James ran, driven by desire, calling out after her. And in this wild and naked chase, he felt almost like a spirit of the forest himself — some magical creature running free at the dawn of time, pursuing love in its most natural and beautiful form.

But even with his mind clouded with need, he had a plan.

Moving to her left and to her right to steer the capricious fox girl, he herded her to the creek where he bathed almost every morning. It wasn't very wide, and it certainly wasn't wild, but it would slow her down.

Enough for him to catch up.

Kesha yelped when she came to the bubbling waters, finally realizing his ploy. She turned on her feet to see James run toward her, grinning as he reached out to take her up in his arms. Then, laughing, she hopped into the creek.

But James was on her now.

He leaped after her, splashing into the water right beside her. She laughed, raised her hands to shield her eyes from the cascade of water, and a moment later he was with her, taking her up in his arms, pressing her close.

"You got me!" she panted, laughing. "I give up!"

James laughed with her. "Good," he breathed, kissing her soft lips.

His hands roamed over her body — cupping her round butt, sliding up to cup her full breasts, and tracing along her flat belly until they found their way down between her legs.

And at the same time, she panted her delight in his ears, nibbled on his earlobes, as her deft hand sunk to grab and squeeze his firm shaft.

"Hmm, James," she hummed. "I love it!"

He smiled as he kissed her, his hand dipping between her hot thighs, winning a yip of pleasure from the fox girl.

In her desire, she threw herself at him, and their lips met once more.

Kissing Kesha was a pleasure of its own that James lost himself in, one hand raking her fluffy tail, the other squeezing her firm butt cheek. He moaned as he tasted of her sweet tongue. They stood thigh-deep in the babbling creek, kissing and nipping at each other.

The increased fire of urgency made Kesha wrap one lovely leg around him, pressing her hot womanhood against his seeking fingers as she moaned with delight.

When their lips parted, Kesha was panting, her eyes closed as she clasped onto him. Her tongue lolled out of her mouth as she wheezed, her eyes fluttering open and closing as she came to a stop for a second.

But James continued relentlessly, his hungry fingers stroking her warm and wet pussy lips. Then he slipped his middle finger between her slick folds, and Kesha yelped with delight as he penetrated her with it.

"Oooh, James," she moaned. "That... ahnn... That's so good."

He grunted with lust as he plunged deeper. Her pussy was tight, but the arousal of their flirting and the ensuing chase had made her juices flow, allowing his probing digit to slip into the depths of her sex. He pushed inside her slowly, his other hand still gripping her fluffy tail.

With a hum of delight, she closed her hand around his shaft again and began pumping him.

James moaned with pleasure as he stood there in the fresh water, his balls just touching the surface, as his sexy fox girl jerked him off while he pleasured her with his fingers. He kissed her lips, her cheek, her neck, until he dipped down to take one of those firm breasts in his mouth and sucked on her perky little nipple.

"Hnnf, James," she purred. "That's it."

He licked her swollen nipple, then let his tongue trace circles around it, winning a gasp of delight from the fox girl as she began pumping a shaft faster.

With a grunt, he released a thick bead of precum, and Kesha's large, green-and-blue eyes dipped down as she bit her lip.

"Oh, James," she hummed. "Look at that... I want to lick it off. Please, can I?"

He grinned. "How can I say no to that?"

With a wicked smile, she pulled back her hands and placed them on his chest, slowly pushing him to the bank of the creek. There, on a grassy and soft stretch, she pushed him to sit down.

"I'm going to make you so happy," she said, a naughty fire in her eyes.

He smiled, then watched as she bent over, her round ass in the air, hovering over his thick weapon.

But he had a naughty little plan of his own...

As Kesha focused on James's engorged dick, getting ready to wrap her plump lips around it, he suddenly shifted forward and grabbed hold of her.

The fox girl yelped and yipped as he lifted her up. She was petite, and she didn't weigh too much, so picking her up and lifting her out of the creek so that she straddled his chest was something that James could manage.

"James!" she exclaimed, giggling and chuckling at his handling of her.

With a grin, he flipped her around once she sat on his chest, making the limber fox girl fight for balance as she almost slipped off.

But now, he had her where he wanted her. Her firm and round ass was close to his face, and she gave a hum of delight as he grabbed a handful of fluffy tail and pulled her butt toward him until her plump and wet pussy lips were hovering over his face.

"Oh, James," she purred. "Oh, my… This is so hot!"

"Sit down," he commanded, his voice firm as he pulled her down by her tail.

"Ah, James!"

Then, her pussy was on his face. He dug into her, ate her out as he relished in the wild, slightly salty taste of her. She slithered down his chest as she collapsed, her face right next to his throbbing dick.

"Kiss it," he grunted, his voice almost drowned by

her slick womanhood.

She purred her consent as her plump lips kissed the tip of his cock, her tongue darting out playfully to lick up the little bead of precum he had for her. And as she leaned forward to get into position, James wrapped her fluffy tail around his fist, squeezed her round ass with his other hand as he brought his thumb closer to her tight little pucker.

She squirmed as he lapped at her pussy, his thumb inching closer and closer to that tight little forbidden hole.

"Oh, James!" She exclaimed as she closed a hand around his shaft and began pumping him hard.

"Please, yes! Please put your finger in there!" Her lips were playing with his cock now, and she gave a lustful moan as she trailed them over his tip.

That moan became muffled as he thrust, pushing his dick between her plump lips.

"Hmm!" she moaned as she gave into it. She bobbed her head as one hand kept working his shaft, the other softly massaging his balls.

James pushed his thumb into her tight pucker, winning another squirm of pleasure from the fox girl. She arched her back, giving him perfect access to her swollen little nub. He began running his tongue in circles around it, occasionally letting it slither down her wet slit.

No doubt she would've cried out in pleasure if she hadn't had her mouth full of cock.

She tightened on James, her orgasm rapidly approaching. But he wasn't done yet. His thumb worked her asshole like a piston, and soon her hips bucked in his grasp and her body shook in spasms of delight as his tongue relentlessly licked her swollen clit.

But to her credit, she didn't stop sucking him off for a moment. She took his shaft as deep into her throat as she could, gasping and gagging as he thrust along with her, sensing his pleasure rise from his toes.

He had wanted to have his way with the fox girl ever since he first caught her outside Corinne's chicken coop — to tame her wildness...

To fill her up with his seed.

He pulled harder on those sexy, fluffy fox tails, pushed his thumb a little deeper, and even let his tongue squirm inside her hot pussy for a moment.

She almost howled with pleasure at that, and her thick thighs began shaking as her entire body grew tense, pressing down on him. And even then, she did not stop feasting on his cock.

Then, with another merciless lash of his tongue, her

body began shuddering. He pushed his thumb deeper, and Kesha practically begged for mercy as she came, shaking and quavering while gagging and sucking on his cock.

When she collapsed, he didn't give her a moment's mercy. He was in full goblin mode now, eager to claim her delicious body for his own and fill it up with his love.

She yelped as he pushed her off him, flipped her onto her back as he rose to his knees, and pulled her in.

Her big green and blue eyes met his, hazy with lust, her tongue sticking out of the corner of her mouth.

"Do it," she purred, arching her back and spreading her legs for him. "Take me, James."

With a grunt of desire, James grabbed hold of his rock hard cock and slid the tip down her wet slit. When he touched her little nub, another shiver of delight — a post-orgasmic thrill — passed through Kesha, and her eyes rolled up in their sockets as she murmured some gibberish.

Then he lined his cock up with a sexy fox girl's pussy and plunged in.

He groaned with delight as he parted her tight walls, and she yipped with pleasure, wrapping her legs around him. It took him three thrusts before he had overcome the tightness caused by her orgasm, and by then he was close to cumming inside her. But he wanted to put it off, enjoy her delicious love a moment longer.

He bent forward, burying his face in her heaving breasts, licking and lapping as he thrust inside her. She mewled with delight, her nails raking his back, opening furrows that Sara had drawn earlier.

The sensation engulfed him — a mixture of pain and pleasure that went straight to his cock as it throbbed inside her, ready to fill her up with his sticky seed.

"Fuck," he groaned. "I can't… I want to cum in you!"

She tightened her embrace, nibbled on his earlobe, and placed her heels on his back to push him deeper inside her.

"Do it," she whispered, followed by a playful nip at his ear. "I want your hot love inside of me. Fill me up!"

He groaned, pulled back, and pushed even deeper. But there was nothing he could do to postpone the pleasure that his limber fox girl gave him, and when he opened his eyes to see her delicious breasts bouncing under the force of his love, he plunged deep and released with a roar of power.

Kesha howled with delight as he blasted a thick rope of potent cum inside her, then pushed him even harder with her heels.

Pure ecstasy washed over James in waves as he emptied his balls, her pussy sucking every drop out of him as he bottomed out inside her.

When he had fired his last, James practically collapsed on top of Kesha. With a hoarse giggle, she enclosed him in her arms, wrapping her three fox tails around him as she kissed his cheeks and his neck.

"That was delicious," she whispered. "I should've done this with you a lot earlier..."

He chuckled, still panting for breath. "I agree," he grunted. "But then again," he added as he returned her fiery kisses. "I do enjoy the chase."

She laughed. "You'll be doing plenty of chasing once I move into the cabin."

"I hope so," he murmured, letting his hands roam over her delicious body, slick with sweat from their intensive bout of lovemaking.

They lay like that for a while, in a tight embrace, as they shared passionate kisses and caressed and stroked each other.

The late afternoon sun shone down on them, warming their bodies despite the cold dip in the creek, and James slowly felt a laziness settling in.

Finally, he lay down beside Kesha, and the fox girl snuggled up against him, hugging both him and her own fox tails as she rested her pretty head on his chest.

"I'm happy we did this," she said. "I hope will be doing a lot more of it."

James stretched, then let his hand drift to her full head of hair, scratching her behind one of her fox ears. "Oh, we will be doing a lot more of this. Don't you worry about that." He chuckled.

She rose, folding her arms on his chest and resting her chin on them as she studied him.

"I think I like you, James Beckett," she said.

He smiled at her, his hand still playing with her fuzzy ear. "Likewise, Kesha," he said. "I think we will have a lot of fun together."

Chapter 47

James surveyed his cabin with a rising sense of contentment.

The expansions were done, and he had used his Board Crafting spell to make a workbench and several shelves for his tools in the workshop. With the same spells, he had made shutters and window frames for the expansions and the workshop.

But there was more he wanted.

He was keen to get a real bathroom — and the art of Sigil-carving that he had learned from Astra would hopefully help him get things like running water, hot water, refrigeration, and even electricity in the long run.

And he'd like a study where he could retreat to if he needed to work, and maybe even an extra living area. Things might get crowded, so a little space to retreat whenever he or anyone else wanted a little quiet would do just fine.

A bout of laughter came from inside the cabin, and a broad smile made its way to James's lips when he heard it.

Sara, Corinne, and Kesha were inside, enjoying breakfast and — apparently — getting along pretty well. That was good, but James hadn't been particularly concerned about Kesha getting along with either Sara or Corinne.

No, the difficulty may lie in her relationship with Lucy.

James was yet to break the news to Lucy about the affection that had grown between him and Kesha. He was not sure how she would take it, but Lucy had proven herself to be loving and understanding. He would talk to her soon and discuss these events with her.

After all, with her organizing the upcoming barbecue to introduce him to the rest of the townsfolk, they would probably spend a lot of time together. And James was looking forward to that.

He hoped that, in the process, Lucy and Kesha might in some way reconcile their differences and grow closer to one another as they became part of the same family once again.

Either way, he wanted them all under his roof before fall came to herald the cold months.

It would arrive soon; James sensed the nip in the air.

Soon enough, temperatures would dip, and it would only be a matter of time before the leaves would turn brown and golden, although the pines would remain green and full of life.

Before that time came, he would need to sort out heating the cabin and make sure they were comfy and toasty for the cold season.

He would also have to help Corinne with the harvest before things got too cold. But with his new spells, he could ease the logistical side of things by simply teleporting her produce to Lucy's general store, where it could be sold to the townsfolk. That would buy Corinne some time. And he might even get Kesha to help out at the farm a little — maybe a little compensation for the chicken coop.

And as his gaze drifted to the tree line, his women laughing merrily in the background, his mind also went out to the red-eyed creature in the forest. To Hind and to Astra. The foundations below the cabin and the things that he might still find there. There was something happening in the woods around Tour, and he expected time would bring it to his doorstep.

James was, after all, the High Mage of Tour.

He smiled before turning back inside, to the warm light and to the laughter of his women.

Life would not get boring anytime soon...

THANK YOU FOR READING!

If you enjoyed this book, please check out my other work on Amazon.

Be sure to **leave me a review on Amazon** to let me know if you liked this book! Like most independent authors, I use the feedback from your review to improve my work and to decide what to focus on next, so your review can make a difference.

If you want to stay up-to-date on my releases, you can join my newsletter by entering the following link into any web browser: https://fierce-thinker-305.ck.page/45f709af30. You can also join my Discord, where the madness never ends... Join by entering the following invite manually in your browser or Discord app: https://discord.gg/ex5rEJdtwu.

<u>Jack Bryce's Books</u>

Below you'll find a list of my work, all available through Amazon.

<u>Aerda Online (completed series)</u>

Phylomancer

Demon Tamer

Clanfather

<u>Warped Earth (completed series)</u>

Apocalypse Cultivator 1

Apocalypse Cultivator 2

Apocalypse Cultivator 3

Apocalypse Cultivator 4

Apocalypse Cultivator 5

<u>Highway Hero (ongoing series)</u>

Highway Hero 1

Highway Hero 2

<u>Country Mage (ongoing series)</u>

Country Mage 1

Country Mage 2

A SPECIAL THANKS TO...

Stoham Baginbott and Maikeruu for beta reading. You guys are absolute kings.

If you're interested in beta reading for me, hit me up on discord (JauntyHavoc#8836) or send an e-mail to lordjackbryce@gmail.com.

Made in the USA
Las Vegas, NV
11 December 2023

82417025R00246